TATTLETALES

SHORT STORIES

Harold Raley

TotalRecall Publications, Inc.
1103 Middlecreek
Friendswood, Texas 77546
281-992-3131 281-482-5390 Fax
www.totalrecallpress.com

All rights reserved
ISBN: 978-1-64883-004-4
UPC: 6-43977-40044-4
Library of Congress Control Number: 2020939616

Printed in the United States of America with simultaneous printings in Australia, Canada, and United Kingdom.

FIRST EDITION
1 2 3 4 5 6 7 8 9 10

Foreword

A celebrated philosopher once said that in order to understand anything human we must tell a story. He spoke a profound truth, and it is important to understand some of its implications. Art, including musical and literary art, tells us very little about what we are. That kind of information is the business of science, which teaches that we are mammalian animals, first cousins to the great apes. On the other hand, art has much to tell us about who we are. It reminds us that we are persons, or better said, men and women, who daily add pages to a private narrative, or notes to an inimitable life melody. We are the novelists of ourselves. If we exist at a primary level as biological creatures subject to nature's laws and limitations, on a different plane we live as unique biographical persons whose mission is not to remain at nature's mercy but to humanize the world with artifact and artistry, creed and creativity, song and story. The thirteen tales in this book are modest examples of the high art of being human in a rich alchemy of styles, times, and climes.

Authors Bio

Novelist and short story writer, linguist, philosopher, and professor, Harold C. Raley holds degrees (BA, MA, PhD) in English, Foreign Languages, Humanities, and Philosophy. Named Distinguished Professor, he has taught languages, literature, and philosophy in American and foreign universities. His publications include fourteen books of fiction, history, language, and philosophy, and approximately 150 articles and essays on wide-ranging topics in professional journals and newspapers.

Table of Contents

Scene 1

Chemical engineer Randall Wheeler, 29, returned to Atlanta a day early from a business trip to Houston and got the shock of his life.

The TV was on but the sound was off when he unlocked the door and set his carryon and laptop next to it. His wife Paula was not in the room. Probably in the kitchen, he thought, as he started toward it. Then just before he called her name, he heard voices in their bedroom.

"Darling, this can't go on any longer," said a man's baritone voice he did not recognize. "You can't stay married to a man you don't love. You love me and I love you. We belong together."

"I know, darling," Paula answered him, "and you know how much I want us to be together. I want that more than anything in the world."

Randall froze in horrified disbelief. Three days earlier on the eve of his trip Paula, 26, had shown him in every way a woman can that she loved him. At least he thought so. He left the next morning totally happy in his marriage and manhood, but sorry to see the sadness in Paula's eyes despite her brave smile.

When I get back, he had promised himself, I'll get her the best gift I can and treat her to the most romantic evening of dining and dancing in her life. But that was then. Now he was staggered by what he had just heard and didn't know what to think. Was it possible that Paula could pretend a love she didn't feel? Maybe I don't know her at all. My God, has she been faking it the six months we've been married? She loves acting and theatre, but is she that good?

"Then one way or another we have to make it happen!" the baritone stranger said angrily. "And soon! I can't stand the thought of you with that man."

"I know, darling, I know. If you feel bad about the situation, think how I feel being with him, sleeping with him and . . . all the rest. I can't bear it any longer, but I don't know what to do. I'm desperate. As if everything else wasn't bad enough, the way I let him set up our finances, he gets nearly everything if I initiate a divorce. What a fool I was. And it was my family's money in the first place. I could fight it in court, but it would be a messy scandal and I still might lose. How can I get free? He just laughs when I suggest a friendly divorce. He's got an ego as big as Texas and thinks every woman worships the ground he walks on. He won't even listen to me."

"Well, by God, he'll listen to me!" the baritone thundered. "Damned creep! I'll get rid of him for you! For us!"

Randall heard the thud of a fist.

"Darling, what do you mean? I hope not what I think I'm hearing."

"You know of any other way? You've already said he won't talk about a divorce. Darling, we've talked around the only real possibility left I don't know how many times and it always comes back to the same thing. He has to go, and if he won't go willingly, then we have to help him make his exit."

"Yes, but it's so . . . so . . . horrible. Darling, are you absolutely sure there isn't some other way?"

"Well, sure, as I said the other day, we could just run off to Tahiti, Aruba, somewhere like that, and live on a tropical beach.

It would be fun for a few weeks then miserable after our money runs out. I knew some people that tried it. After a few months they were panhandlers and human trash. I don't want that for you—for us. What I want, and aim to see to it that we have, is a better life than the hell we're in now. Well, you know what the solution has to be, don't you? Are you okay with it? Are you in? He has to go."

A silence, then Paula's nervous voice: "Okay, I . . . I guess you're right. So, okay; if it has to be that way, then . . . just do it and get it over with. I can't stand any more of this."

Randall retreated quietly to the door, took his bags, closed and locked the door softly but swiftly, hurried out to the car, and drove off in a daze. He had a day to pull himself together and try to make sense of things. His world had flipped too suddenly and drastically for him to keep any semblance of balance.

He drove north and checked into an Alpharetta motel. He had forgotten to eat, but food, untypically for him, was now the farthest thing from his mind. He lay fully dressed on the bed for a long time, staring absently at a faded, lopsidedly hung copy of Monet's *Woman with an Umbrella*, vaguely annoyed at some unspoken level by the breezy motif so alien to the suddenly crushing weight of his circumstances. Much later his thoughts came into focus and he realized his body needed food. The realization was comforting and reminded him of something he had read in a novel: *humanly I'm a wreck, but the animal in me is strong.*

He walked across the street to a fast food restaurant and ordered a hamburger, fries, and coffee to go. Normally he prided himself on his physical conditioning and avoided all three, but tonight was an exception to everything in his life.

Back in his room he mechanically said a prayer, a lifetime habit, then ate and wrote as he sipped the coffee. The hamburger was barely warm, and the fries were stale. Leftovers from the evening batch, he thought. But no matter; he was not in a mood for pleasurable things anyway. He began, then wadded several versions of a letter on motel stationery before he settled on one that he judged appropriate to send Paula. An e-mail would not do.

Paula:

I got home early from my trip and unintentionally overheard a part of your conversation with your lover. I will not mention my feelings at this point since obviously they no longer matter.

You told me when I phoned two days ago that you had some-thing to tell me when I got home. I guess now I know what it was.

I was puzzled when you told your lover that you had asked me for a divorce. I cannot remember ever discussing that possibility with you. In fact, it would be the last thing I would have wanted, but would have granted if that was your wish, as it turns out to be. Paula, please know that I will not stand in the way of your happiness.

As for practical matters, since we have

joint banking and savings accounts, you can have all the money in both. I have the new car now but by the time you open this letter it will be in our driveway and I'll be in the old one. I'll put anything of yours in the new one. As for the house itself, you can have it, the equity, and furniture. I would like to retrieve eventually some of my books, tools, clothes, and personal belongings, but if they offend you, just go ahead and toss them if you like.

I was confused by what you said about your family money. Maybe I misunderstood. But no matter, I agree that whatever money there is in the accounts I leave to you.

There is one thing, though, I cannot agree to: your willingness to be an accomplice to my murder. I would give my life willingly for you in other circumstances, but I cannot let you and your lover stain your souls with the crime of murder. For that reason, I will do everything I can, short of murder myself, to see that it does not happen. I hope it is enough for you that I agree to the divorce and disappear from your life. That should make my death unnecessary and your happiness possible.

I have three weeks of accumulated vacation time. I will get in touch when it's over. Meanwhile, the two accounts should last you well past this transition. The new car is in good condition but will need servicing in a couple of weeks. Ask for Sam if you take it in. The house insurance will be due at the end of next month and the roofer is supposed to show up on Wednesday of this week to unclog the gutters.

That's all I can think of at the moment. I have turned off my cell phone and do not plan to use it for several weeks, if ever again. I'm sure you have no desire to speak to me, and it would be painful for me to talk to you. I will get a new work number for people who need to contact me.

Thank you for these months together. They were the best time of my life. I'm sorry that for you they were the worst.

Goodbye

Randall

He reread the letter, folded and sealed it in a motel envelope, and carefully placed it on the nightstand. Then he looked at the girl in the painting until tears came to his eyes. The pain was like a living thing in the stillness. The caffeine and his calamity kept him awake far into the night.

He felt more alert the next morning despite little sleep. For an instant, he hoped that it had all been a bad dream and that Paula was waiting for him to come home. But the sealed letter was a wakeup reminder of the truth. He skipped breakfast, arranged to keep the room for two more nights, and drove home. Then sure that Paula was still asleep, he quickly exchanged cars. Paula has her own key, he thought, and there's an extra in the kitchen, but I should have reminded her in the letter. Too many things to think of, and I've probably forgotten several. For a moment he stood by their mailbox, looking at the house where he had spent nearly six happy months with Paula. Then he shook his head in finality, dropped the letter in the box, and drove away quickly.

Now what? It was not a good time for Phillips executives, even middle-level managers like himself, to go on vacation. The proposed acquisition of Chenevert Petroleum in Port Arthur, Texas was at the critical stage, and everybody was needed at their post. Then it occurred to him that instead of going on vacation, he could ask to be transferred, temporarily at least, to the Phillips facility in Beaumont. His CEO Jacob Carbone trusted his judgment based on past performances, including his most recent trip to Texas, and would probably approve the transfer. That way he could get away from Atlanta, and Carbone would have a trusted lieutenant on site to serve as his Texas eyes and ears and keep him informed about what was really going on and whether the Chenevert executives were as straight and the company as solid as they seemed to be on paper and at the recent meeting. I'll tell Jacob some, but not all, of the situation with Paula, he thought. Jacob's had his own marital miseries, and not that long ago as I remember. He should be sympathetic.

Carbone agreed to the transfer, but only for a month.

"You keep a keen eye on what those Cajun bastards are up to out there as we get closer to finalizing the deal. Especially that guy Thomas Riviere. I hear he's not above taking money under the table and has the ethics of a Louisiana alligator. You watch him, you hear? We don't need him screwing up this deal with some of the crappy shortcuts they say he takes. There's a lot of money and a lot of bonuses and promotions riding on this merger. So, Randall, I'm depending on you. It's for your own good. You hear me?"

"Loud and clear, boss. You can count on me."

"And on a personal note, Randall, I'm sorry as hell to hear about your problems with Paula. What a lovely girl. From what I saw at the Christmas party, you had her a hundred percent snowed. I can't imagine what changed her mind. You think maybe you two can work things out and get back together?"

"Time will tell, I guess," he said evasively.

"Time, hell, don't you believe it, Randall! Time just makes everything good rust out and fall apart. Quick action and a ton of determination make a better combination. That way you either solve problems or clear their debris so something better can replace it. If you love the girl, you damn well better get your shit together and go after her, and if some bastard's trying to steal her, kick his ass into moon orbit and protect what's yours. By the way, Paula called my office yesterday, asking for your new business number. I told the secretaries not to give it out. It's best for me not to get involved with the personal problems of our employees. It may sound hardhearted, but I've learned that a lot of times you can stir up more trouble trying to help than by staying clear. You understand me, don't you, Randal?"

"Absolutely."

Word reached Beaumont before Randall that he was coming back to Texas as Carbone's point man and snoop dog. It made nearly everybody eager to be on his good side but reluctant to say anything the least bit controversial. His conversations with employees were breezy and superficial with little useful information. Only two gave him anything he didn't already know: a thumbs up from Gus Rye, Chief Engineer and a cautionary warning from Hank Ames, Senior Chemist.

"Nah, Randall, Carbone's got nothing to worry about with Riviere," Rye told him. "He's rough as hell around the edges, but Thomas Riviere is a one tough Cajun who came up the hard way. He came out of the Louisiana swamps twenty-five years ago and made a fortune in oil. But he did it the right way. All those rumors about him are pure bullshit spread around by his enemies that weren't smart enough to beat him in straight-up competition."

But that afternoon chemist Hank Ames stopped him in the parking lot with a different message.

"Randall, I saw you talking with Gus. I don't know what he told you, but I wouldn't consider the Chenevert acquisition a done deal until the documents are signed and duly registered with The Texas Railroad Commission."

"Why do you say that, Hank? You know something that Gus didn't tell me, something that Carbone needs to know about?"

"I may be speaking out of turn and getting my tail in a crack, but what the hell. I'm about to retire and at this point I can pretty much speak my mind. There's a rumor going around that Riviere's considering a rival offer from Occidental Chemicals, that California outfit in Sacramento that's been trying to get a piece of the Texas action."

"But Carbone has already given Chenevert a ten-percent earnest money check and Riviere has signed off on an intent-to-sell document."

"Like I said, I'm retiring so it doesn't matter much to me any way you cut it. But if I were in Carbone's shoes, I'd be real careful with Riviere. They say he pulled a stunt like this several years back and squirreled a chunk of earnest money away in some shady Louisiana investment outfit that he probably owned. I think it went to court, but Riviere has connections high up and got the case shifted over to friendly Louisiana jurisdiction in New Orleans. As far as I know, nothing ever came of it. I doubt the US Marines could get the money back now."

At that moment Gus drove by slowly and waved to them.

The next morning Randall kept his scheduled appointment with the rough-faced Riviere. His impressions were negative as they were at their first meeting, even though the Chenevert CEO was jovial and seemed delighted to personally take Randall on another tour of the refinery. Everything seemed to be in line with the company profile that Randall had practically memorized by now—top-flight engineers and chemists, and excellent technicians. There was nothing he could point to, only a nagging intuition that something was not right. He walked back to his car after all the cordiality, wondering what he would say in his report to Carbone that would justify his suspicions.

As he was approaching his car a thin nervous man came at a trot between cars and bumped into him. Several envelopes flew from his hand. Randall kneeled to help him retrieve his letters as the man apologized loudly for his clumsiness, "So sorry, sir; I need to watch where I'm going!" Then he whispered, "keep the brown one! Yes, that one, the brown one!" Still apologizing, he hurried away.

Back in his hotel suite, Randall opened the envelope. The accounting complexities were a challenge for his chemical engineering background, but he got the message: apparently, Riviere, or someone in company leadership, had been systematically skimming funds from the company for the five-year period covered in the document. Bingo! Randall said out loud. This will change the score big time! I knew something was wrong. If this checks out, not only is Riviere in trouble, but we can kiss the acquisition goodbye.

The next morning as he was skimming through the Beaumont newspaper he saw a secondary headline that got his attention:

> **Chenevert Executive Dies in Accident.**
> "Mr. Albert Thacker, Chief Accountant for Chenevert Petroleum and resident of Sabine Pass died in a ferry accident late Thursday in Cameron, Louisiana. A Cameron Parish deputy reported that Mr. Thacker, who had exited his car during the crossing, apparently fell overboard and was struck by the ferry propeller. He was life-flighted to Lake Charles but pronounced dead on arrival."

Was he the same man that slipped me the envelope? Randall wondered. If he was, I may be in water way over my head. His fears were realized that night as he walked from his car to the hotel. Three men rushed out of the darkness and Randall saw the gleam of a knife blade. He reacted instantly with skills learned as a Green Beret. An expert kick to a kneecap sent the knife-wielding smaller man moaning on his back in the grass and clutching his knee. But the larger men pinned his arms and dragged him to the ground.

At that minute two other men came running and took on the pair. Freed, Randall then took one down with a throat chop and the pair left the remaining assailant unconscious on the concrete. The smaller man got to his feet and tried to run but his leg failed him, and he fell screaming in pain. One of the men silenced him with a rap to the head with what looked like an old police billy club.

Hotel management had called the police who showed up with red lights flashing after the fight was over. Randall and his two allies described what happened. The police were skeptical at first, but then a hotel employee who had witnessed the assault corroborated their story. The assailants were hauled away, and Randall started to thank his rescuers.

"Man was I glad to see you gu—," Randall started to say when the two pinned his arms behind him, snapped handcuffs on him, and started pushing him toward a vehicle.

"Hey, wait a minute! Who are you? What are you doing? I thought you came to help me! Why the cuffs? And where are you taking me?"

"You'll find out," one of them said in a menacingly quiet voice. Now shut up and come quietly with us. If you make any more noise around here, I may have to give you a little sample of what that guy got," he said, tapping the club in his palm.

"Okay, you've got my attention. Now can you tell me what's going on?"

"Better than that, we'll show you. We're taking you to see somebody who wants to see you. We'll be there in a few minutes, so just rest. We're not going to hurt you."

A few minutes later they pulled up to the Holiday Inn on Interstate 10 west of town.

"If you promise good behavior, we'll take off the cuffs. But no funny stuff, okay? We recognized that maneuver you put on that thug. Good move. No, a great move. But we had the same training, so we can do the same if you push us."

"You've got my word. I'm gentle as an angel from here on."

"Fine, see that you stay that way," the man said as he removed the cuffs.

They took the elevator to the third floor. Four doors down the hallway they knocked, and a woman opened.

"Paula! What in the world are you doing in Beaumont?"

"Looking for you, Randall. My friends, Jim and Ben, and I have been on a manhunt, and we finally bagged us the big stag. Fellows, this man is the gentlest person in the world. I'm safe with him, so you can leave us. Please?"

The men looked at each other and grinned. "Gentle, lady? Just a few minutes ago we saw this guy take down a crook with a maneuver that any Green Beret would envy. But if you say so."

"I do say so and thank you."

After Jim and Ben left, Randall stood tense and uncertain about what to expect and what to do.

"Please sit down, Randall. We have a lot to talk about."

"How did you find me, Paula?"

"I didn't. Jim and Ben did. Mr. Carbone and his staff wouldn't tell me where you were, but Jim and Ben have their ways. So here I am."

"Jim and Ben are friends of yours? I don't remember them."

"Not really; I hired them. They're private detectives from Atlanta."

"I don't understand any of this."

"That's why I'm here, to explain things to you."

"But what about your new life, your man friend, or lover, whatever he is, and the divorce and all that."

"Randall, I'm looking at my lover, my only lover. He's sitting right here in front of me." All at once Paula's voice broke and her eyes filled with tears. "Oh, Randall, you wonderful man, don't you know I love you with all my heart? There was never any lover, never any divorce, never any thought of murder. And that letter of yours. Oh my God, I thought I would die when I read it! Despite what you thought I had done, that I had deceived you all this time, you were noble and generous with me. If I loved you before, I loved you more when I saw how you took the high road. I knew more than ever before what a prince of a husband I had, a gentleman in every sense of the word. When I realized what you had heard and put it all together, I was horrified. I knew I had to find you before I lost you for good. No matter how long it took, I had to explain what really happened."

"But I did hear the things you said, Paula, and what the man with you said. It . . ."

"What you heard, Randall, was the first part of a CD of one of our rehearsals: Scene I. I was working hard on my role that night. That's what I was going to tell you when you got home. That I got the lead female role in the play, Murder at Twilight, opposite Jeremy Scott. Can you imagine? You've seen him I'm sure, an experienced stage actor—Broadway, Chicago, three cameo film appearances—and a wonderful person on top of it. But, darling, he's nearly twice my age and happily married to wife Miriam and father of two grown children. I had to do my best acting since I was working with one of the best in the business. I played the part for the six Atlanta performances, but each time my heart was breaking, especially in that scene you overheard."

"Then does that mean that you, that we, are . . .?"

"Still married, still in love, still husband and wife. And husband, if you don't take me in your arms and kiss me this very minute, I think I'm just going to die on the spot."

Randall stood and laughed for the first time in days. "Well, let me be a hero and cure this lovely damsel's distress. And mine too. Let me tell you, Paula, you not only have my love but my gratitude. Until today I thought my life was over, but you have saved it tonight in more ways than one. If you and your detective friends hadn't gone on your 'manhunt' and captured me, I'd probably be in the obituary column tomorrow."

Then he took Paula in his arms and they kissed and loved and talked and loved and caressed and loved and promised and laughed and whispered and slept in each other's arms until the night was old and they were young again.

Early the next morning Randall called Jacob on his private line with the news.

"So that Riviere has been cooking the books and stealing from his own company," Carbone said between muttered curses. "I'm not surprised. I warned the Board about him, but all they could see was the money, not the headaches. I had heard about the Occidental gambit. Not to worry. I've scared them off through my contacts out there and dangled the prospect of a merger down the road to give them something better to think about than dealing with that slime ball Riviere."

"That's not all, boss. There may have been a murder and an attempted murder, an accountant for Chenevert who fell off a ferry and got chopped up by the propeller, maybe the same man that gave me the information—not sure of that—and an attempt on the life of one of your employees."

"Which employee?"

"Me. If it hadn't been for a couple of fellows who happened to come along at the right time, I'd probably be dead."

"You're telling me it was connected to the Chenevert matter?"

"I'm guessing so, but I can't prove it. I suppose no one can. I'm thinking though that somebody at Chenevert—maybe Riviere himself—panicked when they learned that Thacker— that's the dead accountant's name—or whoever it was, had turned incriminating information over to me. But I doubt whether the Beaumont police are interested in digging into the assault on me. Beaumont's not a big city, but it's tough, and the police have more to contend with than street brawls without serious injuries."

"Yeah, right. Glad you're okay. But I want you back here as soon as you can make it. Our jet is at DFW Dallas today, and I can have it swing by Houston this afternoon to pick you up at Hobby Airport around three. Okay with that?"

"Sure, it's only an hour and a half drive. This means the acquisition is off, doesn't it?"

"What makes you think so? No, Randall, you're looking at it the wrong way. Let this be a lesson to you for when you're sitting in a chair like mine. Now's the time to go for the jugular, not back away from a golden opportunity. Riviere or somebody over there dug a hole and fell in it. When we tell him that we have a witness to the accountant's murder and that the law is investigating the attack on you, I'm guessing he or somebody there will panic and cave to our conditions. Chenevert Petroleum is basically sound: good people and prime facilities—I have to give Riviere due credit for that. And it's got the reserves and resources to make us a ton of money in the next few years. We'll hit the scandal angle hard and offer him and his board a little less than we said but sweeten his personal pot a bit and agree to overlook any financial or other discrepancies. That'll give him a way out of troubles and messy investigations, and a comfortable lump of cash to boot. That way he can run back to the swamp a rich, respected man, eat crawdads and alligator steaks, and live like a Cajun king until he's ready for his next scam."

"You said we have a witness to the accountant's murder, if it really was a murder in the first place. What witness are you talking about?"

"I said, if you had listened carefully, Randall, that we'd <u>tell</u> him about a witness. I didn't say we actually had one. I'm guessing he's rattled and not thinking straight. As for the attack on you, hell, for all we and they know, the Beaumont police could still be looking into it and there could be indictments. Now, any more items before I'm off to meet with my screwy Board?"

"Just a couple."

"What are they?"

"For one, I'll have to leave my car over here if I fly back today."

"No problem. Just leave it in airport parking and we'll have somebody drive it back to Atlanta. And what's the other?"

"An extra passenger for the flight back to Atlanta."

"And who would that be?"

"Paula, my wife. We're back together."

"Congratulations, Randall. I'm happy for both of you. You came through on all fronts. And there could be more good news when you get back to Atlanta. But we don't have to rush things all that much. In fact, if you and Paula want to drive back at your leisure, we'll cancel the Houston detour. That way you can take the rest of the week off and I'll see you on Monday. Okay with that?"

"Sounds great. Thanks."

"Okay. Till then enjoy and stay steady, my man."

*****

Post Script: A year later Randall and Paula moved to Beaumont when he was named Vice President and CEO of the newly acquired Chenevert Division of Phillips Chemicals in Texas. Both are active in church and civic affairs, and as new motherhood duties permit, Paula is involved in regional theatre. They named their three-month old son Henry B. Wheeler. Henry for Randall's father, and B for Beaumont, where by Paula's arithmetic likely he got his start in life.

The Reluctant Virgin

On a country road in western Louisiana far from any sizable town but almost within sight of the Texas border there once stood a modest Catholic chapel. In the waning years of the 19th century and early years of the 20th it attracted believers and skeptics alike, drawn by supernatural claims about an exquisite golden icon which the faithful called "The Reluctant Virgin." The revered icon surely has a much longer history, but the chapters known to us began in March of 1794 during the revolutionary "Reign of Terror" in France.

*****

Lashing his tiring horse a bare league ahead of blood-mad revolutionaries crying for his head, young Count Henri de la Haye reached the Roncevaux Pass in the High Pyrenees Mountains. Riding fresh mounts, his pursuers were soon within sight and closing fast on their intended victim. But luckier in these same dark defiles than legendary Count Roland a thousand years earlier in the reign of Charlemagne, Henri barely outraced them to the border and emerged at last into the relative safety of Spain.

Other members of his family were not so fortunate. Like thousands of other French aristocrats, the de la Haye line, proud descendants of the Valois princes, fell like harvest wheat under the strokes of the busy guillotine. Among the victims were his young wife and infant son snatched away and executed in the middle of the night. He alone was left, and that by a happenstance that many would call miraculous. But that story we must leave for another telling.

The grieving aristocrat made his way to San Sebastián where he boarded a vessel carrying dozens of noble French families into exile in Louisiana. Of landed properties, now he had none; of possessions, few; but among these was a wondrously wrought icon of the Virgin Mary that in happier times reflected both the devout piety of the de la Haye family and the artistic splendor of Renaissance Italy. Many believed the beautiful figurine was the work of the great Cellini himself. Yet the de la Hayes claimed the icon came not from Italy but was brought from the Holy Land by one of their Crusader ancestors centuries earlier.

In time Count de la Haye joined the colony of exiles in St. Martinville on the Bayou Teche, where as far as resources permitted they reconstituted the genteel life they had known in the glorious, decadent France of King Louis XVI. In little St. Martinville they organized operas, parties, plays, and balls, and fancied themselves again in glittering Versailles half a world away.

But unlike many of his countrymen, Count Henri de la Haye soon realized that life in *La Louisiane* could not be simply a make-believe continuation of old France. Here, he discovered, titles and family meant very little. The Acadians (or Cajuns, as the Americans would call them in a later era), among whom they had settled, were rudely democratic and egalitarian, and their French lacked the polished elegance of their Parisian speech. Even worse in the eyes of the aristocrats, they had the disturbing tendency to judge people on their personal qualities, not on ancestral pedigree.

It was more than some of his compatriots could bear, and they thought of nothing else but returning to France, which most of them did in time. But Count Henri embraced the new country and the challenge of a new life. To the strong disapproval of his aristocratic countrymen, he dropped his title and shortened his surname, becoming simply Henri Lahaye. Not only that, but two years later he married an Acadian girl and began life with her on his Vermilion plantation, which he purchased with a combination of generous credit and the modest monetary assets slipped out of France. Within three years his wife blessed him with a son. Not only was he again a father but also a working planter who labored with his own hands, a thing unthinkable for a highborn aristocrat in his native France.

But though a changed man in this new land, he did not change everything. His ancestral piety and devotion to his religious heritage continued and perhaps even intensified, at least in gratitude. For Henri prospered in his new country and condition, and his wife bore him many more children. By 1820 he was one of the richest men in Louisiana. His religious devotion took on a visible aspect. He commissioned the building of an impressive chapel for family worship but made it available also to his workers and slaves, whose numbers, despite his wife's objections to slavery, grew apace with his wealth and prosperity. Not only pious but generous, he sponsored frequent masses and soon added residential quarters for itinerant priests.

The golden icon of the Holy Mother became an object of especial veneration in the chapel, and the belief spread that miracles of healing often occurred in her presence.

Like a biblical patriarch, Henri died in 1850 "old and full of years." His eldest son Augustin took over the vast Lahaye estates. Though less overtly pious than his father, Augustin surpassed him in astuteness of mind and generosity of spirit. Under his guiding hand, the Lahaye estates prospered even more.

So it was that the Lahayes of the New World regained the equivalent of their de la Haye ancestors in the Old. But within a few years it was all destined to change, including the fate of the golden icon.

When the Civil War broke out, the Lahayes cast their lot with the Confederacy. Augustin himself raised and commanded a company of dragoons under General Beauregard. They were decimated at Atlanta, and Augustin himself was killed. His brother René replaced him as head of the Lahaye properties. But only for a few months. After the surrender of the Confederate armies, brigands and former slaves plundered the Lahaye holdings and burned its buildings, including the chapel. Thus, the terror of revolutionary France was revisited on a new Lahaye generation.

Seeing that all hope was lost, René buried the golden icon and refused to reveal its location even under torture and eventual strangulation at the hands of the outlaws. The few Lahaye survivors fled for their lives, their properties passed into other hands, and the stories of the icon and its miracles faded into legend.

A generation passed.

*****

In August of 1888 Douglas Cotton, owner of the old Lahaye planation, hired Bob Terrell to enclose the site of the chapel with barbed wire. Cotton was religiously indifferent, and it annoyed him to see "superstitious Catholics," as he called them, trampling his property, praying for some residual blessing from an icon stolen or destroyed many years earlier.

Bob hated work of any kind, and none more so than digging

post holes in rock-hard gumbo soil in the hot, dry summer. But he needed all the money he could lay hands on. Within a month at most Bob planned to strike out for Texas.

Not that intended to go alone. His mistress, Annie Scroggins by name, would accompany him. He and Annie had gone over their plans several times and self-righteously compiled a list of reasons to justify their illicit love affair. She complained of her preacher husband's suffocating moral rules and restrictions that sucked every last jot of joy out of her. Women were by nature perverse, Amos Scroggins preached and cited the stories of Eve and Jezebel to prove his case. He even reproached himself for desiring her and occasionally giving in to his own carnal urges.

*****

"Honey, Amos tells me all the time I'm a whore, says that all women are, and he makes me feel like one," she complained to Bob. "Then he expects me to act like a saint in front of the church people."

As for Bob, he was tired of farming, tired of his stringy-haired wife who complained day and night and pretended sickness whenever the possibility of intimacy came up. Not that he really wanted intimacy with her, he hastened to assure Annie.

"Besides all that, she can't cook a lick," Bob groused, "and you never heard a woman moan and groan every time I take a notion to have a little drink."

"She just don't know how to appreciate a good man," Annie assured him with a giggle and a kiss, "but, lordy, I do every time we're together."

In short, to hear them tell it, neither was to blame for the failure of their respective marriages. They convinced each other that they deserved better and with a clear conscience could run away for a happy life together.

Bob grinned as he considered his prospects, including a deal he had dreamed up to cheat miserly Douglas Cotton out of some extra money for their Texas escape. The day before he had offered to sell his wagon and team to Cotton for the ridiculously low price of fifty dollars. The shrewd Cotton considered the deal, but first had to know why Bob wanted to sell.

"Aw, Mr. Cotton, I reckon I'm gonna get out of farming and go into the logging business, and it'll be a help to me if you can take them off my hands."

"Well, Bob, I tell you what. I'll buy them from you, but I won't give you a nickel over forty dollars. That's my only offer. You can take it or leave it."

"Mr. Cotton, you know as well as I do that my wagon and team is worth way more than forty dollars. But I'm in a tight and under the circumstances I reckon I'll take the money. Only thing I ask is that you pay me now so's I can clear up some debts. And one more thing: if you could see your way clear to let me haul some stuff over to my new place. It won't take me but two or three days to move the stuff and get the wagon and team back to you. And I'll finish the postholes tomorrow before I leave."

Cotton grumbled about releasing the money before he had property in hand, but the deal was too profitable to turn down. Reluctantly he decided to trust him. Terrell, of course, had no intention of keeping the bargain.

The next day Bob was chuckling to himself over the deal when the posthole diggers struck an object. At first, he thought it was a cluster of clam shells or a chunk of rock salt that sometimes turned up in the area, but as he dug around it with his hands, metal began to gleam. When he reached to pick it up, he realized that it was too heavy for rock salt or clam shells. Then it hit him: the gold icon! He had heard stories about it but always supposed like everybody else that no one would ever find it again.

His first impulse was to take the icon and run home with it. But then on second thought, somebody might spot it. No, better to stay calm, he told himself. The best thing was to cover it with dirt and leave it where it had been all these years. He and Annie would pick it up on the way to Texas.

The icon changed their plans. Instead of waiting any longer, they would get started that very night, if Annie could slip out of her house.

It so happened that Amos had to go on a pastoral visit that night, which made it easy for Annie to get away with most of her clothes and some of her things. They loaded her things in the wagon and giddy with excitement, headed for the icon. With that much gold they could start life in style out in Texas. And Cotton's forty dollars would help.

Everything went as planned. Bob hopped out of the wagon and retrieved the icon, wrapping it in a sack and hiding it under their belongings. Then he jumped in the wagon, popped the mules with the leather reins, and they were off.

They rode for three days, nervously looking over their shoulder and camping only when both they and the team had to rest and take food. Now though they were beginning to breathe a bit easier. In fact, by the third day Bob thought they had already crossed the Texas border. But he did not know the region and had mistaken a bayou for the upper Sabine River. They were still in Louisiana. In any case, Annie, who suffered from exhaustion and diarrhea all day, begged him to stop for the night.

At daylight the next day they were ready to make their way

deeper into Texas. Bob rapped the mules with the reins and they lunged forward. But the wagon did not move. He lashed the mules harder. The wagon creaked but did not budge. Bob jumped down to see what was blocking the wagon wheel. He saw nothing. He shortened the reins in his left hand and used the loose ends with his right to give the mules a severe lashing. They strained forward; their harness squeaked, but still the wagon did not move.

"What is it, honey? Why won't the wagon move?" Annie asked nervously.

"I'll be goddamned if I know, woman!" Bob snapped. Annie's maladies, complaints, and the stresses of running away were getting on his nerves.

Annie was shocked and hurt. Bob had never cursed in her presence or spoken to her in that tone of voice.

Bob beat and cursed the mules, but they could not move the wagon. He was still alternately cursing, whipping, and pleading with the team hours later when Douglas Cotton and half a dozen of his men and a couple of deputies overtook them.

Bob protested indignantly to the amused posse that they were in Texas and beyond the reach of Louisiana law.

"You would be, Terrell, if you had made it a few more miles," Cotton informed him as he unstrung a bullwhip from his saddle. "But you're still in Louisiana, and you're gonna stay in Louisiana till I decide whether to hang you from the nearest tree or skin you alive with this whip. The deputies here don't care one way or another. They said it was up to me."

Their runaway scheme now in shambles, Annie and Bob each tried to blame the other. Bob, she said, had begged her to go with him to Texas, had forced her into the wagon and stopped her every time she tried to get away. Bob said it was the other way around, that she had played up to him and talked him into something he never really wanted to do. The more they accused each other the more the men grinned and fingered their ropes and whips.

Still, it was a mystery to all why the wagon would not move. For Cotton and his men had no better luck than Bob. Finally, the reason, but not a rational explanation, was discovered when they uncovered the icon and removed it from the wagon. Without it the mules easily moved the wagon. With it, the team could not budge it. Suddenly Robert Hebert of the Catholic faith, spoke in a hushed, awe-filled voice:

"The Holy Mother doesn't want to be moved from this place. This is where she wants to be. The old people tell of things like this happening in other places. Mr. Cotton, the icon is legally yours and I take orders from you, have for going on ten years, but if I was in your place, I wouldn't try to go against powers that are bigger than all of us. And one more thing: she stopped Bob and Annie from doing more dirt."

Nobody could argue with Hebert, not even skeptical Douglas Cotton. While he was mulling over his options word of "the reluctant Virgin" spread quickly throughout the area. A delegation of Catholic faithful led by a priest appeared and asked to speak with Cotton. They had quickly found a wealthy sponsor and several dozen contributors, Father Pierre Landry informed him, and were willing to pay him anything within their means for the right to the icon. Cotton reasoned that since apparently the statue could not be moved—though he was still unwilling to admit it had anything to do with the supernatural—he would hear their best offer.

"Too low," he said without hesitation when they offered. "Add a thousand dollars and she's yours."

Father Landry paled over the amount, but after several moments of whispered consultation with his parishioners, he nodded and smiled. "It's more money than we have, Mr. Cotton, but not more than our faith. At the moment I cannot tell you where the extra thousand will come from, only that we are certain God will provide. Give us till sundown."

Father Landry's conviction came true. The money was collected and paid, and the deal was done. The Virgin had found her residence. By chance, or otherwise, this event, both sublime and sordid, occurred on land already belonging to one of parishioners who donated acreage for a new sanctuary. In the meantime, Robert Hebert asked permission to stay several days, alternating with local men to stand guard over the icon until better provisions for her dignity and safety could be made.

As for Annie, they allowed her to walk home to Amos, to whom she made her lying excuses. To her surprise, he did not punish her, at least not physically. Hadn't he always said that women were whores by nature anyway? There's the proof, he said. Later she was obliged listen to Amos preach embarrassing sermons on the topic.

After horsewhipping Bob to within an inch of his life, Cotton offered to let him live, provided he surrender the forty dollars along with the wagon and team. Bob bellowed his acceptance of the terms and thus ended up poorer than before, losing the respect and earning the scorn of everyone in the Vermilion region. But he had not lost everything: he still had the same stringy-haired wife who now had more reasons than ever to whine and nag.

As for the immovable icon, for many years she remained in her place of honor and veneration in her sanctuary, where she moved multitudes to a deeper faith and, if the accounts are true, occasionally healed the lives and cured the maladies of certain people.

Then one night in 1922 the sanctuary burned to the ground. Robert Hebert, who spent his later years seeing after the Sanctuary and protecting the golden icon, could not explain how the fire started. He and others searched through the debris but did not find the icon. No one ever knew for certain what happened to it. Many believed it was stolen, but Robert had a different opinion.

"She finished her work in this place," he said sadly but firmly. "I know in my heart she has gone on somewhere else, somewhere where people are suffering and need her help."

The End of Time

On Friday morning, June 17, 1948 a decrepit 1931 ton and a half Chevrolet truck with a Tennessee tag crawled like a crippled beetle up Higdon Mountain in northeast Alabama. Reaching the top, the driver pulled over in a cloud of blue smoke and hissing steam from the uncapped radiator.

"Hey, honey, we made it up that mountain and we're nearly there!" Herschel Benefield, 23, said excitedly to his new wife Maxine, 21. "Higdon's Crossroads is about two miles ahead, and my Uncle Charlie Hardin's place is just this side of it, white cinderblock house on the right."

"Well, I'm glad. I was scared to death on that steep curve down there that this old wreck was going to stall and roll backwards off that bluff with us in it."

"Yeah, I was too, honey, to tell you the truth. Ole Ed Higdon that lives across from that curve tells about a lot of accidents, and a good many end up in his yard or garden. We lucked out, but I betcha we burned a quart of oil coming up that stretch, and probably half the water leaked or boiled out of the radiator after the cap blew off. Now we'll have to wait here till the engine cools off, then try to make it on to Uncle Charlie's house. I just hope we can get there before this ole rattletrap dies on us completely. I've poured all the oil and water I brought with us into the thing, but with the radiator leaking the way it is and the oil about gone, the engine block could crack or freeze up. And if it does, that's all she wrote."

"Herschel, we have to get there this morning. If we don't have

Reverend Forest's tent set up and the signs out when he gets here tomorrow, there'll be holy hell to pay, and me and you'll do the paying. You've seen how he gets when things don't go the way he wants them to. Besides all that to worry about, I'm about to starve and I need to go to the toilet real bad."

"Don't you worry none, honey. We'll have Malcolm's ole tent and signs up and ready. And you can wait a little while longer on breakfast. But if you can't hold out on your other business, you can do like I'm fixing to—head out yonder to the bushes."

"Hershel, I'm not going to squat down like an ole hen out there in the woods and get chiggers and spiders all over me. I'll wait till we get to a proper toilet."

"Suit yourself," he said as he trotted off toward the bushes.

Like a balky mule, the old truck refused to budge when Hershel came back to start it.

"Dadburn thing's still too hot. We'll have to let it cool off some more."

But when Maxine complained again about breakfast and the toilet, he ran the battery down trying to start it and had to get out the old crank he kept under the seat. After hand cranking the engine until his arm was nearly ready to fall off, there was a promising sputter.

"Pump the foot-feed a couple o' times, Maxine! But don't flood the carburetor!" he yelled excitedly. "I think she's about to crank up!"

Sure enough, the old engine belched and backfired, then began firing on four or five of its straight-six cylinders.

"What's wrong with it?" Maxine asked as Herschel hurriedly pitched the crank under the seat and slid behind the wheel. "What's making it skip like that?"

"Well, in my expert opinion, honey bunch, just about anything you want to name. But let's get moving while it's still running."

A mile ahead, steam and smoke started swirling again, and as Herschel pulled into the dirt lane to Charlie's house the engine clanged, backfired, and died. He clutched it, shifted to neutral, and let it come to rest astraddle two rows of Charlie's cotton.

"Here we are, sweetheart, we made it to Uncle Charlie's!" Herschel said with a hearty laugh, banging his fist in triumph on the metal dashboard. "Well, just about made it. We ended up around a hundred yards shy of Uncle Charlie's house you see up there on the hill. But it's the end of the road for this ole wreck. For one thing I think it may have just slung a rod and it's mired up to the axles in this cotton patch. Come on, doll, you run for that toilet behind the house and I'll go rouse up Uncle Charlie's folks and see if they can scrounge us up some breakfast!"

As for the old Chevrolet, it sat there for weeks axle-deep in the cotton patch, one corner of its bed sticking out a bit into the lane, until the events in this story were over.

*****

Late the next afternoon a powerful 1947 black Buick Roadmaster whined effortlessly up the same highway and pulled into Charlie's front yard. Charlie, wife Noxie, sons Henry and Jasper, and Maxine came out to greet evangelist Malcolm Forest.

"Welcome to Higdon's Crossroads, Reverend Forest," Charlie said, extending his hand. "We're so glad you could come down from Tennessee to hold a revival here in our community."

Malcolm ignored Charlie's offer of a handshake; instead he folded his long arms across his chest and addressed Maxine.

"Maxine, come here. I have some questions for you."

"Yes sir, Reverend, what is it?"

"Where's Herschel?"

"Oh, didn't you see him? He's down yonder working on the truck. It broke down on us."

"I've told that husband of yours how to take care of that vehicle, but with him it's in one ear and out the other."

"He thinks it may have slung a rod."

"Amid all the breakdowns and rod-slinging, did he get the tent up and the signs posted according to my instructions?"

"We did, Reverend Forest," Charlie broke in, "me and my boys hauled the tent and equipment in my truck this morning and set it up down at the crossroads and got the signs posted all over the community."

"I didn't see any on my way in."

"We put up all we had."

"Maxine, that means you forget to put the extra batch in the truck. Didn't I tell you they were on my desk?"

"Yes sir, you did. I'm sorry. We got in a hurry and went off and left them."

"The work of the Kingdom requires diligence and attention to detail.

You're a married woman now, Maxine, not a girl any more. I pay you and Herschel to work responsibly in the ministry. See that you both do so, or changes may become necessary."

"Yes, sir," she said, hanging her head.

Forest turned to Charlie. "Charlie Hardin, you say your name is, I need information on certain points."

"Yes sir, I'm Charlie, this here's my wife Noxie, and our two boys over there are Henry and Jasper. We're all ready to help in any way we can. Noxie here can do—"

"You can start by pointing out my quarters," he said, cutting Charlie off. "I was told it's a separate building a bit away from the house."

"Yes, sir. It's that little house you see down yonder past the garden. My mother lived there till she passed away last yea—"

"It will have to do," Malcolm said, ignoring anything else Charlie had to say. "After I take my early supper, see that no one disturbs me until tomorrow. It is important for me to study the Scriptures, pray, and align myself with the movement of the Holy Ghost. We must all be ready tomorrow to begin our pressing Kingdom work."

"Yes, sir," Charlie said with subdued awe in his tone. Forest's baritone voice had startling, unexpected inflections and rumbled like distant thunder. Even the most trivial things he said got people's attention like an oracle of the Almighty. There was no Southern small talk in the man, and his brusque manner and overwhelming presence had everybody scrambling to please him.

His description followed suit. Picture an exceptionally tall, lean man of fifty or so with long, sinewy arms; large, heavily veined hands; and thick, rebellious salt-and-pepper hair that stuck out at odd angles as though a storm had whipped it into permanent chaos. Combine these features with a long, hooked nose; boney face and corded neck; bushy untrimmed eyebrows; and intense black eyes set close together, which, to quote one awestruck woman, "can look holes right through you." In a way that no one in Higdon's Crossroads ever thought to put into words, Malcolm Forest reminded them of an Old Testament prophet, newly stepped out of the Bible into this lesser world to thunder forth divine judgments and warn of wrathful punishments.

By the end of the day Higdon's Crossroads was a beehive of buzzing gossip as the excitement built steadily toward evangelist Malcolm Forest's opening sermon Sunday night.

"I hear tell that three hundred people got saved at his last revival up in East Tennessee, somewhere close to that town called Cleveland." Mabel Jenkins said to her cousin Clovis Maccabee.

"Yeah, I heard that too," Clovis said. Some say it was more like four hundred and that it's like that at all his revivals. I went down to the crossroads a while ago to look at that revival tent, and I betcha it will hold four hundred people. But I don't know where in the world they'll find that many folding chairs."

"Oh, they say they've rented them from the school, now that it's out for the summer. The question is, will there be folks to sit in them? How many people you reckon will show up?"

"I couldn't even guess, but everybody I've talked to says they're going. And I reckon we'll go too."

"You going to regular church in the morning?"

"Yeah, I reckon so. What about y'all?"

"I guess so, though Fred's already grumbling about the revival, says that going to church every day of the week and twice on Sunday is a little too much. "He says if we keep this up we'll be sprouting angel wings and sporting halos. You know how he likes to make fun of nearly everything except them old radio programs he listens to all the time, specially the ones on Sunday evenings."

"Mabel, you need to tell your ole rascal of a husband to quit listening to those sinful programs and spend more time reading the Bible and thinking about spiritual matters, specially on Sunday."

"You tell him that, Clovis. I've tried for the longest to get him to stop his smart-alecky talk and turn off some of those old shows; and had about as much luck as I would learning pigs to fly."

Paul Yates, Pastor of Higdon's Crossroads Holiness Church, was probably the only person worried about revival instead of being simply excited or indifferent. He had seen other revivalists leave communities confused by false teachings and sometimes in spiritual shambles. In fact, he had done his best to rebuild the Holiness Church in Higdon's Crossroads after a split five years earlier under the former minister when half the congregation left over the doctrine of "double damnation." He knew from painful experience that theological controversies were like a fire in dry grass: easy to start, hard to stop, and impossible to undo completely.

That Sunday church attendance was down to thirty-five, half the usual number. He was apprehensive about the revival, but nothing could have prepared Preacher Yates and Higdon's Crossroads for what was coming.

*****

Higdon's Crossroads, 7 pm, Sunday, June 20, 1948: 440 souls scrouged in the revival tent eagerly awaited the arrival of Evangelist Malcolm Forest. 7:10: fifteen more people pushed their way in. Young men and boys gave their chairs to women and elderly folks and sat on the grass inside or outside the tent; no sign of the evangelist. 7:15; still no Forest. Then, at 7:18 the tent flaps behind the makeshift pulpit parted, and to a low murmur of excitement and intense scrutiny, in stepped black-clad Malcolm Forest. Striding to the pulpit that elevated him several feet above the congregation, looking neither to his right nor to his left, he laid an enormous Bible on the pulpit. Then for a long moment he studied the upturned faces in silence, and when the tension, silence, and apprehension had reached their dramatic peak, he spoke. And this is what he said:

"Men and women of Higdon's Crossroads, I read on your faces and discern in your thoughts that you have come here tonight expecting to be entertained. Know from the start, lest there be misunderstanding of my mission, that entertainment is not my purpose. Far from it. I am come not to amuse you but by the grace of God to bring you a message of extreme urgency. Why you were chosen first to hear the message God has given me, I cannot say. The Almighty works in mysterious ways and seldom where and when we think He will. Consider yourselves blessed that He has chosen this community. Yet know of a certainty that mine is not a soothing oracle of peace but of certain doom and inescapable destruction for those unwilling to heed the warning that God has decreed should be told here. But for others, perhaps fewer in number, yet wiser and more willing in spirit, this is a message of divine love and a chance for salvation. A last chance. By what I shall say to you tonight you will be convicted in your understanding, mortified in your spirit, chastened in your soul, and for those enslaved by sin, frightened out of your wits. How you respond tells how you stand with God in the closing days of this world and in eternity thereafter. For I bring you a revelation of the last days, the end of time, as it was foreshadowed by the prophets of old, foretold in the very words of our Lord and Savior Jesus Christ, and now at the end of time made known to you."

The evangelist paused and turned his face upward as though caught up in some enrapturing vision. The congregants held their breath. Then he turned a page of his Bible, concentrated on it for a moment, and spoke in a tone differently modulated and in a much lower register that nevertheless had its own intensity and penetrating power.

"Men and women of Higdon's Crossroads, think not that you can conceal from me your sinful thoughts and wicked deeds. God has given me the gift of discernment. What you would hide in your sinful hearts and keep from public notice God makes evident to me. Lest you doubt me, I shall tell of sinful dealings but give no names. For I was not sent here to accuse, nor to excuse, even less to belittle, but to preach repentance before time runs out. Tonight, a man sits among you who makes light of the Christian faith and prefers his paltry worldly amusements to the majestic saving grace of Christ, from which he drifts ever further as his mockery of the faith grows more disrespectful. Another, who knows that I have read his heart, claims a good name in the community but lately sold an ailing animal to a trusting neighbor. Still another today committed adultery with his neighbor's wife. And the young woman who took money from the elderly woman's purse must return it at once. All these and others have placed themselves in peril of hell fire. All these transgressions must stop and stop now. For here at the very edge of world doom, you risk damnation by committing them. And I tell you that little time is left to repent of them. In each case and in others unmentioned, you know who you are and how you have sinned. I know who you are and could call you by name if I chose. But most important of all, God knows who you are and what you have done. And he will soon call you by a name that only he knows to give an account of your deeds. For God created you and knows you much more than you know yourself. If you have not repented of your sins on that great and terrible day of the Lord when Jesus returns to judge the world, he will cast you into the flames of hell. That day draws ever nearer; the clock ticks away the brief hours and minutes that remain. On that day no sin will remain hidden. For as the Bible says, everything hidden shall be revealed. Even now the dark shroud of sinful concealment is being lifted and evil deeds are coming to light."

Once again Evangelist Forest did a panoramic scan of the faces as the agitated congregation privately squirmed while individually trying their best to appear outwardly calm and, above all, innocent. All felt guilty, for all had fallen short. It was as though they had been exposed publicly in the nude for all the world to see their nakedness. There seemed to be nowhere to hide from this evangelist who claimed to know at a glance every ugly thing hidden in their life. Now Forest resumed his sermon with the full-throated resonance of his powerful voice:

"Men and brethren, what shall we do?" he cried in a vibrating rumble, almost a roar, that petrified the congregation. "This was the cry that went up in Jerusalem when the people realized to their horror and despair that they had crucified the Savior of the world. And it is the cry of all people over the ages who must finally confess on their knees that by sinning and shunning God they have taken their evil part in the suffering and death of Christ. Let all in the sound of my voice know that the answer to their question remains the same now as it was then: Repent and be baptized every one of you in the name of Jesus Christ for the remission of your sins. The Apostle Peter announced in the Book of Acts the mighty consequence arising from this repentance: 'And ye shall receive the gift of the Holy Ghost.' But hear this and heed: mankind's circumstances are more straitened in our day. We live at a different time in history, a time that grows very short. It has been revealed to me that the end of time is fast approaching. Therefore, we must act, you must act, and act quickly, before the short count of days runs out. Tomorrow and in the following days we have left, I shall tell you in stages what God has revealed to me about the last day and when it will come, yes, when it will happen. That knowledge, hidden for ages, God has also made known to me. I shall not tell you today when it will happen, for you would panic and serve neither man nor God in your terror. It is a secret, a burden, that I alone must keep until all things are in readiness. Step by step according to God's plan we must prepare ourselves for the end. And the first step is this: those of you who are sunk in the satanic wickedness of this world must repent and be washed in the cleansing blood of the Lamb. If you do this and receive baptism, your sins will be forgiven you in time to avoid the everlasting fires of hell. But do not wait, there is no time left for waiting. Waiting itself becomes a sin; to wait is to risk agonizing torture forever in merciless, pitiless, red hot hell! Come, therefore, to this altar, which though rough and unadorned like the stable where Jesus was born, yet as a rude manger served him when he came into the world, so this rough altar can serve us now as we make ready to leave it. For the servants cannot presume to be better than their Master. Therefore, come! Come and be gathered into the blessed fellowship of God and his Kingdom! Come, come quickly to the altar while you may!"

Under the magic of his seductive voice and finely crafted phraseology, the congregants quickly flocked to the altar, succumbing to his rhetorical skills and vivid verbal imagery. Whether they were now fully committed to God we cannot know, but obviously by the time the service ended, they were, without apparent exceptions, fully under the hypnotic control of

Malcolm Forest. They came forward by dozens and by scores to kneel at the altar, sobbing and sorrowful, joyful and jubilant, stricken and repentant, praying and praising.

An hour, two hours, and nearly three passed. For the congregation, the revival experience was too life-altering to let the mundane pressures and petty realities of common chores reclaim their attention. When the last congregants finally filed out, aflame with divine arousal, the wee hours of the morning had begun. A later generation might describe the dramatic advent of evangelist Malcolm Forest as a "paradigm shift" for Higdon's Crossroads. But that kind of sophisticated language and analytical thinking it implied lay many years in the future. The present hour was both compressed and expanded beyond all markers of conventional time. Everything they had ever done, thought to do, or failed to do culminated that evening.

The next night over five hundred people—nearly all the residents of Higdon's Crossroads—filled the tent and spilled out across an open field to the edge of the east-west Henson Road at its intersection with north-south Higdon Highway. Again, and with even greater fervor, they responded to Malcolm Forest's evangelical wizardry as enthusiasm fed on a flood of thrilling fears and rising expectations. After the sermon, upwards of a hundred fifty came forward and knelt at, or near, the roughhewn oaken altar, there to place their immortal destiny in the hands of the Almighty. Services the following nights were even longer and of greater intensity. By midweek the sermonizing, singing, testifying, and weeping extended into the early morning hours. On Thursday several congregants began to speak in tongues; others writhed on the ground lost in ecstasy, as drunk on supernatural illumination as the buzzing insects were intoxicated by the brilliance of the swaying electric lights. The stale tent air, which might have gagged neutral observers with its rancid odor of sweaty, unbathed bodies packed together in the mid-summer Alabama heat, to the enraptured worshipers seemed filled with a divine grace flowing down from supernal realms.

After ten days of revival, Malcolm and the strongest Elders baptized more than three hundred souls in Earl Powell's cattle pond. Herschel lined them up in proper order, men and boys in one line and women and girls in the other. Maxine had towels ready for them as they emerged dripping from the water. Later, after changing into dry clothes in separate sections of Earl's barn, the congregation prayed, sang, and devoured a mountain of food the women had prepared.

But with evangelical success came the practical problem of space. The revival tent was much too small as people began pouring in from other communities. So far, the next wave of expected summer rains had held off, and some, who now thought to sense a divine nerve in everything, said it was a miracle. No one spoke openly against the notion, but some pointed out that since miracles are the unpredictable acts of God and not subject to the will of men, why not consider a practical solution to the problem: the Holiness Church? It stood empty as the congregation, along with nearly the whole community, was swept up in revival fervor. Some noticed that Pastor Yates had not attended the services and took his absence to be disapproval.

"We need to ask Preacher Yates where he stands," said newly repentant Fred Jenkins. "Any preacher that won't attend services like we're having has got to have something wrong with his religion."

"I agree we need to find out where he stands," Charlie Hardin said, "but let's not judge him until the Church Elders speak to him."

"Well, that's fine by me, but I still say it's a community disgrace to have that big church standing up there empty, and all these folks down here crowded in a tent or sitting out there on the ground."

Charlie had a sudden inspiration: "Why don't we ask Reverend Forest what he thinks about it. I think it would be best to do what he says. The Lord gives him direct inspiration."

The idea gained traction as the day went on, and late that afternoon a delegation of elders, plus Fred Jenkins, Charlie Hardin, and his brother Melvin showed up at the revivalist's cottage to seek his counsel.

"Men, this is a matter best settled among yourselves," Forest told them. "The early Church chose deacons and elders to deal with practical matters like this, while the Apostles busied themselves with teaching and spreading the Gospel. We are charged in our late time to do likewise: I to preach the Gospel, you to lend support. But since you have disrupted my daily prayer and meditation, I will remind you also of what you seem to have forgotten: that the earth is the lord's and the fullness thereof. The cattle on a thousand hills and the fruit of the fertile valleys are his. From this the principle should be clear to you: He has universal dominion over his creation and prior claim to whatever is needful for his purposes. On this principle you need to make all your decisions. And I advise you to do so."

"Does that mean we need to move the revival into the church building?" wondered elder Earl Powell as they walked back to their vehicles.

"That's what Reverend Forest just told us, aint it?" fellow

elder Jacob Hendrix commented, "unless I misunderstood him. Sometimes it's hard for me to understand some of the words he uses, and the way he uses them. But I know he speaks the truth."

"Well, to me there's no two ways about it," said Fred. "That's exactly what the Reverend meant, though he was talking Bible principles, not specifics. Now you men are the church elders and have the say so, but if I was in your place, I'd vote to take over the church for the Lord's work. And since Pastor Yates has not been to a single revival service that we know of, I'd tell him that he needs either to join in or get outta the way."

When these choices were put to Pastor Yates in more polite language, he reached in his pocket and pulled out the church keys. "Here you are, men," he said, handing them to Earl Powell. "I'll have a letter of resignation ready for you in the morning."

"A letter won't be necessary, Paul. We know you're a man of your word. Truth is, we wish you'd stay and be a part of what's going on in this community."

"If I thought it was God's work, I would be the first in line, but I'm afraid it's something else."

"Like what? Earl asked.

"I won't say more than I've said, Earl, and I'll have that letter ready in the morning."

"I am truly sorry you feel that way, Paul. But if you do, then I guess it's best you leave. But we don't need a letter."

"But I do, Earl. I prefer to do things in proper order. We all understand how things stand now, but other people down the road might not and there could be misunderstandings."

"Well, if that's the way you feel about it, then we'll do it your way, and we'll treat you right on the money."

"I'll make today's date my last paid day as Pastor, if that's all right with you elders."

"We can add something in appreciation for what you've done for the community."

"That's good of you, Earl, but no. You may discover that you'll need the money much more than I do. I can manage; I hope the community can."

With Pastor Yates gone, the tent came down and services shifted to the church building. Even though it was also too small to hold the burgeoning crowds, the century-old sheltered eating areas on the east and south sides could handle most of the overflow. Although the setup was by no means ideal, with the church windows and doors open and Malcolm Forest's mighty voice, good ears could hear his message at least a quarter mile away on a quiet evening. Overall, the new location was more impressive than the bare crossroads venue and lent an appearance of permanence to what started out as a week-long revival.

The move seemed providential, for as the allotted week wound down the congregants clamored for an extension and begged Forest not to leave them. He was coming tantalizingly closer to telling them his full and final revelations. Still he would not rush.

"These revelations, hidden for ages, cannot be revealed in haste," Forest cautioned. "Everything must proceed by steps and stages according to God's timing, not ours. In that regard, my plan was to conclude this revival this Sunday. But man proposes, and God disposes. And we must yield to His will, not insist on imposing ours. My work here is not finished. For that reason, dear brothers and sisters of Higdon's Crossroads, I shall remain among you perhaps to the end of this world, for time is truly short. His will be done for us all. He is the Potter; we are the clay, and by his hand he shall shape our destiny as he will."

July entered its second week, but instead of devoting themselves to the intense labors of middle summer as they had in former years, the farmers of Higdon's Crossroads neglected their fields and spent their days at the revival that now ruled their lives.

"What good is it to work ourselves to death in the fields, when this old world is about to end?" reasoned Earl Powell. "Best we all pray and get ourselves ready for the day Jesus comes."

The congregation generally agreed with Earl, though some worried privately that their crops were being neglected. Their old habits urged them to work; their new outlook told them such things no longer mattered. Their conflict drove them to cluster even closer around Malcolm Forest. He was their compass in these frightful times, and nobody questioned his spiritual authority. And if they had doubts, no one dared say them openly.

By the middle of July Forest had narrowed the predicted end of time to August, just weeks away. But he added: "If enough people repent and join the faithful, the Almighty may grant this world more time. As God promised to spare Sodom and Gomorrah if Abraham could find a bare handful of faithful believers, so He may extend time if we are united in devotion and loyalty to Him. Therefore, pray, pray without ceasing that our families, relatives, friends, and countrymen may join us in Heaven."

"But Reverend Forest," they asked, "how will we live and what will we eat until the end time comes, specially if it's longer than you first thought?"

"Oh, ye of little faith," he said, shaking his head. "Don't you know that Jesus, the Good Shepherd, will provide pasturage for his flock? But to settle the doubts of those whose faith is still weak, take the earliest Christians as your model. Didn't they pool their holdings and share everything in common? So, if you have food, bring it here that others may eat; if spare clothing, bring it that all will be decently dressed; if money, likewise bring it, so that nothing needful from this world shall be lacking. Share all things equally, as the believers in the days of Peter shared all they had."

"What about the money we borrowed from the bank to make our crops?" Melvin Hardin wanted to know.

"It is a moral principle that we should be honest in all our worldly dealings," Forest reminded them. "But it is a higher principle that all things belong to God. The cattle on a thousand hills and the fruits of the fertile valleys are His. Now as the world comes to an end the higher principles must prevail. Therefore, make no exceptions but turn everything over to Him."

"But, Reverend, tell us how we do that," Melvin wanted to know.

"The best way to serve the Son of Man is to serve the sons of men. And who are these, you ask? All these assembled here, your brothers and sisters. The riches of God are the riches of his faithful servants. Jesus withheld nothing, not even his own life. We must do likewise, offering ourselves, our fortunes, our belongings, all that we are, including our very lives, to the Kingdom of God. And having become members of the Kingdom through repentance, baptism, and the sacrificial gift that Jesus made of himself, we are heirs to its riches. Therefore, hold back nothing, and nothing shall be withheld from you, but give all that you are and all that you have. The secular world no longer holds a claim over you. You are free by the will and power of Almighty God."

The congregation took his words to mean that they were now debt-free and could do as they chose with their money, borrowed or otherwise. Accordingly, they contributed all they had to the common fund, being first admonished by Forest not to hide a portion and suffer the fate of Ananias and Sapphira as told in the Bible. In this way the sum came to several thousand dollars. No one knew exactly how much, for it was handed over to Malcolm Forest, in whom they placed all their trust.

But if the people of Higdon's Cross Roads were convinced that Forest spoke the truth, the worried bankers who lent the money were not. As August approached and hundreds of acres of cotton and corn lay abandoned to weeds and grass, they came out to the Church to remind the assembled farmers of liens and mortgages.

Speaking for the group, Earl Powell declared: "We don't care about such things anymore."

"Are you saying, Mr. Powell, that you men don't intend to repay the loans you made in the spring?" Banker Edwin Morris of Scottsboro Bank asked him.

"What we're saying, Mr. Morris, is that the old world is about to end, and we're concerned with more important things, as you city men oughta be too."

"Who told you that?"

"Reverend Malcolm Forest. He's running a revival here in Higdon's Crossroads."

"Hmmm, I've heard that name. Is he by any chance from Tennessee?"

"Yes, sir, and he has run big revivals up there. But ours is the biggest yet," Earl said proudly.

"Well, all I can tell you is that you should be careful with him. I hope you folks haven't turned any of the money you borrowed over to him. If you have, you may have been duped. He's a great preacher—they say he was once a professional actor—but there are rumors about him up in Tennessee. Now as far as the world coming to end, it may, and it could come at any time. Who knows for sure? We appreciate your religious views. I'm a church-going Christian myself; but come fall, if fall comes, we'll be expecting the loans to be repaid or there will be consequences that you won't like. That's not a threat, just a business fact."

As the bankers drove off, a wave of doubt and dismay clouded their confidence. Their old familiar world of toil and trouble, lately dismissed and nearly forgotten, had returned in full, frightening force to puncture their idealistic balloon and to suggest that they had fallen victim to their own gullibility. Immediately a delegate hurried over to Charlie Hardin's place for reassurance. But Malcolm, the money, and his Roadmaster Buick were gone, never to be seen again in Higdon's Crossroads.

*****

As he drove away with books, papers, and the revival funds riding next to him, Malcolm came as close to feeling satisfied with his performance as it was possible for him to experience in these limited circumstances. For he was never totally pleased with anything he did, nor anything done for him. As a young man he dreamed of performing theatrically before thousands and unleashing the full power of his towering rhetoric. But enemies and intrigues, he recalled bitterly, had dashed his dreams. Revival ministry became a fallback position for his skills, but he chafed under the restrictions of themes and audience level. Things had gone as well as could be hoped for in Higdon's Cross

Roads, but he was not deluded by the limited scope of things that ended, like several other, in deceptive manipulations. No longer did he take pleasure in the sordid pattern. But the closest he could come to justification of his deeds was the argument that what he had done was more than simple fraud. Theatre and poetry were fictions; by what flimsy logic did the dreary remainder of the world claim exclusive right to decide what was true or false? Much of what he taught the congregation was biblical and true in the context of life as they knew it. The fact that he had purposes of his own did not negate the central truth of the message these simple people wanted to hear. But it had been a local challenge and a trivial triumph, less than he longed for, far less than he had always longed for. In earlier years he gave no thought to moral shabbiness, but in time he began to crave accomplishment and the permanence of things that really mattered. He had made too many shameful exits like this. Was he destined never to hear prolonged applause when the final curtain came down?

"Vanity of vanities," he said to himself in his best stage voice. "Vanity of vanities," he repeated as he sped down Higdon Mountain. "Even the things I say now are false. My world is a colossal void. Finally, and for once at least, I am being honest, and it is worse than what I was before."

He looked into the future and saw nothing rewarding, beautiful, or true. But the less he saw, the more he hurried to get there. He could feel his life accelerating to a finale. The steep curve was just ahead. He still had a choice: the brakes or the accelerator. Now his life was racing toward the end. He did not hesitate but pressed the pedal to the floor, and the Roadmaster soared into the void with a roar of power. He hated the limitations and half-way things that had frustrated him all his life. "Do it totally, do it right," he had said to himself the night of his first and only New York performance. But the audience disagreed and reacted to his supreme effort with catcalls and boos. But did they really know? What right did they have to ruin everything? The greater part of him died that night.

The acceleration caused the Buick to overshoot Ed's garden entirely. Landing half way down the slope, it bounced hard, rolled over several times and ended wheels up in the hollow two hundred yards below his house. The next morning Ed thought he heard a car horn blowing down in the ravine and went out to check. He saw nothing and was about to go back inside when on an impulse he hobbled past the garden to look at the slope below it. That's when he spotted metal pieces and black paint marks on the rocks. I guess I need to get down there to see what it is, he sighed, afraid of what he might find and dreading the torture another trip down into the steep ravine meant for his aching knees.

Malcolm was still alive and feebly pressing the horn when Ed reached the car and got a door open. Then gasping to tell Ed something, he died.

Ed was stunned when he saw the thousands of dollars in the box and scattered around the car. To keep or not to keep it, that was the first question that came to mind. But what would I do with that much money? he thought to himself, summoning arguments against temptation. I have enough to eat and clothes to last as long as I do. And I'm too old to try new things. Maybe if I was younger or Mollie was still alive, he let himself dream and remember for a moment. But no, he thought, shaking his head. It probably belongs to them people up at the Crossroads, and I've got to get somebody to deal with this dead man. He must be that preacher that run off with the money that I heard about yesterday. I reckon I'll just carry the money up there and give it back to them. That way they can send somebody to take care of this corpse. I can't by myself. But no, that could get me into all kinds of trouble. First thing the folks up there would probably do is accuse me of keeping some of the money. No; the thing to do is get the sheriff out here real quick before somebody else finds this wreck with a dead man in it. The sooner I can turn everything over to the law and get shed of the whole thing, the better off I'll be. Maybe the money will get back to the right folks eventually, though I doubt it. When law people get ahold of money or property, they figure out all kinds of legal ways to keep it. Just like they done us back in Grandpa's day when all the land around this part of the country belonged to us Higdons. For an instant his ancestral bitterness flared up, but then he thought better. No use worrying about that now. It ain't none of my business anymore. I hope the folks up there can save their farms. I got nothing against them, even though they're livin on land that's ours by rights. Course if they had any sense they wouldn't be in this mess to start with. But then I guess you could say that about most folks.

*****

With Charlie's help and a junkyard motor and radiator, Herschel got the old truck running again and out of the cotton patch.

"What about the tent and all? Can you haul it off?" Charlie asked, anxious to get rid of reminders of what they had been through.

"No, I don't ever wanta lay eyes on that ole tent again! Y'all can burn the damn thing for all I care; or give it to Uncle Melvin if he's got any use for it. Ever since Malcolm run off with their money, these folks been trying to shove some of the blame on me. But I told two or three of them right from the start to be careful with that silver-tongued devil—you included, Uncle Charlie. You were right there with them all the way. But nobody would listen. Forest was paying me and Maxine, so we couldn't say too much. I'm just glad it's over. Malcolm was always preaching about the end of time, scaring people half to death and taking their money when the truth was he didn't know any more than the rest of us about things like that. But you know, in a way he was right. It was the end of time and it happened about when he said it would, but it was the end of his time, not ours.

"Well, I guess I've said about everything I need to and then some, Uncle Charlie, so we'll be going. You got everything packed and ready, Maxine? Folks, we appreciate all you've done for us and sorry things didn't work out better. I imagine it's gonna be a mess trying to settle up the money Mr. Higdon turned over to the law. (Do you reckon he kept a little bit for hisself?) No telling what that pack of lawyers, bankers, and judges will decide to do with it. Probably nothing good, but I hope all you folks around here can keep your farms. Now I doubt we'll be down this way again. So, bye and good luck and give our best to Uncle Melvin. And bye to you Aunt Noxie, Henry, Jasper. Now come on, darlin', let's go home to Tennessee!"

Vengeance Is Mine

At 8 o'clock on a Monday morning in early April of 1878, the iron doors of the Alabama state prison swung open and for the first time in a dozen years out stepped Gil McCormick.

For a moment he paused, squinting in the unaccustomed sunlight and realigning himself with the outside world. Then ignoring the warden's advice and outstretched hand, Gil shifted a small satchel of belongings at his belt and without a backward look set off at a brisk pace to keep the oath he had sworn twelve years earlier to kill Nate Tidwell.

His hatred of Nate, as intense as their friendship had once been, and his sworn oath to kill him for his treachery had sustained him through all the long years of digging in the prison coalmines. He had seen many lesser men come and go: most to die from the hellish ordeal of the mines, first in spirit and then in body as they wasted away to coughing skeletons, consumed by the coal dust.

But Gil's strength and spirit were undiminished. In the early years the guards beat him for insubordination and surly backtalk, but they could not break him. Later they treated him with grudging respect and stayed clear of his massive fists that could break jaws and crack ribs. The day he walked out of prison at thirty-five he was stronger and infinitely harder than the twenty-three-old they had sentenced. He feared no man and trusted no force but his own. As far as he knew or cared, his family and relatives had long since died or left Winston County. And if he ever had thoughts about God, they evaporated in the mines. He lived only for one purpose: to deal death to Nate Tidwell. And afterwards what? Gil did not know or care. For him there was no "after," only the all-fulfilling moment of revenge that left no room for consequences and second thoughts.

He had relived the bitter truth of Nate's betrayal countless times during imprisonment. As Winston County sharpshooters during the Civil War, they switched sides and fortunes with the ebb and flow of the conflict in the Unionist-leaning North Alabama hills, at times siding with the Alabama Home Guard that sporadically rode up from Tuscaloosa to recruit for the Confederacy and hang deserters, then turning back to the Unionists when it was to their advantage.[1] But as the war neared an end and the Home Guard disbanded, Nate swung over to the Unionists for good, while Gil, now more outlaw than soldier, continued to raid and plunder without regard for cause or military protocol.

The war ended, and Nate rode home to family, farm, and respectability. On the other hand, Gil was branded an outlaw and frustrated Winston County authorities posted a $250 reward for information leading to his capture.

---

1. Historical note: In 1861 Winston County seceded from the State of Alabama and declared itself the "Free State of Winston." For many decades it was the only republican county in otherwise solidly democratic Alabama. To varying degrees, counties along the Appalachian Mountains shared these unionist sympathies, though many men chose not to fight on either side. For more than a century Alabama pursued a punitive policy toward Winston County for its unionist attitudes and republican leanings, refusing to build and maintain passable roads through the area. Oddly enough, however, this neglect eventually worked in its environmental favor. Today, much of Winston County lies within the Bankhead national forest and attracts visitors to its hiking, hunting, fishing, and scenic venues.

For a few months Gil and his band hid out in the Winston County hills and caves which they knew like the back of their hand. But with the restoration of order in the North Alabama counties, one by one his men were killed, captured, or driven away. Finally, only Gil was left and now the authorities were closing in on him too.

He made his last stand in a hidden cave near Nate's farm. Out of loyalty to his old friend, Nate supplied him with food and ammunition as Gil's supplies ran low. But Nate's wife Eura was becoming more and more worried about the dangers Gil posed for her family.

"Nate, the law's gonna catch him sooner or later, and when they do, they may arrest you too for helping him."

"He's my friend, woman. I can't turn my back on him. You oughta know that. Gil saved my life once or twice in the war."

"I'm not asking you to turn your back on him. But just think a little, husband. If they can take him alive, it's true he'll probably serve time in the pen and all, but at least he'll be alive. That way he can do his time and get a fresh start in life. He's still a young man, but the way things are going, one of these days they'll corner him and shoot him dead. Now, Nate, which way would you rather have it for Gil, killed or captured?"

"Now, Eura, that's not a fair way to look at it. You're twisting things and you know it."

"That's exactly the way it is, Nate. It's not that Gil has a lot of choices, does he? And neither do we, for that matter. And there's something else to consider."

"What?"

"The money."

"What money?"

"Why, the reward they're offering: 250 Yankee dollars, that's what. Somebody's gonna claim that money when they run Gil down, and it might as well be us as somebody else. You know we need it with all the hard times we're going through. And we've got the kids to think about."

"Now, Eura, if you think I'm gonna take money for turning Gil in, you've got another think coming. I'm not gonna do a lowdown thing like that, no matter how hard up we are."

"Nate, you wouldn't have to come right out publicly and tell the law where he is. All I'm saying is when Sheriff Blackwood comes around here again a body could just give him a little hint, a word here and there. There's a lot of ways to tell things without saying them in so many words. And remember this, Nate: when it's all said and done, you'd be saving Gil's life. The Sheriff knows he's around here close and pretty soon he'll figure out exactly where. And one more thing."

"What?"

"What's to keep Gil from naming you as his partner?"

"Gil wouldn't do that."

"How do you know that? Gil may not be the same man today he was when you rode with him back in the war. No telling what all he's done since then. You have to realize, Nate, that if a man robs and steals long enough, it gets to be second nature with him and he'll do anything to anybody—even his closest friends. So, do you want him dead, or alive with a chance to make something of his life?"

"Well, I don't want him to get shot. You know that. It's just that—"

"Then you have to do one of two things," she said cutting him off. "Either help the law capture him or keep on doing what you've been doing until Gil's dead and they arrest you for covering for him. The first way we all come out to the good; the other way, the law will shoot Gil and you could go to jail yourself."

Against his better instincts, Nate let Eura put the idea in his head that turning Gil in was the best thing to do. And once she turned his thinking in that direction, the idea took on a life of its own. Two hundred and fifty dollars was a lot of money, and there was Eura and children to think about. The more he thought about it, the more Nate convinced himself that it was the right thing to do. After all, Gil had brought it on himself. He could have stopped the raiding and plundering like all the other men in Winston and neighboring counties. War was one thing, and they had gone through its dangers and hardships together; but robbing people and calling it war was something else, maybe even something underhanded. Nate ended up blaming Gil not only for his own troubles but also for the predicament in which he had put his closest friend. He asked himself, what right did Gil have to put me at risk? Even though it went against the grain, he reasoned that it was a man's duty to help see that the guilty — friend or not — had to answer for their crimes. And besides, that way I could save his life. Eura's right about that.

The next time Sheriff Ed Blackwood and his deputies came searching, Nate showed them the trail to Gil's hiding place and reminded the Sheriff of the reward.

"Don't you worry, Tidwell, you'll get your blood money if we catch him!", Blackwood said, giving him a withering look and spitting tobacco juice in the general direction of Nate's boots.

Soon afterward Blackwood and his deputies cornered Gil. He held them off until his ammunition was exhausted, wounding one man in the leg and breaking another's ribs with his fist. Gil himself was bleeding from the clubbing it took to finally bring him down.

"How'd you find me?" he asked Sheriff Blackwood through bloodied lips. "Somebody had to tell you. Who was it?"

"Gil, that's for me to know and you to guess. The only thing I can say is that some of your friends ain't as friendly as you think. You figure it out from there."

Gil understood that he meant Nate. It had to be Nate. He was the only one who knew where Gil was hiding out. And so was born his abiding hatred for the man who was once his closest friend. But now it was time to kill him—and anyone else who tried to get in the way of his revenge. The trial judge could have as readily given Gil twenty or thirty years of prison time. But why bother? No inmate had ever survived more than eight or nine years in the prison mines. In effect, twelve years was a death sentence with time to spare for an ordinary man. The difference was that Gil was no ordinary man.

*****

The young woman was in despair. Hours earlier the right rear wagon wheel had worked loose and fallen off its axle. It would be dark in another hour and there were no houses or travelers on this forested section of Brushy Pond Road. Even though she found the loose axle nut a little way back down the road, she was not nearly strong enough to line up the heavy iron-rimmed wheel, much less leverage the axle with a stout pole and prop it into position with rocks. The job would probably take two strong men.

She waited, again scanning the deserted road in both directions and hoping somebody would happen along to help her. But now night was closing in on her and she had not seen a soul. She fought back tears of frustration and fear for her own safety and was anguished at the thought of her parents alone, hungry, and helpless in the dark house. What was she to do? Could she unhitch one of the mules and ride it home, leaving the other tied to the wagon? But neither mule had been broken to ride and probably would buck her off if she tried. What was she to do? In total weariness of body and spirit she sagged against the inclined wagon bed and tried to think clearly about her options.

A rustle in the bushes along the road startled her. With a surge of terror that brought a gasp from her throat, she suddenly made out the silhouette of a man in the dark foliage. Knowing she had spotted him, he stepped forward without a word.

The powerfully built, dark-bearded man towered above her. His leather coat that reached nearly to his knees was ripped down the left side and tattered at the bottom. In his left hand he clutched a shiny new 30-30 Winchester rifle that seemed a stark mismatch with his grimy appearance and ragged clothing.

"Mister . . . sir, . . . she said fearfully. "I broke down, as you can see. The wagon dropped a wheel and I can't fix it. I'm not stout enough by myself, and nobody lives on this stretch of road to help me. And I need to get on home. My parents are waiting on me. Daddy'll be worried about me. They're both real bad off and I need to get there to help them, mister. And I need to get this wagon and team back to Preacher Yates. I promised I'd have them back by dark."

The man came forward without responding, propped his rifle against a bush, checked the wagon, unhitched the mule team, tied them to a sapling by the roadside, and examined the wheel and axle. Then he began unloading the six sacks from the wagon bed.

"What are you doing, mister. I need to take these sacks home. They're food and stuff for my folks. They need them."

Without answering her, he dropped the last sack and rolled the wagon wheel into position and braced it against his knee. Then he reached down and lifted the axle with one hand and with the other maneuvered the wheel until it slid into place. He grunted and pointed to the axle nut she was holding. She hurried to hand it to him. He screwed it on with both hands as far as he could, then with a rock pounded it for several more turns until it was tight. Then he checked and tightened the other wheels and tossed the sacks back in the wagon bed. Finally, he rehitched the team and motioned for her to get in the wagon. Once she was seated he handed her the reins.

"Mister, oh I am ever so much obliged for your help! And I have to say you are the stoutest man I've ever seen. The way you just lifted that axle with one hand and all and put the wheel back on with the other. My goodness, mister, I've never seen anybody that strong. Can I have your name, sir, so I can tell my daddy now you helped me out?"

"Tell me your name," he said finally in a tone that was not to be disobeyed.

"I'm Creola Tidwell, Nate Tidwell's daughter."

He stared at her with an intensity that caused her to avert his gaze.

"Where's your daddy?"

"At home. We live several miles over yonder close to the Piney Grove community, you know, where the Corn Road dead ends at the Danville Road right where the counties join."

"Nate used to live over close to Pine Torch Church," the man commented.

"Then you know my Daddy? We had to leave the old home place some years ago," she explained. "I was just coming from over that way with these things when the wheel fell off."

The man turned to leave.

"Mister, you didn't tell me your name. I'm hoping you can come by the house, so my Daddy can thank you in a proper way for your help. I don't know what I'd have done if you hadn't happened along when you did. I do thank you kindly again, sir."

"I'll be by," he said as he picked up his rifle. "You can tell your daddy that. He'll know who I am," he added as he stepped into the woods.

For a moment she heard the crackle of his steps on the dry leaves. Then they stopped. He's probably watching me from in there, she thought with a thrill of terror. She popped the reins on the mule rumps and urged the team to a trot. Strange man, but he did fix the wagon. Still and all, she thought in panic, I don't want to press my luck. Whoever he is, he's a hard man. And stout as a horse. He could snap my neck with one hand if he wanted to. No telling how dangerous he might be. And Lord help me if he took a notion to come after me. She glanced back in fear but saw only the deepening gloom of the forest.

*****

It was still dark the next day when Nate Tidwell awoke to the cold sensation of a rifle barrel rammed against his stomach.

"It's you, aint it, Gil?"

"I'm back, Nate, back to kill you for selling me out."

"I've been expecting you since Creola told me about the wagon wheel and the big man that fixed it for her. I figured it was you. Never was but one man around this country stout enough to do what she says you did."

The door to the other room opened and scrawny Creola rushed to her father's bed.

"Mister, what're you doing? Why are you holding that rifle on him like that? You stop that! Daddy's a sick man and nearly blind besides. And his heart's too weak to stand that kind of treatment!"

She tried to turn the rifle barrel away, but Gil pushed her aside.

"Stay outta my way, girl, I've got something to settle with your daddy that's got nothing to do with you."

"If it concerns Daddy, it does. I take care of him and Momma."

"Where's she at?"

"In yonder, in the other room."

"You go fetch her. I wantta talk to her too."

"You can't talk to her, mister. She's—"

"You bring her in here like I told you, or I'll just shoot Nate right now."

Creola was right; Gil couldn't talk to Eura. Nor could anyone else. Her eyes were vacant and her face expressionless except for a grimace that vaguely resembled a faint smile. She hummed a toneless song in a world cut off from this one as she caressed a dirty rag doll.

"What's the matter with her?"

"She went simple in the head the winter Katie died of pneumonia," Nate explained. "I reckon she doesn't rightly understand anything a body says to her."

"You had a boy too, older than the girls. Where's he at?"

"Matthew just left us one day. Didn't tell us where he was

going and we aint heard from him since. Just couldn't take the hard times any longer, I reckon."

"What's the matter with you?"

"I was working for Preacher Yates, fixing pasture fences, and his bull gored and stomped me so bad I couldn't ever walk again. And all I can see is shadows and the difference between light and dark. Gil, lotta times I wished the Lord God had just finished me then and there, and never understood why He didn't. Creola here has had to move me around and do everything for me and her mother since then. Reverend Yates lets us live here outta the goodness of his heart. And I guess he feels some responsibility for what his bull did to me. Gil?"

"Yeah?"

"You gonna shoot me, are you?"

"That's was my reason for coming back here. Been aiming to for all the twelve years I dug coal in the prison mines."

"No, mister," said Creola said, "I'm not gonna let you hurt my daddy, or my momma!"

"Creola, honey, you stay outta this. Gil, just shoot if that's your pleasure. I was wrong to turn you in, and I'm still man enough to take what's coming to me. You'll be doing me a kindly thing, the truth be told. But when you shoot, just shoot us both, me and Eura. We've been more trouble to this saintly girl than any human deserves. And none of what you hold against me is her fault. So just shoot the both of us and let Creola go free. It'll be the kindest thing you could do for her."

"No, Daddy, don't say awful things like that! You and Momma are all I've got! I don't know what this man has against you or what happened back yonder in the war, but he don't have the right to take his spite out that way. Nobody's got that right.

Getting even is the Lord's business. It says in the Good Book somewhere, 'Vengeance is mine'."

"I run my own business and don't put much stock in what you call 'The Good Book'. It wasn't any good to me all the years I spent digging in the mines. Still and all, I never had it in mind to kill anybody but you, Nate. And like I said, that was my reason for coming back here."

"Gil, if you kill me and leave Eura behind, you'll just be punishing this innocent girl. But if we're gone, then maybe she can get out and have a life for herself. What's she look like anyway, Gil? Is she pretty enough to get married?"

Gil glanced over at Creola's bony, tear-streaked face and emaciated body.

"Naw, she aint pretty. She's not much of nothing, to be honest with you, so skinny and beat down she'd have to stand up twice to make a shadow."

"Gil, is there anything you could do for her, like help her get on her feet a little after I'm gone?"

"No."

"But you helped her the other day when the wagon broke down. Couldn't you help her just one more time, for old times' sake back when we were buddies?"

"Stop your pleading, Nate. I'm not beholden to her."

"I thank you again, Mr. McCormick, for your help the other day," Creola said defiantly, "But ugly and beat down, as you say I am, I don't need your help now. I can take care of Daddy and Momma—and myself. So I'll just ask you to get outta our house and put an end to all this killing talk!"

Gil raised the rifle barrel from Nate's stomach and was silent for a moment.

"What are you gonna do, Gil?" Nate asked with a quiver in his voice.

"I'm thinking I oughta kill you, like I said."

Gil pointed the rifle and pulled the trigger. Creola screamed. Eura crooned a little louder and clutched her doll tighter. Nate grunted and went limp.

"You killed Daddy! You murderer you, you killed my daddy!" Creola screamed and threw herself across her father's body.

"Quit your whining, girl. I didn't shoot him. Bullet went down through the mattress and into floor planks. Didn't touch him. He aint worth killing, neither one of them, the shape he and Eura are in now. I came here to kill a man, not a crippled-up excuse for one. It wouldn't be right and wouldn't give me any satisfaction. If there is a God, he got even with him first, I reckon, before I had a chance to. Well, so be it."

With that he turned, kicked the door so hard it almost twisted off its hinges, and disappeared into the woods behind the house.

Nevertheless, it was another shock to Nate's failing heart and he died a few weeks later. Somebody told Creola that Gil had appeared and stood at the edge of the woods bordering the cemetery but did not go inside the church to hear Preacher Yates deliver the funeral sermon or go to the graveyard to witness the burial.

*****

A week later Creola heard a cowbell and hammering out at the barn. She went to look and found Gil. A mule team hitched to a new two-horse wagon and piled high with plows and implements was tied to a fence post. A white cow trailing on a long rope behind the wagon was pushing her head through the fence to get at the tall grass.

"Just what do you think you're doing here, Mr. McCormick?"

"Fixing me a place to sleep."

"A place to sleep? You can't sleep here! This is our place and you're not welcome. Haven't you caused us enough grief already?"

"Creola," he said, pointing with the hammer, "first thing, you take that cow down yonder to the creek to drink and then turn her loose out there in the pasture. She needs to graze, and the grass is good. And then you get yourself in the kitchen and cook me some breakfast. Here, I brought a bucketful of eggs and meat up from Danville. And bring it out here when it's ready."

"I'm not taking orders from you!" she said, pushing the bucket away. "And I'll tell you again, this is our place and you can't stay here!"

"And you eat all you can yourself," he said, ignoring her outburst. "We're gonna try to put some meat on your scrawny bones. We've got a lot of work to do to fix up this place. And then when you get done with that, you trot over yonder to old man Yates' house and tell him I'm running this place now. Tell him I'll pay him a hundred and fifty dollars a year for the rent of this land, but no thirds and fourths on the cotton and corn. You got all that straight, Creola?"

Creola led the cow to the creek and then turned her loose in the lush pasture. Then she went in the house and took Nate's old shotgun from its rack. She loaded it, thought for a moment, then took the shell out and replaced the gun in the rack. "I'm not gonna do the same thing that man was fixing to do to Daddy," she said to herself.

She started a fire in the stove and cooked the biggest breakfast in her life. After feeding her mother and herself, she carried enough scrambled eggs and ham for three men out to Gil. Then she went to convey his message to Preacher Yates.

"It's fine with me if it is with you, Creola," he said. "I told your father that you all could have the run of that house and farm for as long as he lived. And now I'm telling you the same thing. But if Gil McCormick wants to pay me a hundred fifty dollars a year to farm it, so much the better. We've got more land here anyway than my boys and I can farm. But here's some sincere advice, Creola: you watch yourself with Gil McCormick. Don't cross him if you can help it. He's carrying some deep grudges and is liable to take them out on anybody that even looks cross-eyed at him. You'll need to cut him a lot of slack and step wide of his pathway. If he's anything like he was back in the old days, he can kill a man with his fists or shoot him over a trifle. So be careful. I don't think he's all bad, but right now we don't need to provoke him. I'll need to talk to him about several things, but it's not yet time."

By summer Gil had over thirty acres under cultivation, Creola labored mightily herself. With abundant food and milk, she had gained weight and was beginning to look like a presentable woman. Periodically, Gil would disappear for days at a time but always returned with food and supplies. Creola wondered where his money came from, but he did not answer her occasional questions. Probably he's got money or gold he stole buried somewhere, she thought to herself, but recalling Preacher Yates' cautionary words, felt the wiser course was not to press him.

*****

Eura died in the fall. People wondered—and gossiped— about what Creola and Gil would do now that both her parents were gone. Gil never mentioned his own family, but after the church service one Sunday Preacher Yates told Creola in answer to her question about it, that Gil's mother died while he was in prison and his father left Winston County for parts unknown not long thereafter. The good Reverend, concerned about gossip and community morals, now decided it was time to talk to Gil about some things, including the situation with Creola.

"Not that it's any of your business, Yates," Gil informed him, "but far's I'm concerned, Creola can stay where she is, and I'll do the same till I take a notion to do something else. And just so you'll know, she gets half of the crop money. So, this is the way it'll be: she lives in the house and I sleep in the barn. I aint got no manly intentions towards her if that's what you're frettin' about."

"Have you ever thought about taking a wife, Gil?"

"A wife? I don't need no wife. I've got along without one all this time, and I reckon I can manage by myself from here on."

"Creola's a good woman. You could do a lot worse. And you're going to get old in time and you'll need somebody like her. You won't always be as strong as you are now. And you saw how she took care of her parents."

"She's not the easiest woman to look at, don't you think?"

"Well, I'd say that depends on who's doing the looking. And, Gil, as far as that goes, you're no prizewinner yourself in the looks department. Anyway, there's a lot more to a woman than her looks. And in case you haven't noticed, she's looking a lot better than she did four or five months ago. Back then she was half starved. I give you credit for feeding her. You give all these things some thought."

Gil snorted and went on his way. Old fool, trying to tell everybody what to do, he said to himself. But several times in the following days the wise old preacher's words came back to bother him. And one day Creola saw him staring at her in an odd way.

Fall came. Gil and Creola picked ten bales of cotton, which over a month-long span he hauled down to the Danville gin and sold to a cotton broker. True to his promise to Preacher Yates, he paid him a hundred fifty dollars and later handed Creola a hundred ninety dollars as her share.

"For me? All that for me? Lordy mercy, I've never had that much money in my whole life. Why, thank you truly, Mr. McCormick."

"I told old man Yates I was gonna split the crop even with you."

"But you didn't tell me."

"Didn't get around to it. But said or not, that was my aim all along."

"Well, that's all right, and I'm glad you kept your promise and thank you again. But from now on you need to tell me things, Mr. McCormick."

He hesitated for a moment. "Well, there is one thing I would say to you."

"And what would that be?" she asked, surprised at the softness of his voice.

"I wish you would stop calling me Mr. McCormick all the time. My name's Gil. I aint never been a 'Mr. McCormick.' You can just call me Gil, you hear?"

"I hear you, Mr. . . . Gil," she said laughing.

The corn was next to be gathered. But the harvest turned out to be so bountiful that there was not enough room in the barn to hold it. Gil started building a shed on the side to handle the overflow. That's when Creola came back from church one

Sunday and discovered Gil unconscious with a heavy timber across his chest.

She revived him with a bucket of cold water. Gil pushed aside the beam and got to his feet, but staggered and nearly fell again.

"You sit down here, Gil McCormick, and let me see what kind of shape you're in. It looks like that beam gashed your head and caused a lot of bleeding. I know you have a hard head but that oak beam is a little bit harder. And you ought to be going to church on Sunday anyway, not working like it was a week day."

"To me every day's the same. Sun comes up in the east on Sunday just like it does any other day. And I ain't got time to fuss over a little bump on the head," he protested as he started to rise.

"I told you to sit while I look at that gash! Now you mind me, you hear? And I would advise you not to talk smart-alecky about holy things. "The sharp tone of her voice startled him, and he settled back and let her examine the wound. Then she left for a moment and returned with a wet rag and a bottle of horse liniment.

"Close your eyes, Gil" she ordered as she washed away the splinters and clotted blood. This may sting a little, but it'll get the healing started right away."

It was all he could do not to let loose a stream of profanity as the vile liquid seared his exposed skin like a branding iron. But Creola was right. By the next morning Gil was back to half strength and completely healed a few days later.

Two weeks later with the shed finished and the corn gathered, Gil went up to the house and called Creola.

"What is it, Gil? What do you want? That place on your head bothering you again?"

"No, my head's fine, best it's been in a long time. Now, what

I need is for you to run over to Preacher Yates' house and tell him to come over here. I need to talk to him. And tell him to bring his Bible."

"His Bible? What for?"

"You'll both know when he gets here. Now go, girl."

Reverend Yates was as mystified as Creola. On their way to her house they both speculated whether the blow to Gil's head had something to do with it. The mystery deepened when Creola told him that Gil had been acting a little different lately.

"What is it, Gil, what can I do for you? I brought my Bible. Creola said you wanted me to."

"You can find some place in it where it talks about marrying and such like. I thought about what you said to me a while back, and I have decided that now that the cotton's picked and the corn gathered, maybe it is time for me to get married."

"Gil," laughed Preacher Yates, "it takes two people to have a wedding. Where's the woman in this arrangement?"

"Well, can't you see her? She's standing right there by you, Preacher. It's Creola, that's who. Remember, you recommended her to me. Now will you quit wasting time with foolish talk and marry us?"

"No."

"No? After all that talk you won't marry us?"

"Not unless and until Creola says so. So how do you feel about all this, Creola. Are you willing to marry this man, knowing he may be more bear than human?"

"Well, Reverend Yates, let me think about that for a bit before I give an answer. To be honest about it, this was the last thing I ever expected to hear. Gil, you once said I was ugly. Is that what you think of me? Do you want to marry an ugly woman that used to be so scrawny that I remember you saying she had to stand up twice to make a shadow?"

"That was before I got to know you."

"You didn't answer my question."

"Now you've fleshed out."

"Still haven't answered my question."

"Well, yeah, I reckon I do."

"Do what, Gil?"

"Thunderation, woman! You won't have it any other way but in plain words, will you?"

"That's right, Gil, I want to hear it in plain words. So, tell me plainly what you want of me."

"I reckon I want to marry you. Will you?"

"Will I what, Gil McCormick?"

"Will you marry me, Creola Tidwell?"

"That depends."

"Depends on what?"

"On how you answer me one more question, Gil."

"Damnation! You've got more questions than fleas on a dog's back!

All right, what is it?"

"Do you love me?"

"Woman, I can't talk about things like that, specially not with another man listening to my words, and a preacher to boot. It's too womanish."

"It's all right, Gil," Reverend Yates laughed. "We preachers know a thing or two about love."

"But she meant that other kind of love, like between, you know, a man and a woman."

"Oh, we preachers know about that kind of love too. It's all part of the same package God gave us. So, don't mind me. You just answer Creola's question."

"Well, what was it again? Y'all are both coming at me from so many directions my head is spinning."

"Gil, I asked you a simple question: do you love me?"

"Well, I never thought of it in a straight way like that. So, I don't know if I can answer in just one little word. I've got to where I like having you around. I've gotten used to your face and the way you talk. I like your cooking and the way you walk. And the way you make sense—most of the time. I reckon you can't fix a wagon wheel, but you work hard and you know how to take care of people. I can fix a wagon and do stuff like that, but I aint the best when it comes to talking and taking care of people."

"I think I'm hearing a 'yes' in all that. Wouldn't you say so, Reverend Yates?"

"I'm hearing the same thing, Creola. And you, Gil. Are you saying you want to spend your life with this good woman? Will you cherish and protect her all the days of your life till death do you part?"

"I reckon so. Yeah, I guess that's what I want."

"And you, Creola, do you agree to love and cherish this man all the days of your life till death do you part?"

"Well, getting a straight answer from Gil is like pulling teeth, but what he says is close enough to suit me. Yes, I do agree, Reverend Yates. I will marry him."

"Then I now pronounce you man and wife."

"Man and wife? You mean you just married us?"

"Yessir, I just did, Gil. But we need to get some neighbors to sign as witnesses. So you'll have to repeat the words over at my house in front of them. But yes, Gil, consider yourself married to this fine woman. And congratulations! If anybody can, Creola will make a worthwhile man out of you. You're strong, without a doubt the strongest man I've ever seen. But in another way, this young woman is as strong as they come. And hers is the kind of strength you need."

"I thought there was more to marrying than just saying a few words."

"There is, Gil, a lot more. The real test starts today and goes on as long as your earthly life together lasts. So, you be good to Creola. And you both be good to each other."

✶✶✶✶✶

Post Script: Gil and Creola lived another year on the Yates farm, long enough for their first daughter, Susie, to be born. But then disgusted with neighbors who would not forgive him his prison past, Gil persuaded Creola to move out to Texas. With their departure direct knowledge of their life ended. But shortly before his much-lamented death three years later, Preacher Yates got a letter from Creola thanking him again and telling him that God had blessed them with another child, a little boy they named Gilbert. She added that the McCormick family was doing "tolerably well" out near Tyler, Texas. "Gil," she wrote, "is like a new man out here. Texas suits him. It's big country, like him in a way, I reckon, and he feels more at home here. People around here don't care what he used to be or what he done back yonder. They treat people according to who they are and what they do today. And we try to treat them the same way. Lots of people around here are just like us, gettin' fresh starts. Gil has let go of a lotta hurt out here. I'm workin' on him about goin' to church with me and the young'uns. He's still holdin out and plays like he's mad when I talk about it; you know how mule-brained stubborn he is. But I can tell he's glad we go. I think he'll come around when sees that other men he knows do. And if for no other reason, for the kids. You oughta see him with them, Reverend, big as a bear and gentle as a lamb. He still talks rough sometimes, but he's good to me."

Aliens

The aliens were gaining on him. Lights flared in the predawn mist and the explosive blasts of their weapons followed. He mourned silently for his fallen companion, the last of his six crewmembers. But he could not stop, not even to make the sign of the sacred icon over her body. The aliens were too close. He could hear their excited cries as they found her body and picked up his tracks where he had just forded a small stream. Now he could see in the growing light a jagged ridge of hills rising sheer above the forest canopy. Perhaps its fissures and recesses would give him enough time and concealment to make his final report. It would be an account of catastrophic system failure, loss of the crew, and failure of the mission.

He had no illusions about his own chances. The aliens were on familiar ground while he was exhausted by the planet's crushing gravity and increasingly confused by its excessive oxygen. He had discarded his breathing apparatus soon after the aliens and their beasts picked up his scent. With great effort he could breathe the thick atmosphere, but he knew he was doomed as soon as the planet's lethal microorganisms entered his lungs. He would not see his own world again. Most of all he regretted that he did not reach the tenth level of maturity in which he would have been allowed to consume the sacred paternity food, father offspring, and die immediately thereafter with great honor and celebration according to the ancient rites. He had progressed through nine mutations during the nearly five hundred planetary revolutions of his planet around its star. But now one revolution and a successful mission short of full maturity, he would join his crew in death.

He had never questioned the cultural mandate to explore alien worlds and learn of other life forms. Many expeditions had been lost in the ages since the explorations began. All were honored, and he had no doubt that the mission under his command would be similarly praised. It was a comfort, but honor and duty demanded unwavering adherence to protocol till the end. He must do all that life and strength permitted. The fate of future missions could be compromised if he failed to send his final report.

These aliens, though primitive, were cunning and their beasts ferocious beyond anything he had experienced during his many voyages. The oldest chronicles told of similar creatures in the Zeta Sector, but many in the Expeditionary Corps suspected that the stories were pious fables intended to bolster courage and emphasize obedience to the prime expeditionary imperatives, not accounts of real events from their elder history. The willful destruction of life was too absurd and foreign to their thinking to be believable, even though leaders taught their novice commanders that it had once been a feature of their own prehistory.

Momentarily the pursuers lost his trail and veered off toward the deeper forest foliage. He could sense the frustration in their cries and snarls of their beasts. In the brief interval he found a crevice in the sheer rock. It was too narrow for his body, but he forced his way in, tearing flesh and permashield uniform alike. What difference would a cut and tear make now? The toxic microbes were already constricting his throat so that each breath was a heaving, rasping torture.

Now the beasts picked up his spoor again. His time was short but hopefully sufficient. In the growing light and fading consciousness he completed the intricately encoded report and sent it homeward in staged, musical intervals via his Command Messenger. No biological enemy had ever broken the code. Only the master computers on Alpha Planet were equal to the task of deciphering its fifty-five phased, binary stages. Now only four brief but essential tasks remained. The first was to set the craft's automatic controls with the Command Messenger so that it would start spinning crewless through the interstellar void to Alpha. The second was to press the destruct sequence buttons on the Messenger itself. By Prime Directive, advanced systems were not to fall under the control of violent aliens advanced enough to misuse them for destructive purposes. The third was to perform the rite of the sacred icon for himself and his fallen crewmates. And the fourth, to die.

He completed all the tasks only seconds before the beasts burst snarling into the crevice and began tearing his lifeless corpse apart.

*****

"Sheriff Tatum, I'm tellin' you, I've seen some gruesome things in my time, but nothing as ugly or smelly as that thing the dogs drug outta that hole up there in the rocks. It's got to be a demon straight outta hell, like the others we shot down by the river or the ones the dogs tore apart. But this one was longer with extra tentacles like an octopus. I'm guessing it was their leader." Deputy Henry Williams wiped the sweat from his brow. His hands were still shaking so hard that he had trouble pulling a cigarette from a new pack. "No telling how long I'll have nightmares about that thing," he mumbled. "But let me get the camera outta my car and take some pictures."

"Pictures? Pictures of what?" asked Tatum.

"Why, of the aliens, or what's left of them. And the UFO. For the record and the report," Williams replied, his face reflecting his puzzlement.

"Henry, forget the camera. Go tell the men to come down here. All of them. And be quick about it. We don't have a lot of time."

"Yes sir, right away."

"Men, listen carefully to what I have to tell you," Sheriff Tatum said as his deputies gathered around him. "What you thought you saw out there today you didn't see. You got that? You didn't see anything out of the ordinary."

"But, Sheriff," Williams protested, "the UFO across the ridge, the bodies of those things. Whatta you mean, we didn't see anything?"

"Men, I'm telling you, for your own good and the good of Henderson County, our official report will state that we found nothing out of the ordinary in this incident. Probably just some game poachers that got away. Listen, the military will be crawling all over this place later today or tomorrow. And you don't want to tell or show those bastards anything they don't want to hear or see. If you do, there'll be hell to pay, and we'll do the paying. And the same goes for any other federal folks. You don't screw around with anything or anybody the government sends down here to snoop around. And two other things."

"What's that, Sheriff?" Deputy Bo Filmore asked.

"I want you men to sack the bodies and anything else these creatures had, weight them with rocks, and drop them in the river. And be quick about it."

"But what about the UFO, sir, Henry asked? We can't hide it."

"It's gone," deputy Don Wilson explained. "Me and Bo saw it lift off a few minutes ago. Disappeared in an instant."

"Well thank God for that. One thing less to worry about."

"You said there were two things," Bo reminded the Sheriff. "What else besides the bodies and all?"

"The other thing is this: if any of you decide to get cute and sing a solo to the military or the Feds, don't count on me to back you. All you'd get from me or my office would be a denial and your dismissal. So, do we understand one another on all points?"

"Yes sir," they all answered

All except Henry.

*****

The military came that afternoon and other governmental officials arrived the next morning. Military personnel scoured the area, but all they found were some odd tracks and a few scraps of strange fabric at the crevice, along with a faint nauseating odor. Both groups questioned Sheriff Tatum and his deputies, and satisfied with their responses, eventually left. Asked about several reports of UFO sightings, Tatum dismissed them as airplanes, Venus, or overactive imaginations.

"We get them all the time, and usually by the same kooky citizens," he said, shaking his head. "Just something we have to deal with."

He exchanged a knowing look with the lieutenant who nodded in acknowledgment.

But Henry Williams was deeply troubled by Sheriff Tatum's orders. For days he struggled to reconcile his sense of ethics with his loyalty to Tatum and his fellow deputies. But after two weeks ethics won out and he began telling what he had witnessed; first, to his wife Marge and eventually to anybody who would listen to his story. Marge suffered patiently for weeks, all the time begging Henry to stop the nonsense. But he would not. Friends and family began avoiding him, and finally, despairing of the whole situation, Marge took their two children and left him too. True to his word, Sheriff Tatum fired Henry when he found out what his senior deputy was doing. Things went from bad to worse after that, as Henry, now alienated and broke, became the butt of jokes and an object of scorn. Nobody would listen to him, much less hire him. Luckily, he was eligible for medical and psychiatric care through the VA as a Vietnam War veteran. After evaluation by medical experts, he was granted a small pension, barely enough to keep bread on his table. He begged Marge to bring the children and come home, but she refused.

"Henry, I'm sorry, but we're staying here with my parents. I tried to help you, but you wouldn't listen."

"But, Marge, what I saw was real."

"Real or not, I don't care anymore. I've had it with you, Henry. You thought more of that crazy story than you did our family's reputation and welfare. I can't forgive you for that. All you did was hurt our family and embarrass a lot of people in this county. Now just leave me and the kids alone."

*****

Post Script: But maybe some good came from what everybody took to be Henry's delusional story: he probably did more than anybody else in Henderson County to convince folks that there are no such things as aliens and UFOs. After all, who could be naïve enough to believe in the existence of things that, in addition to sensible local authorities, every responsible government in the world has officially denied?

Second Sight

The arrival of English siblings Virginia and Nigel Langford, 19 and 21, respectively, in August of 1938 transformed what had been a slow summer for the collegiate set of Urbana, Ohio into an exciting late flurry of parties and picnics. In his toney British accent Nigel, who delighted in everything American, approvingly described the golden-hued countryside of lakes, orchards, maturing corn fields, and ripening pumpkins as a "season of mists and mellow fruitfulness." Several of the American students were snobbishly pleased to recognize the famous verse from Keats.

The Urbana young people enthusiastically admitted the attractive English pair into their inner circle. These included Julianne Hopkins, daughter of Episcopal clergyman Malcolm and wife Stella Hopkins whose church was sponsoring the siblings and housing them in the parsonage; George Hallisey, son of local banker Luther Hallisey; Henry Fowler, whose father Malcolm Fowler owned Fowler Lumber and Construction Company; Jennifer Wainscot, daughter of Samuel Wainscot, a prosperous grain dealer whose main office was located in Dayton, but fortunately for the group, he preferred to keep his primary residence in Urbana. Fortunately, for despite her physical frailty, Jennifer was the wittiest and brightest girl of the circle. Citing Byron's famous verse, hard-smitten Nigel said that "she walks in beauty." Then there was Hugh Ulrich, who with the unambitious indolence of the rich lived with his uncle Frederick Ulrich whose wealth was obvious but its source a mystery. Lastly, the group included James and Helen Farnsworth, whose parents Harvey and Norma owned Urbana's department store. Other young people were often invited to join the circle for the larger parties but not usually included in the cozier gatherings.

A paragon of English beauty with sky-blue eyes and fairest of complexions, slender, blonde Virginia quickly stirred romantic hopes in the young men. But despite their genuine affection for her, some of the American girls could not easily suppress a certain envy and even jealousy of beautiful Virginia. Not that these qualities took root and prospered. Virginia was so kind to all that soon she won over the girls nearly as completely as she mesmerized the boys, especially Henry Fowler who could not take his eyes off her.

It was much the same with handsome Nigel. Quickly dubbed "the poet" for his repertoire of verses suitable to every place, person, and emotion, he charmed without malice and extolled things American without the belittlement often characteristic of Englishmen in America. On the contrary, Nigel declared after only a few days in Urbana that he could foresee making his permanent home in America. On the other hand, Virginia could not imagine living her life anywhere but in England.

"Life will prove to be prosperous and happy for you here," she told Nigel, "and I heartily endorse your idea of settling in America. But as for me, I must soon return to England. My life, such as it is destined to be, must be there."

Despite his insistence at the time that she explain her remark, only later did Nigel understand fully what seemed to him to be her overly fatalistic tone regarding her own prospects.

One evening the group gathered at the Farnsworth home to

celebrate Jennifer's nineteenth birthday with music, presents, and dessert. But she did not appear for her party. The waited for nearly an hour, but still Jennifer did not show.

"I talked to her this morning on the telephone," Helen told the group. "She was having another one of her coughing spells, but said it was nothing serious and that she would be here with bells on. You know the way she talks. Life is one big party for Jennifer."

"*Elle ne viendra pas,*" Virginia said almost in whisper to Nigel.

"What did you say, Virginia?" Julianne asked. "I didn't catch what you said."

"She said that Jennifer is not coming," Nigel explained. Then after a pause he added: "She spoke in French. We used to spend our summers in France, and probably would have again this year were it not for the political tensions on the Continent that have our father worried. Anyway, Virginia and I fell into the habit of speaking French amongst English speakers. For purely knavish reasons at first, I should add. It's frightfully impolite of us to do so, but it allows us to communicate without revealing certain things in English-speaking settings. One could say it's our code language. Very rude of Sis in this case with you, our dear friends, but I fear there is something she would rather not reveal."

"But what is it, Virginia?" Helen asked her. "This bunch knows just about everything about everybody in our group. And we'll get all pouty if you know something about Jennifer that we don't, and you won't tell us what it is."

Virginia shook her head and said softly, "It's nothing, just a momentary impression. Please forgive me. Nigel is right. It was rude of me to speak French before you, my dear friends, though I know some of you have taken French courses at your universities."

"Hey, I have,' James said cheerfully. "I took a year of French at Ohio U and can't speak a word of it."

"But tell us why you thought Jennifer wasn't coming," Helen insisted. "How would you know that? Because it turns out you were right. It's so late now that I doubt she will show up."

"Virginia . . . sees things, senses things at times about people and what will happen to them," Nigel explained. "but she doesn't always tell what those impressions of the future are. She has a bit of second sight, a touch of clairvoyance. She's had the gift all her life."

"Second sight! Clairvoyance! Wow! Isn't that something like being a fortune teller, or a palm reader?" George asked. "Golly gee, what a neat gift to be able to know what people are up to and see things about their future. Wowee! Tell us some things you see about us, Virginia."

"I don't believe in fortune telling and things like that," Henry said. "How can you know something that hasn't happened yet? it's spooky. You don't really believe in that stuff, the gift, as they call it, do you, Virginia?"

"It's not a gift, Henry, as George and Nigel mistakenly call it, but a burden, rather a curse than a blessing. Oh, Nigel, why did you have to say anything about my . . . peculiarity?"

"Sorry, sis. I was just trying to clarify things. And you did speak first," Nigel said weakly, for once at a loss for words and appropriate poetic verses.

Jennifer was forgotten in the excitement as everyone except Henry crowded around Virginia to learn about their future. She told them a few things. For example, that James would transfer from Ohio University to an East Coast school.

"Hey, I've been making plans to transfer all summer, but I

hadn't told anybody except my parents. I want to change majors and go in a different direction. But, Virginia, how did you know?"

"I sensed it, but don't ask me how," she said sweetly. "As I said, it was just an impression."

Then taking Helen by the hand, she told her that she would be married by Christmas.

"Married? But I'm not even engaged, Virginia, I don't even have a steady boyfriend, much less a formal fiancé."

"It will happen rather suddenly. Soon you shall have one. Indeed, dear Helen, you've already met him."

"But who, when, where?" Helen asked excitedly. "Tell me about him."

Virginia smiled. "Helen, all I can say for now is that you will think him handsome and love him dearly. Be patient. He is near, and you shall soon know his name."

"Oh, good gracious! How can I be patient now that you've told me this? Tell me more, please, pretty please, Virginia!" Then suddenly she squealed, "Oh, my Lord, I think I know who it is! I just put two and two together. If it's who I'm thinking it is, I met him just last Sunday. And is he cute! Is he the one, Virginia?"

"That's all I can tell you for now, except that you shall be happy with the husband Providence will thrust into your life."

She informed others of pleasant, innocuous things: an unexpected trip to California for one, a new automobile for another, a delightful letter in the mail for a third, a change of residence for still another, and so on till everyone had something to be excited about. All, that is, except for Henry, who wanted no part of it. As they were saying goodbye, Virginia took George aside.

"George, I see that you and your family will be going to Colorado in autumn. There is something I wanted to tell you, but not with others present."

"Why, yes, the family takes a yearly fall trip to our place out there in the mountains. It's beautiful in the fall with all the colors. But everybody knows we always go there. I suppose somebody in our group mentioned it to you. So why your reluctance to talk openly about it?"

"George, I caution you not to go mountain climbing this year."

"But why not? We always climb some of the lower peaks. I'm an old hand at it."

"I foresee the possibility of some sort of injury. It's not clear what it will be, but please do other things and stay away from the slopes."

"I promise I'll be careful, I always am. So, don't worry. I'll be fine. As said, I'm an old hand."

Virginia was unconvinced by George's lighthearted reassurance but said nothing more about it.

Later, as they were walking back to the parsonage, Nigel asked Virginia whether she would share what she had foreseen concerning Jennifer.

"You are attracted to her, aren't you, Nigel?" she asked.

"Powerfully so, Sis. Indeed, so drawn to her that I am on the point of declaring my feelings to her."

"Don't, Nigel," she said, tightening her grip on his arm, "don't say anything to her about your feelings, even though I sense she already knows."

"But why not?" he said, stopping under a street light to look her in the eye. "She's a wonderful girl, and I dare imagine her at my side, forging our life together here in America. I told you before that I hope to settle in this bountiful land. The prospects, economic and sentimental, are exactly what I am seeking."

"And I encourage you to do so, but not with Jennifer."

"But why not? She's so beautiful, witty and wonderful, and I dare think she cares for me."

"Of course she is, Nigel, and she cares deeply for you, but—"

"But what?" he asked as they strolled on.

"It's late for us to be talking out here in the street. Come along, Nigel. Julianne is already inside, and we should be, too. Father Hopkins and Mrs. Hopkins will be concerned about us."

"I shan't go inside until you explain your reservations about Jennifer."

"Please, Nigel."

"No, not another step until you tell me."

Virginia sighed deeply. "It's just an impression."

"That much I know already. But what sort of impression?"

"You are forcing me say things I do not wish to say."

"Not another step until you do so."

"Jennifer is ill, Nigel."

"I know that, but she will soon recover. She has had this condition before, she tells me, and always recovered nicely. And so she shall again."

"No, Nigel, not this time," she said softly as tears came to her eyes. "Her illness is advanced. She is about to leave us."

"Leave us? In what way? Is she going away for treatment?"

"In a manner of speaking, yes. Oh, Nigel. I must say it directly without misleading you: Jennifer is about to die."

"Die?" Nigel said with a look of horror on his face. "No, Sis, this time you are most certainly wrong. I'm in love with her. She cannot die. In our short time in America she has become the centre of my life."

"My impressions are sometimes wrong, or wrongly understood, as you know, dear brother, but not in this case. Some of my impressions are unequivocally clear, and this is one of them I must say with more regret than I can express in words. And we must accept it, you must accept it."

"No! No! I will not accept this monstrous thing you tell me! Jennifer must live. With her 'the world's great age begins anew, the golden years return.' The words are Shelley's, but the reality has to be mine, else life for me has no meaning at all."

"I would do anything to change the course of events for you and Jennifer, if only I could somehow do so. But I cannot. Truly what you call my gift is my curse."

"I shall not accept it."

"Come, Nigel, it's late. At least you cannot deny that fact. We must not break the rules we agreed to with Father Hopkins when we came here."

The next day word came that Jennifer was in the Dayton regional hospital. Her friends piled in two cars and rushed down to see her. Between hacking coughs, she was bright and witty as always. Her friends lavished encouraging assurances on her, insisting that she would soon be well and on her feet. But she was thinner, and a pallor had drained her face of color. Virginia saw plainly that Jennifer struggled to keep a cheerful face. She could see the shrouding death shadow already beginning to settle around her.

On the way back to Urbana, Jennifer's friends convinced themselves that she would soon recover. But a few days later they learned that her parents had committed her to an Illinois clinic for specialized treatment. News spread that the prognosis was grim. By the time it was diagnosed for sure, her tuberculosis was too advanced for successful treatment.

Three weeks later Jennifer was dead. Her death and funeral cast a pervasive gloom over her friends. Death, they assumed and thus did not say, was out of place with the young like Jennifer. By the very right of life as they believed, death was, or ought to be, the expected and acceptable fate of the elderly. Yet in the midst of their youthful fun and gaiety death had rudely trampled the rule, intruding like a thief to steal their joy and darken their days. They would try to live their lives as happily as before, but they would no longer trust life completely.

The summer parties and picnics ended, and anxious to recapture their carefree ways, some of the friends quickly scattered to campuses to recover them. For others happiness was too strong in any case to be daunted. Helen was ecstatic about her approaching Christmas wedding to Tim Morris, Hugh's cousin, and George was relieved to learn that his leg, shattered in a fall into a crevice in the Colorado mountains, should heal completely. College is okay, his doctor told him, but no roughhouse running or jumping for a few months, and no more mountain climbing, at least for a year.

Nigel began a deep bereavement. And to the gloom of his private life was added the disturbing news, relayed in his father's latest letter, that Great Britain appeared to be edging ever closer to war with Germany.

"I shall return home," he told Virginia. "Father's post about the likelihood of war reminds me that I must set aside my personal grief as best I can and prepare myself to do my duty for Mother England. In any case, without Jennifer, there is no longer any meaning for my life here in America, as I once thought. She is what anchored me to this land."

"Don't return to England, Nigel, Virginia begged him. Stay here. Jennifer's passing was a tragic loss, but in time you will meet another girl and have a happy life here. This is the place for you. England is your past; America, your future."

"Virginia, I cannot stay here. I know you sense things, dire things perhaps, that you will not freely tell me. I also have certain forebodings, but my mind is made up. No matter what the future holds back in England, I shall accept it."

"Then, dear brother, if I cannot persuade you to remain here, we shall return to England together. For that was always my intention, as I told you earlier."

"But, Sis, with more reason, it is I who now counsel you to remain in America. It is obvious from observing him in your presence that Henry is in love with you. And from all I have seen of him he gives every sign of being a person of excellent character and steadfast devotion to you. And to include a circumstance that would be of particular interest to our parents, his family appears to be quite comfortably set financially."

"He is what you say, Nigel, and I do care for him also, but for reasons that only he should hear, our relationship must not progress beyond friendship."

"Then you must speak to him soon, sis, for he has already approached me about his feelings for you. In our conversation I told him about my plans to return to England. He was greatly agitated at the thought that you might leave also. So, Sis, prepare yourself for an earnest conversation with him. I fancy he will show up soon."

Sure enough, the very next morning Henry showed up and

with the barest of preliminaries, declared his love to Virginia and asked her to marry him. But as gently as she could, Virginia rejected his proposal.

"But why, Virginia? You surely know I love you. I have made no effort to hide my feelings and couldn't even if I tried. If practical things matter to you, then let me say that my family is financially comfortable. And if you wish it to be so and as a sign that my love for you is true, I will go to England to show your parents who I am and formally ask your father for your hand in marriage."

"Oh, Henry, I have no doubts about your sentiments or your sincerity. And I do care very much for you, too. In these few weeks you have shown yourself to be a gentleman with everyone and a good friend to Nigel and me."

"Then tell me what obstacles stand in the way of my love for you and I promise I will do everything in my power to resolve them."

"There is only one insurmountable reason why I must say no, Henry."

"Well, what is it?"

"Marriage would not work for us. Eventually you would not accept me as I am."

"Oh, but I will accept you, always, always. That I will swear to you on a stack of Bibles!"

"I have no doubt about the sincerity of your intentions. But sadly, no, Henry, my peculiar gift as some call it, though I prefer to describe it as my burden, would become an annoyance and an embarrassment to you. I know you speak with all the sincerity of an honest, truthful man who would make any woman a wonderful husband. But I speak with equal sincerity when I say that sooner or later our differences would divide and separate us."

"But Virginia I also have habits and weaknesses that no doubt I would have to change for the sake of our marriage. And that I am willing, more than willing, to do."

"Believe me, so would I if it were possible. But the difference is that what you call 'habits' or 'weaknesses'—though I have observed none such in your behaviour—are unlike my condition, which for better or worse is who and what I am and cannot be changed. No, Henry, regretfully but for your sake and mine, I must not marry you. And my decision is final. Please accept it and do not ask me again. It is painful for me to reject your proposal, but I must for both our sakes."

"I don't understand."

"But Henry, I understand only too well."

Henry left puzzled, hurt, and angered by what he took to be Virginia's unreasonable decision. Hadn't she admitted that she also cared about him? He was too American to accept fatalism as a reason for anything, especially where love was involved. If two people loved each other, he argued to himself and anyone else who would listen, then any obstacle can be overcome.

But in the end, it was no use. If Henry was insistent at first and persistent till the last, Virginia was unwavering in her decision. The ordeal almost broke her will. Without confessing her deeper feelings to anyone, not even to Nigel, she was deeply in love with Henry. Her vibrant youth cried out for his love, but her foresight said no. Finally, she was reduced to a single surmise: because she loved Henry so deeply, she could not subject him to the emotional wreckage she foresaw for him if she relented and married him. But it was all she could do not to selfishly give in to the temptation to say yes to Henry.

At night she wavered, wept, prayed, and reaffirmed her resolution. But not without a lingering, accusing bitterness against her destiny.

"Why, dear God, did I not foresee for Nigel and me, what I can so often foretell in the lives of others? We came to America innocently hoping for enjoyment and good things. Now we shall both return to England with broken hearts. How I wish now that we had never set foot in this country."

A week later amidst goodbyes and well wishes from the few American friends who had not yet scattered to their respective colleges, Virginia and Nigel boarded the Dayton train for New York via Chicago, and eventually on by liner to England. For them America was over, but their stories are not finished for us.

*****

In January of 1945 Mrs. Helen Farnsworth Hallisey got a heavily censored and long-delayed letter from her husband, Dr. George Hallisey, Major, US Medical Corps. Obviously he was stationed in England, but exactly where cannot be determined because of the redactions.

Dearest Helen:

I trust this letter finds you, my darling, and our dearest little Peggy well and happy. It would be impossible to tell you how much I love and miss you both. Since being promoted to the rank of Major and assuming my new position at ____________ hospital, my situation is as good as one may expect under these trying circumstances. The climate here in _________ is sunnier and my arthritic knee acts up less than it did in _________. (Next time I may listen when a clairvoyant tells me not to go mountain climbing.)

I was sorry to hear about Hugh's death in the Pacific Theater. He always downplayed himself and pretended not be much involved with ordinary matters and people, but he was a brave man under all that put-on.

That thought leads me to an odd but sad circumstance that will certainly interest you and our friends back home. You remember our English friends Nigel and Virginia _______ from back in '38. Would you believe I have seen both in recent weeks? Nigel was a patient here when I first arrived. He survived Dunkirk but was gravely wounded in what they call the "Battle of the Bulge." He's quite the hero and has more medals than I could count. His prognosis remains somewhat problematic. Although physically he is able to take daily walks and generally care for himself, he seems to have fallen into a sort of melancholy world of his own. He acts, or did when I last spoke with him, as though he were much older and even a bit senile. I am a medical doctor, not a psychiatrist, so I cannot comment further on his mental state. He was discharged just last week and sent home to continue his recovery. But if you were to see him today, you would think him at least twenty years older than he was when we knew him back in our college days.

As for Virginia, she was on the nursing staff here for a few weeks but was recently reassigned to _________ France where the need is greater. You recall that she and Nigel both spoke French. I regret to say that she has also greatly aged, one could say at an unnaturally fast pace. Her hair is completely white and her delicate complexion, which we all admired, is now thin and wrinkled like that of a person several decades older. She asked about all her Ohio friends, and specifically about Henry. I cannot describe her reaction when I confirmed what she already seemed to know: that he married Julianne Hopkins and that they have two beautiful children. Was there something between them? I seem to recall some talk of it. In any case, she sent her greetings and well wishes to her American friends and asked me to give them one of Nigel's poems. I include it with this letter. I don't remember much about poetry from my English classes, but I suppose it is an ode of sorts to Jennifer. I think we all knew or learned that Nigel was deeply in love with her and that her death was the main reason he returned to England. Will you see that friends in Urbana get a copy? Virginia wanted all of us to have one.

In closing, my dearest Helen, I think of nothing but returning to you, little Peggy—I try to guess how big she must be by now—, dear relatives, and friends in old Urbana. Ask everyone to pray for the maimed and wounded and for a quick end to this barbaric war. Our side is winning in Europe, but every day it lasts is a day too long. We don't get much official news about how things are going in the Pacific War, but from the scuttlebutt I hear it seems that we are making progress there too. God grant that before long the killing will be over.

With all my love,

George

Jennifer: in Memoriam

About this lake I must have walked a hundred times or more,
Beyond the grove and down the slope, and then along the shore.
I search for things that never were, and yet must ever be,
Recalling dreams that time forgot, of love, of you and me.
The beauties that adorn this lake cannot console my heart.
For why did we, to union born, live out our lives apart?
Within what realm, in shadows grim, did fate our course decree
That we, the heirs to morning light, should never morning see?
Though twilight falls in swift descent and darkness wins this day,
An age will come, a morning dawn, when love shall have its sway.
Then earth's old curse of war and wrong must all dominion yield;
And healed of hurts, reborn from death, our life again we build:
No love is lost, no beauty spent, though time may give them pause.
A balance holds all things in trust till God reveal their cause.

Nigel

A Man of his Word

On a Wednesday afternoon in mid-April, 1922, Wesley Stokesbury, 21, waited as usual for teacher Helen DuMont, 20, to dismiss her first-grade class at the Natchitoches Elementary School. Then together they strolled the short distance to the gate of her two-story, white-columned house at the edge of town. After lingering as long as she allowed, he said goodbye and with her lovely image flooding his thoughts, headed happily toward his house a half mile north of the River Road. Down the road a way he climbed under the barbed wire fence and took his usual shortcut across the pasture, first making sure that "Ole Romper," Fulmer DuMont's prize bull, was nowhere around.

Wesley and Helen had been friends from childhood and classmates until they both finished ninth grade in 1917. Helen went on to High School and then spent a year at College in New Orleans before returning to teach first grade in her old elementary school. Further schooling was out of the question for Wesley. By that time his father James was hopelessly alcoholic, and Wesley had to work their thirty-acre farm east of Natchitoches.

Her image abruptly vanished as he reached the north fence without any sign of the bull and heard his mother screaming and his father cursing. There was a dull thud followed by a second, weaker cry of pain and terror. Wesley knew what was going on and what he had to do to stop it. It was an old, ugly story, repeated many times before, but today enough was finally too much. He would not let it happen again. He scrambled under the barbed wire, ran through the open back door to his bedroom, grabbed a double-barreled, twelve-gauge shotgun, loaded both chambers, and kicked open the door to his parents' bedroom.

He saw a grisly scene. Mildred Farley Stokesbury, 44, was fetally curled up on her side, her arms crossed defensively across her battered face, while husband James Stokesbury, 45, waved a blood-splattered, straight-back hickory chair over his head ready to hit her again.

"You hit her again and I'll shoot," Wesley said quietly.

"You get outta here, boy! This ain't none of your business!"

"You hit her again and I'll shoot," Wesley repeated in the same quiet voice, leveling the shotgun at his father's midriff.

Something in Wesley's tone got through to the drunken James. In earlier years Wesley had pleaded with him not to hurt his mother. But in his violent drunken rages James paid no heed to the boy, or anyone else. Several times city constables or parish deputies had arrested him for assault and destruction of property, but Mildred always refused to press charges. She blamed herself; in some way she could not understand or correct, she had failed James. As for James, nothing was ever his fault. "I do as I damn well please," he said, "and that goes double for my own house!" But this time it was different. Instead of a boy, a man's voice was now speaking to him, and even in his drunken fury James knew there was lethal intention in Wesley's words. He hesitated, then slammed the chair against the wall and stepped away from his wife. Mildred groaned and got to her knees. Blood dripped from her nose and her right eye was already hideously blue and swollen shut.

"She ain't hurt, just putting on a show. But next time, by God, she'll know better than to spend my money! Anyway, I didn't aim to hurt her. It's just that she makes me mad with her whiny complaining and the way she hides my money. On top of that, a man takes one little drink, and she's on him like a chicken on a June bug. I'm the man of this house and what I say goes!"

"Not this time! What goes is you! Get your things and get out of this house! And don't come back! Don't ever come back!"

"Wesley," his mother pleaded, "put the gun down! He's your father! You're his son! Please, Wesley, don't even think about doing what you're saying! You can't have your father's blood on your hands!"

"I don't want his blood on my hands. I'm sorry it runs in my veins. But he can't stay here. One of these days he would kill you, or I would have to kill him. How many times has he promised to change, and how many times has he gone right back to drinking and beating you? Momma, get his things together and put them out on the front porch, or throw them out in the yard. I don't care which. This man is going to leave, or I'll have to shoot him. He'll decide, but he's not going to stay here!"

"Son, you can't . . ."

"I can, Momma, and I will if I have to. Now get his things or he'll leave without them."

"Wesley, put the shotgun down," James said with a travesty of a smile. I promise I won't ever hit your momma again. And I swear I'll never touch a drop of liquor again. I'll quit drinking. I swear it!"

"Wesley, put the gun down and listen to him. We're supposed to forgive. That's the Christian way. Anyway, it's all my fault. I said some things that made him mad. I'll try to do better."

"Momma, you always say that, but you didn't do anything wrong, and I want you to quit saying you did. He's to blame. He's made that same promise a thousand times and you still believe him? No, Momma, he's got to go. He's never kept any promise he made to us. But I can tell you one thing. I will keep my promise. If he ever shows up here again, I'll have to shoot him. I can't let him stay here, not now, not ever again."

"Son, please . . ."

"No, Momma, no! Quit trying to defend him and go get his things! He has to go!"

"Mildred, you just go ahead and get me my damned things and see if I give a good goddamn! I don't aim to stay here and be insulted by this sorry boy of yours! You always took his side anyway, and look what it got you, a boy who's got no natural respect for his father! What mother would let her son take a gun to his father and throw him out after he's agreed to every goddamned thing y'all want him to do?"

"It's too late for talk, now it's time to walk. So get out, with or without your things. And I'm telling you right now, don't show up here again!"

Wesley trembled with rage and conflicted emotions as tearful Mildred gathered James' clothes and pleaded in vain with her son to put the gun down. James blustered and threatened, then promised to change and asked for another chance. But Wesley kept the shotgun leveled at him. In the end James cursed both of them and the world in general, slammed the door so hard that the windows rattled, and disappeared from their life.

Less than two weeks later he was dead from a brutal beating and knifing by an unidentified assailant, or assailants. Only the murderer ever knew who killed him. Mildred and Wesley, Fulmer, Martha, and Helen DuMont, Reverend Buford Yates, Tom and Marie Bougeois, Louis and Inez Tremont, and a few other townspeople attended the funeral on Saturday in late April. Several of the Catholic mourners were a bit tense being in a fundamentalist Protestant church, but in human tragedy and friendship they all overcame their differences. Reverend Yates of Christian Assembly Church preached a short sermon on God's forgiveness and his firm belief that in his final minutes James repented of his sins and was restored to heavenly grace. "Remember, brothers and sisters," he reminded the small congregation, "we believe that once saved, always saved, and for much of his life James was a faithful member of this church." Wesley was empty of feelings and could think of nothing meaningful to say to his weeping mother. Racked with sobs and with a world of grief and pain in her voice, she bent over the body in the open pine-plank casket and asked softly, "Why, James, why couldn't you have changed back when it would have mattered to us?" Despite his resolve not to show his emotions, tears gathered in Wesley's eyes as the pine-plank casket was lowered into the grave and the first shovelfuls of red dirt and gravel rattled on the boards.

The following Tuesday Fulmer DuMont drove his buggy out to the Stokesbury place and informed Mildred that a week earlier James had sold him their farm. The tract was once a part of the 300-acre half section his great great-grandfather Jacques DuMont had bought in 1796, and Fulmer had always wanted to restore it to the original DuMont estate.

"Mr. DuMont, this is the first I've heard of it. I didn't sign any papers, and I would never have agreed to the sale. This land and house were all Wesley and I had left. And I don't see how James could sell the place without my agreeing to it. I thought there was something called 'community property' law."

"Well, Mrs. Stokesbury, I thought so too, and I guess there is. So I asked lawyer Ben Boudreau about it. He looked into it and told me that in his opinion the sale is legal and binding. Seems that there was some confusion about the original sale and deed, and ownership was never clear to start with, whether my family or James had title to the land. In any case, James had claim to the land before you married him and his is the only name on the 1890 deed. You have to understand that James came to me with the offer, otherwise I wouldn't have approached him. Now I'll be glad to take you into town to talk to Mr. Boudreau if you want."

Mildred sighed and shook her head in resignation. "No, it wouldn't change anything, and I don't have money for lawyers and legal stuff like that. So we'll just have to leave things the way they are. It's true that James had the farm when we married. He told me his granddaddy bought it from your folks way back yonder in the 1800s and that there were some questions about the transaction that were never settled."

"That's the way I understand it, too. Some of the old deeds are confusing because of the differences between the French and English languages and land measurements—*Arpents* and acres, things like that. Anyway, I wanted to come out and tell you about it. I'm real sorry about the troubles you've had and now this."

"I just don't know what we'll do now. All we have left are the team, wagon, and plows. I reckon there's still a few bushels of corn in the crib. James didn't leave us any money and had none on him when he died, they tell me. Did you pay him in cash money, Mr. DuMont?"

"I did, $1,000 in ten new hundred-dollar bills, but I guess we both know what happened to it. I'm sorry I couldn't turn the money over to you, but legally it was his. And I hate to tell you, but the team, wagon, animals, and farm implements were part of the deal. James threw them in with everything else."

Fulmer didn't tell Mildred that James had offered to include the house furniture, but he wouldn't accept it.

Mildred shook her head. "I understand, and yes, we both know there's no question about what went with the money. Every penny James could come up with always went for liquor or gambling—or worse things. No reason to drag all that up again. My problem is that we don't have anywhere to go. The folks I have left don't live in this part of the country and couldn't help me even if they did."

"Look, Mrs. Stokesbury. This is part of what I wanted to tell you. I'm not asking you and Wesley to move out of the house. For the time being I don't have any pressing need of it, though Cyrus Hardoin, my overseer, may want to keep some farm implements in the barn. You and Wesley can live here rent free if you want to, at least until you figure out something better. You can have the corn that's left in the corncrib and the use of the outbuildings just like always. I'll leave you and Wesley the cow, hogs and chickens. Go ahead and tend your garden spot, too. And I was thinking that since this year I'll be needing more field hands, Wesley could work for me like he has in his spare days for the last few years. You tell him to come by the house tomorrow evening around five or so. I want to talk to him about it. He's the man of the family now and needs to hear it from me, man to man. And if you're willing, Mrs. Stokesbury, Martha tells me she may ask you to help some with her housework. I guess you heard that her colored maid Hannah Meeks has moved out to her sister's in Dallas and left Martha without housekeeping help. But I reckon she'll talk to you about all that. I know all this is hard on you and we want to be fair with you."

"Mr. DuMont, you don't know how much I appreciate what you're saying. Wesley and me, we need the work, and we want to do whatever we can to show our appreciation. Thank you and God bless you both for your good intentions. I don't hold what James did against you. You and your family will be in my prayers."

"Well, I'm glad you feel that way and thank you for it," Fulmer said with some embarrassment. "Now, I'll say good day to you and be on my way."

When word spread that Wesley had run his father off with a loaded shotgun people forgot his many reasons and remembered only the single threat to shoot. Before he was murdered, James told a twisted version of what happened that put all the blame on Wesley and Mildred. That plus the normal gossipy exaggeration of events persuaded some people that Wesley was probably directly responsible for James' death.

"I know James Stokesbury was a drinking man and could be mean as a sore-tailed bear when he was drunk," storekeeper Tom Bourgeois said, "but that don't give that boy the right to pull a gun on his daddy. I reckon he's twenty or twenty-one and nearly a grown man, but if my boys Robert or Joel had done that, grown or not, why I would've taken that shotgun away from them and broke it over their head."

"I see it the same way you do, Tom," cane grower Louis Tremont said as he trimmed his last wedge of chewing tobacco with his pocket knife. "James used to be a good worker when he was sober but mean as hell when he got to drinking, which is about all he was fit for these last few years. But then again we don't know what aggravations he had to put up with, do we? People tell me there's more to the story than what Mildred and her boy are telling. I do feel sorry for her though. She seems like a good, soft-spoken woman and all in public, but then again we don't know what she's like when the doors are shut, do we?"

"No we don't, Tom, and that's the thing. James Stokesbury was not a perfect man. Hell, no mortal man is—except me of course," Tom grinned, "But a man has the right to have the say over his own household. Folks are saying now that the boy might even have been the one that killed his daddy."

Tom shook his head. "I've heard that talk too and that's why I've told my kids to stay away from him. I don't want them around somebody like that. Why, even if he didn't kill James, he was just one pull on the trigger from being a murderer. And his own daddy, too. Riotous living, as Father Vincent said in his homily last Sunday, runs in that family and trouble follows them like their shadow. You remember old Henry Stokesbury, James' daddy, don't you? He was as much of a wino as James was, maybe worse. And somebody told me that the family was prosperous way back before the Civil War. Now I don't like to speak ill of the dead, but old Henry, and maybe some before him, started that family down the road to ruin and I guess now James has finished the job."

"Yeah, and alcohol got his daddy killed just like it did James. They never did find out who knifed old Henry either, did they?"

"No, they didn't. You remember that all kinds of rumors circulated about money he owed to some gamblers down in Baton Rouge but nothing the law could use as evidence. There was talk that Ben Judson, that lumberman up in Mansfield could've been involved. That man's as mean as a Mexican scorpion. But could've been anybody. He ran with bad company just like James. He cheated and gypped everybody he could in

Natchitoches and other places around this part of the world. And I was one of the ones he swindled way back when I was just starting out as a young storekeeper. Never saw a penny of what he owed me, and it was considerable. The only good I got out of it was a lesson to be more careful with credit. I reckon he ended up with more enemies than fleas on a dog, and to tell the truth, James turned out to be just as sorry. And I'll bet you money that boy Wesley will be just like them. I heard a doctor say one time that drinking runs in families. And besides all that, I was always told that the Stokesburys have Indian blood, and it shows with their black hair and darker skin and all, and they say Indians can't handle liquor."

"Well, hell, Tom, you don't have to be a doctor to know that stuff. You can see it in families all the time. But I reckon you're right about the Indians. I remember my great grandpapá on my mother's side, Antoine LeBrun, saying they couldn't hold their liquor, and he would never offer them wine. Some of them and a few of the Natchez tribe still lived in this part of the world way back yonder when he was a boy. That was before they were killed off or the government sent them out to Oklahoma Territory. Speaking of Indians, while you're up there by the counter, Tom, hand me another pack of that Red Man chewing tobacco, yeah, that's it, the one right there on the right, and then I'll be getting on back to the house."

"What's the story on the Stokesburys anyway, Louis? Wasn't your family connected with them in some way?"

"I was told it started way back with my great great-grandfather. He started out in Quebec, so they said, and then sorta turned wild after his first wife died and lived for several years as a trapper and hunter back in Cherokee mountain country. I think they called men like him *"coureurs de bois"* or something like that. My grandpapá said it mean "wood runners." I guess that's where he first met up with the Stokesburys. Later he moved down here, settled, and married again. When he heard the Stokesburys were looking for a new place to settle, he had them move here. Great Great-Grandpapá must have been a pistol in his day. My *grand-maman* told us that he ran away from Quebec with a girl from a high-class family. And she told me, too, that a long time ago, back in France, that the Tremonts, or Trémonts, as the old folks used to call it, were high society folks and members of the nobility. So Tom, you don't have to bow, but you need to be more respectful when you talk to me."

"That'll be the day. But ain't it always the same story? Women just keep a young man's life in an unholy mess. What did the old folks used to say every time a fellow got in trouble, *Cherchez la* woman, or something like that."

"As I remember, it was Cherchez la femme. Look for the woman."

"Yeah, that was it. Look for the woman. Too bad we forgot all our good old French language, ain't it, Tom? My Grand-Maman could still speak it and tried to teach me, but I didn't want to learn. But anyway, women get a man into more trouble than he can ever get out of."

"And if you think about it, don't we do the same for the ladies?"

"I guess so. Seems like that's the way God set up creation. Well, I'd best be getting on. I got me a man coming over to look at my cane harvest and a couple of fattening hogs, and I'm hoping he'll make me an offer to take all of it. How much do I owe you for the tobacco?"

"Fifteen cents."

"Fifteen cents? That's three pennies more than last time."

"Yeah, prices have gone up a little."

"I don't see how common folks are going to make it with prices going up all the time. But things are always against plain folks. Anyhow, stay in the traces, Tom and I'll see you next time."

"Same to you, Lou, er, Sir Lou, I reckon I should say."

Wesley showed up at the DuMont house at five the next afternoon. Fulmer opened the door and told him to come with him down to the barn. Helen was nowhere to be seen.

"Wesley, I'll say again that I'm real sorry about your father," Fulmer said, fumbling with the Georgia latch on a stable door and more nervous than he wanted to show.

"Momma said you wanted to talk to me," Wesley responded, ignoring Fulmer's comment.

"That's right, Wesley. She probably told you that James sold the place to me."

"Yes sir, but she said you would let us stay on in the house."

"I did tell her that, but I wanted to talk to you about that and some other things, now that you're the man of the house."

"We're obliged to you, Mr. DuMont. Daddy didn't have any right to sell the place without telling us. But I guess what's done is done. Anyway, if you'll let us stay on, we'll take good care of the place."

"I know you will."

"Momma said you might want me to work for you."

"That's right, Wesley. You may have heard that I'm planting a lot more cotton acreage this year—nearly two hundred fifty acres—plus my usual acreage in cane, and I'll need more field hands. What I'll want you to do mainly is tend the thirty acres your family has farmed over the years. You know the land and the team, and the plows are already there in the barn and outbuildings, so that makes it easier for you. Now then, if you have time to spare, I'll ask you to help out in my cane fields. As you know, Cyrus Hardoin is my overseer, so you'll be working under his supervision. Of course, you've worked under Cyrus before."

"Yes sir, when I could these last five or six years, both in cotton and corn, and some in the cane. I always tried to put in an honest day's work for him. I guess you know I've already planted early this year and was lucky enough to miss the late frost. I've got a good stand of cotton and corn already. Momma and me had just enough money to cover the fertilizer with money she saved up last fall and kept from Daddy. He beat her up when he found out about it. That's why I had to run him off, to keep him from killing her."

"I know, Wesley, and that's a shame. But here's what I can offer you to make things as right as I can with you. The land and everything planted on it is mine by right of ownership. That was the agreement I made with James. But I don't know if you and Mildred knew about it."

"No sir, he didn't tell us anything. We didn't know the first thing about it."

"That's what I figured. But to be fair to you I'll hire you on come Monday when the main planting starts. And, as I said, you and your mother can stay on in the house rent free. And like I said, you can keep the hogs, cow, chickens, and the garden spot for your use. I believe that's a fair arrangement, not perfect but the best I can do under the circumstances. You're a hard worker, and I want you to see to it that the land gives us a good crop.

That's why I want you to work for me again. Cyrus speaks well of you, Wesley. As for the money, I'll pay you the going wage for a man, two dollars a day in the growing and gathering seasons, except Sunday and rainy days, just like all the other hands. And I keep short accounts—pay off every Friday. You check with Cyrus about anything you need and help with the chopping, hoeing, and gathering. Does all this sound fair to you?"

"Yes sir, Mr. DuMont, and I'm much obliged to you. I promise I'll do my best. Now if you don't need me for anything else right now, it's late so I reckon I'll be on my way, Momma being the way she is after . . . But again, I thank you for the chance. I'll do what Mr. Hardoin tells me."

"Uh, yeah, Wesley, that's good. I'm glad that's settled, but now there is one other matter I have to talk to you about before you leave."

"Yes sir?"

"Wesley, I know that you and Helen played together when you were little kids and that here lately you've been walking her home from school after she's finished her teaching. I need to talk to you about that."

"Is something wrong?"

"Not with you, Wesley, just the circumstances. I hate to say this, but I'll have to ask you to keep your distance from Helen from now on."

"Is it because of the drinking in my family? Or our religious differences?"

"To be honest with you, Wesley, it's the drinking, not the Church. Helen likes you. As far as that's concerned, we all like you, but you both are getting on toward marriageable age and . . "

"You don't want her to end up with a man from a family like

mine. Is that what you're telling me?"

"Wesley, I've got nothing against you personally. You have proved yourself to be a hardworking boy—young man—and Helen tells you were a smart student back in your schooling days. But to be honest with you, the family reputation is against you, and I can't run the risk where Helen is concerned. She's my only child since our baby girl Betty passed away in the flu epidemic in '17, and I have to do all I can to protect her and give her every chance at a good marriage. So, I hate to do it, but I'll have to ask you to stay away from her. Now Wesley, this is what I'm asking you to do: give me your word that you'll do what I ask. And I believe you are a man of your word. That's the one and only condition I place on our agreement to let you and your mother stay on the place and work for me like I said before. Now if for some reason you can't agree to it, then I'm afraid I'd have to ask you to move out. As I said, Wesley, I have nothing against you personally, but my first obligation is to my daughter. I hope you can see things from my side. I try to be fair to everybody, but my daughter comes first."

Wesley was silent for a long moment as he stared at Ole Romper stalking back and forth by the far pasture fence next to his house.

"Wesley, what . . . ?" Fulmer started to ask.

"Yes, sir," he interrupted, turning back to face Fulmer, "I understand your reasons. Mr. DuMont, and I give you my word that I won't talk to Helen any more. But just let me say one more thing."

A flicker of concern wrinkled Fulmer's broad face as he closed the Georgia latch. "And what would that be?" he asked cautiously.

"I just want you to know that if there's ever anything I can do for you or your family, Mrs. DuMont and Helen, I promise I'll do it. You have all been good to us and I would want to do what I can if ever you are in a bind. I want you to know that."

"I appreciate that, Wesley," Fulmer said with relief and a condescending smile, thinking to himself that such a circumstance would never come about. "I don't like asking you to do this and let me say here and now that I hope life is good to you. You've had a hard life and Lord knows you and your mother may be in for more hard times down the road—for that matter, who knows what we all may be in for—but I hope you always stay on the right course. If you keep the faith and work hard, I believe the Good Lord will see you through. Wesley, I know what I'm talking about. I had it pretty hard myself growing up in Henderson Swamp down south. But no need to go into that story now."

They shook hands and went on their way. Wesley took his customary shortcut across the pasture and for once he didn't look to see whether Ole Romper was close by or not. Today was different in a lot of ways. There was a finality in his life, but he did not know exactly what it meant or what would follow, only that it was painful. A lot of doors had slammed shut and the world was closing in on him. He was having to pull back in retreat on all sides. Now, suddenly, Helen was beyond his reach. Wesley meant to keep the promise he had made to Fulmer. But despite his resolve, his eyes teared over and he clinched his fists in anger as he silently said goodbye to her and surrendered his boyhood ideals and the future he had dreamed about. From now on, he thought to himself, he would have to take care of his mother and face the ugly world as a man. His young life was over in everything but years. Despite all, though, the transition had a certain upside. He needed the full strength of manhood. What hurt—and probably always would—was losing the girl who had always been the center of his world.

At that moment he saw the yellow glow of the kerosene lamp Mildred had just lit. The lamp and emerging starlight were the only lights left. Ole Romper watched him from his favorite spot by the fence, but except for a snort and a swish of his tail made no hostile move. For once Wesley felt no fear of him and perhaps the animal sensed the change in him.

With few exceptions, his former friends and schoolmates kept their distance. True to his promise to Fulmer, Wesley stayed away from Helen. He wondered if Fulmer had explained the situation to her. It would be years before he spoke to her again, though at times he yielded to the overwhelming desire to sneak a glimpse of her from a distance.

Helen was always on his mind, but loneliness drove him to talk to other girls. Judith Fontaine twice invited him to escort her, first to a picnic and then to a party. She was pretty and talkative, but afterwards Wesley did not follow up and Judith turned to other boys. Months later she married Brian Bordelon of Colfax. News of her wedding saddened Wesley, not because of any feelings for her but because it was another reminder life was passing him by.

A similar isolating separation happened at Christian Assembly Church that Mildred and Wesley had attended since he was a child. James was a member until alcoholism replaced his religious faith. After a few Sundays of stares and cold treatment, Wesley pleaded excessive farm work and told Mildred that he would not be going back to church but urged her to go for both of them. She said she understood, but her eyes glistened with tears. Wesley was everything she could desire in a son and it grieved her to see him entering manhood without the normal youthful entertainments and friendships. He did not speak again of Helen, in fact spoke little about anything, but she guessed what Fulmer, or maybe Helen herself, must had said to him and with a mother's wisdom understood his silence and sensed his pain.

Wesley devoted all his time and energy to the fields, and the crops prospered. At first Cyrus balked when Wesley asked for extra guano for the fields.

"Son, we've never used more than three or four hundred pounds to the acre and that at spring planting, never any extra in the middle of summer. This stretch of land, especially this side of the Red River, is pretty rich to start with. You use more than that and you'll burn the corn up and the cotton will be all stalk and no bolls. I don't recommend it."

"Mr. Hardoin, I understand what you're saying, but along about the first week in July I'd like to try about a hundred and fifty pounds of fertilizer an acre extra and see what happens. I could be wrong, but I believe it'll pay off."

Wesley had read about the beneficial effects of extra fertilizer and the negative thinking of Southern cotton farmers about its use, but he thought it best not to mention book knowledge to crusty old Cyrus.

"Well, I reckon I can spare you that much. Fulmer told me to give you what you asked for. But if it don't work, we'll both have to answer to him."

Wesley applied the extra fertilizer in July. Rains came three days later and by laying-by plowing at the end of the month both the cotton and corn had taken on a deep green, vigorous luster and sagged under the weight of bolls and ears. As the cotton field began to turn white in the last ten days of August it was apparent that Wesley was right about the extra fertilizer. Old Cyrus shook his head in disbelief when he came out to have a look.

"Well, *sacré bleu*, just look at that field, would you! I wouldn't have believed it, son, but you have the best cotton and corn in this part of the Valley. They say old dogs can't learn new tricks, but by George, I'm ready to take back what I said to you in the spring. If this works, and it looks like it will, next year I'm going to recommend to Mr. DuMont that we do to two hundred acres what you've done to thirty."

When the final harvest was over, Wesley's twenty acres of cotton yielded forty-six bales of cotton, over twice the average harvest. And the corn bushel production was equally impressive. The following year, Fulmer took Cyrus' advice and added the midsummer fertilizer following Wesley's example. Even though the rains did not come at the best times, the cotton yield was still fifty percent higher than normal. Fulmer was delighted with both the profits and his enhanced reputation as the top cotton farmer in that end of the parish. Wesley's field yielded thirty-nine bales in a drier season than normal and nearly the same bumper crop of corn as the year before. On a late October Saturday Fulmer came out in his brand-new Model T Ford to talk to Wesley.

"Wesley, I just want to tell you how pleased I am with what you've done. For two years in a row you have had the top yield around this part of the parish, and our overall production is over half again as much as it was two years ago."

"I'm real pleased it turned out that way. I'm glad you and Mr. Hardoin let me use the extra guano, and the credit goes to him. I believe it more than paid for itself."

"Man, you bet it did! Now, Wesley, is there anything else you know of that will let us get even bigger yields?"

"Well, Mr. DuMont, I've been thinking about that, and I do have one thing we might try?"

"Yeah, and what's that?"

"I don't know much about cane, but I wonder if we're not thinning out the cotton and corn too much. Now that we're using more fertilizer, maybe we could leave more stalks. I believe it might pay off."

"But what if it didn't? Wouldn't too many stalks crowd too much and stifle everything?"

"Maybe, but what if we tried it on just a couple of acres? Then if it didn't work, it wouldn't affect the harvest that much. But if it does work, then the next year we could do the same thing to more acreage."

"Well, it sounds reasonable, but I still have my doubts. But I guess we wouldn't be taking a big risk if we first tried it on just a few acres."

"The way I figure it, eventually we might not have to chop by hand at all."

"I don't follow you. What do you mean?"

"We could just put a different plate in the planter, one that it would spread the seeds apart a little more. If it worked, just think of the money and time you could save if we didn't have to pay for all that chopping."

"But they don't make planter plates like you're talking about, do they?"

"No sir, not that I know of, but why couldn't we make our own?"

"What do you mean? How could we make our own?"

"Well, sir, I don't mean make them from scratch, but we could modify the factory-made ones, maybe plug every second hole or third hole in the rotation, something like that. If you want me to, I have thought of a way to rig up one for you and Mr. Hardoin to look at."

"I wish you would. But first, Wesley, I need to talk to you about something else."

"Yes sir?"

"I'm not going to keep it from you that you've made me a lot of money with your idea about the extra fertilizer and I'm beholden to you."

"Well, I'm just glad it turned out that way, and I give credit to Mr. Hardoin for letting me do it."

"What I'd like to do is offer you the job of working directly under Cyrus. It would mean more responsibility but a higher pay, too, three dollars a day instead of two. Cyrus has been my right-hand man for a good many years now, but he's getting a little long in the tooth and can't put in the hours he could when he was younger. I know he likes you and I believe you could work together, under his supervision of course. What do you think?"

"I respect Mr. Hardoin a lot, and if you ask me, he seems to still be much of a man. But if it's something you want me to do, I'd be glad to give it a try. But I have to say I don't have any complaints about doing what I've been doing."

"And you're good at it, and that's all the more reason to tighten up your traces a link or two. So, unless you tell me different, come next Monday, you'll be working with Cyrus. You can think of yourself as 'underseer' to my overseer," he said, a smile creasing his face, "something like a deputy overseer."

"I have just one question, Mr. DuMont. Is Mr. Hardoin okay

with me? Like I said, I respect him a lot and wouldn't want to do anything that puts him in a bind."

"Wesley, I've talked with him already, and he's happy with the idea. There are older men, good men, who work for me, but you seem to have a special knack for seeing new ways to do things, ways that make money and do us all a lot of good. That new Model-T Ford car you see sitting out there in the yard is one result of your good thinking."

"I'm glad."

"Tomorrow, me, Martha, and Robert Bourgeois, Tom's son, are driving Helen in it. She's having a reunion with some of her old classmates down in Alexandria. It's a long way, forty or fifty miles at least, but that's a fine automobile."

Wesley nodded without comment, but the mention of Robert Bourgeois was like a stab wound. Long after Fulmer left, he felt residual emotional tremors. He had not spoken to Helen since James' funeral and had seen her only from a distance, but he reasoned that eventually Robert or someone like him would come along and that in the natural unfolding of life someday she would marry. Still, his heart rebelled against what his head told him. Helen was ever present in his thoughts as he worked in the fields, her image undimmed by separation and time. But he had given Fulmer his word not to see her any more, and he would die before breaking it. It was all he had left. Even though he did not say so in words, not even to himself, there was a wounded pride in him. He was determined to prove to himself and everybody else in Natchitoches that even though he was the son and grandson of drunkards, he was his own man who lived by his private code of honor. But to say so would seem like dismissive arrogant boasting that nobody would believe. Only in the slow pace of life would he be able to show it. He could not foresee what it meant, only that it did not include the happiness with Helen he once dreamed of, at best only a grim, silent satisfaction. But that he could endure, or at least told himself he could. He sensed rather than reasoned that a day might come when his determination would be put to the test. He had set his life course for the years ahead, patiently living them one day at a time. But even at that early stage he was aware that someday the wild card of chance could trump his well-laid plans. But it was nothing to be concerned about. He was too still young to see it as anything but a time too distant from the present to be real. His life appeared to be still too spacious and his days too many ever to be overtaken by the slow approach of remote years yet unborn.

The events leading to James' death, which many in Natchitoches first attributed to the same ancestral flaws in Wesley that had brought the family to moral and alcoholic ruin, in time were reduced in the collective opinion to a small blemish on his growing reputation as a successful farmer and man of influence in his job as Assistant Overseer to Cyrus Hardoin. Just as his perceived defects were once exaggerated, now in the fickle swing of public opinion so were his virtues.

"You know, Tom, I never did believe all those tales they were telling two or three years ago about Wesley Stokes," Louis Tremont said as he cut a slice from his Red Man Chewing Tobacco with his Barlow knife. "That man was always a hard worker as a boy and now as a man he's just about the best cotton farmer in this parish. I reckon if he had to get tough with his daddy, why it was to defend his momma. James was a mean one when he took to the bottle, which was every chance he had."

"Yeah, I agree with you, Lou. People talk out of turn and

make mountains out of molehills. Wesley comes in the store a lot, always friendly and never late in paying for what he buys. I've never heard him use swear words and doesn't drink at all. And you remember when everybody was saying he would follow right along in the tracks of his daddy and grandpa? Shows you how much judgment some folks have. Not a thimbleful of sense, as my grandma Marie-Agnes Meuniere used to say." "Somebody told me yesterday that a farm agent and some agricultural experts along with some bankers, have been out to talk to him about how he manages to get so many bales to the acre."

"I don't doubt it. He's just about made Fulmer DuMont a rich man. And done all right for himself, I reckon. Did you see that new car he bought?"

"Who, Wesley?"

"No, Fulmer, it's some kind of truck, not a car, a Chevrolet I think. I saw it yesterday. Shiny as a new silver dollar. And he's still got his Model-T Ford. I doubt you'll catch Wesley Stokesbury spending money on motor cars. They tell me he saves about everything he makes. Somebody at the Bank let it slip that he's got an account with over a thousand dollars in it."

"Speaking of the DuMonts, what's this I hear about your boy Robert and Fulmer's daughter breaking up? Last I heard they were about to get married."

"Well, that's what we all thought. They've been going together for two or three years. Robert wanted to get married some time ago, but Helen wanted to teach school a little long. So one year turned into two and still no wedding. Times have changed, but the school people still don't want married women for teachers. That makes it hard to keep teachers; they keep marrying and leaving the teaching business to start families of their own. Oh, here comes Mrs. Cora LeBlanc Let me wait on her."

"You go right ahead. Well, *bonjour*, Mrs. LeBlanc. How's your family getting along?"

"*Très bien*, I reckon, Mr. Tremont. Bill has the miseries again. Gets them every year about this time. Coughing, sneezing, runny nose, and all."

"What do you reckon it is?"

"We don't have the slightest idea. Last year we took him to Doctor Bentley down in Baton Rouge and he told Bill he probably had what they call an allergy."

"A what?"

"An allergy, they call it. I really don't know what it is, Mr. Tremont. Dr. Bentley said it was a kind of irritation caused by plants or animals that affects the breathing passages. I told Bill it might be the cedar trees out in the front yard. He likes to sit out there on the porch with that old dog of his when the weather's good, and that powder and stuff comes blowing in the house. I told him he ought to cut the cedars down just to be on the safe side."

"Did he?" asked Tom.

"Lord no! You know how stubborn Bill is, as hardheaded as a balky mule. He got mad and said that Dr. Bentley didn't know his head from a hole in the ground—and some other things I can't repeat."

"Is he taking any medicine?" Tom wondered.

"Well, he claims he isn't, but he's got something hidden out in the storage shed. I see him slip out there every now and then when he thinks I'm not looking. That's why I've come down here to the store, Mr. Bourgeois, to see if you might stock something that could help him."

"The only two things I can think of right off hand are garlic powder, which I have on the shelf, and honey, which I don't stock. Directions on the powder will tell you how to fix it but do add a dash of Cayenne pepper to it. But I would advise you to go over to Delbert Brown's. He just put up about fifteen jars of fresh clover-based honey, as pure and clear as it can be. But do what you can to keep Bill out of the smokehouse. I imagine we all know what he's got hidden out there, and you don't want him to get in the habit of nipping that stuff too often."

"Well, I'll try it. Bill coughs and sneezes so much that nobody can get any rest at our house."

"Have you thought about locking him and his old dog in that shed you talking about?" Louis asked with a grin.

Cora stared at him for a few seconds before catching the humor. "You know, Mr. Tremont," she said laughing, "that's not such a bad idea. It might make my life a lot easier if I could put him and that old hound of his in there together. They're both too old to hunt anyway. About all they're fit for these days is to get in my way. How much do I owe you, Mr. Bourgeois?"

"Nothing for the advice about the honey, Mrs. LeBlanc; thirty-five cents for garlic powder and a penny tax. Got to keep the government in business."

"Yeah, they've always got their hand out, don't they?" Louis commented, "For all the good they do us."

"Uh huh, well, I best be getting along. Good day to you both and do give my kind regards to Inez and Marie."

"Yes, ma'am," Lou and Tom said in unison.

"Mrs. LeBlanc is a fine woman," Tom said as the door closed behind her, "maybe a bit hot-tempered, though, so I hear."

"Yeah, that she is, so they tell me. Horace Dutreau is neighbor to them, as you know, and he told me once that she and Bill have had some arguments so loud they could damage your eardrums."

"I guess we all have our faults—except me, of course," Tom said with a grin.

"Yeah, you wish. Well, I'd best be getting back to the house. But I just remembered, you never did tell me why your boy and that DuMont girl broke up. Inez couldn't tell me."

"Well, Marie and I couldn't get much out of Robert," Tom said, his grin fading, "but as best I understood it, they had a falling out over Wesley Stokesbury."

"Wesley Stokesbury? What did he have to do with it, if you don't mind telling me?"

"I don't know for certain. Robert never has liked him for some reason. Maybe jealous of him. You know the Stokesbury boy used to talk to her before Fulmer DuMont put a stop to it. Well, I guess Robert said something about him that the girl didn't like, and she took up for him. That made Robert mad. One thing led to another and first thing you know they broke up."

"Don't you reckon they'll patch things up? Young people say just about anything that pops into their minds these days. It was different back in our day."

"I have my doubts that they'll get back together any time soon. Robert's already talking to Cyrus Hardoin granddaughter Margaret. She's been after him for the longest."

"I guess she's a good girl, if you can stand the Hardoin clan. You reckon he's just trying to show the DuMont girl that other girls like him so she'll come a running back?"

"It could be that, but I'm thinking there's more to it. The fact that the girl kept putting off the wedding tells me a lot. Anyway, me and Marie are staying clear of the whole thing. I've got enough worries without trying to settle young people's spats."

"Probably the smartest thing to do. Well, I better be getting on back to the house. Stay in the traces, Tom, and I'll see you next time."

"Same to you, Lou."

Tom was relieved that Lou had not asked him for a Coca cola that he never paid for.

In the fall of 1924 Mildred started coughing and losing weight. Wesley was concerned but she insisted that nothing was wrong. "I always get a cold in the fall."

But then one day her coughing worsened. She began spitting up blood and was too weak to do housework for Mrs. DuMont. Over her objections, Wesley hitched the team to the wagon and took her to see Dr. Bentley. His preliminary diagnosis was ominous. "Mildred, Wesley, I'll be honest with you. I'm afraid it could be tuberculosis, consumption the old people call it, and I've seen several cases lately. I'll be in a better position to say for sure when we've had a chance to examine the specimens I took. I don't have the equipment here in my office, but the hospital across town does. It probably will take the better part of the week to get the results."

To nobody's surprise but contrary to everybody's hopes, Mildred's tuberculosis was confirmed. Dr. Bentley was vague about possible cures.

"You might think of moving to a place like Arizona," Dr. Bentley advised. "The desert climate seems to help some people, and then there's the coast. Others report that the salt air is beneficial."

"I can't even think of such places," Mildred said, "I can't afford to move away, and even if I could, I wouldn't. I've lived here most of my life, and here is where I'll die."

"No, momma, you're not going to die!" Wesley protested, disturbed by her fatalism, "We'll get you well and strong. You'll see."

But Wesley was wrong and Mildred's mortal premonitions were right. She could not keep her food down. She lost weight and declined rapidly and within weeks took to her deathbed. But the cause was more than tuberculosis. When Dr. Bentley responded to Wesley's desperate request and drove his Buick up to see her, he found the symptoms of stomach cancer. As she edged closer to the end, her mind wandered and several times she was delirious with high fever. But one day when her mind was clear, she confessed her feelings to Wesley.

"When James died, I started dying too. Until then I hoped he would come back, and we could live together as a family. I know, son, Lord God how well I know, that he was a bad husband and father, but I loved him anyway and was never meant to live without him."

She silent for a moment, staring into space. Then she turned and placed her hand on Wesley's arm. "Son, there is one more thing I need you to do."

"What's that, momma?"

"I want you to write to my folks back in Blount County, Tennessee. Let them know about me. Tell them I'm sick but happy and that I've had a good life. There's an old address in there in the dresser drawer. I don't know if any of the family still lives there or not. But maybe a letter will get to them. Just put it in care of Harris and Dicey Farley. They're your grandparents, if either one is still alive."

Mildred had never talked about her family, and after several years Wesley stopped asking her about them. He guessed that over their objections his mother had run away and married James.

Many weeks later the letter returned unopened. "Dead," I guess, Wesley thought to himself.

Wesley second-guessed himself as Mildred grew weaker. "Maybe I was the one that should have left," he thought. "But then he would have killed momma. I thought I was doing the right thing, but maybe I was wrong. Maybe I should have just walked out and left them together. Maybe I didn't have the right to do what I did. But then I couldn't leave momma."

After obsessing for several days over the contradictory options, he convinced himself that an ideal resolution of his dilemma was out of the question and in any case the consequences could not be undone. He had done what he thought was best under the circumstances and so eased his conscience and put the matter to rest, though sometimes at night he would wake up and rehash it.

A week later when he brought in her breakfast, Mildred did not respond. He touched her arm and knew by the alien feel of her skin that she was gone. He sobbed but after a while was comforted by the realization that she had died in her sleep and her suffering was over. Then, suddenly, the temporary relief gave way to a feeling of absolute and utter loneliness. Mildred was the remaining tether that had tied him to the world, like those he sometimes attached to the young mules to keep them from jumping the low barnyard fence and wandering into the fields. Now he felt the subdued dread of abandonment, which unwise people mistake for freedom.

Unlike James' funeral, Mildred's was packed with church members and townspeople. She was praised as a faithful

Christian woman whose life was hard but her example was inspiring. Preacher Yates spoke of her many acts of kindness and charity and assured the congregation that Mildred was now at peace in the Heavenly Kingdom. "Brothers and sisters, this parting sermon is sad for us in this sinful world yet easy in a way to preach. Mildred already preached it for us by the Godly way she lived." With that and many condolences to Wesley from the congregation, she was laid to rest beside James. But Wesley bought her an iron casket.

As for Wesley, he was far from any peace of mind in the following days. Helen and her parents attended the funeral, and at the sight of her and the sound of her voice—the first time she had spoken to him in over two years—his old feelings rushed forth like a reopened wound. She was lovelier and more mature, transformed in ways he could not describe from the pretty girl of former times into the beautiful woman who told him how sorry she was for his loss. She meant Mildred, of course, but for Wesley even at that moment of grieving he was aware of an even greater loss. He loved Helen and despite his promise to Fulmer, could not imagine not loving her, even though now she had moved beyond him and his small world to higher circles he could not reach. Everything separated them—money, church, social class. There was only one possible remedy and it was clear to him before the funeral had ended: everything that had been meaningful had left him, and now he must leave Natchitoches.

But then, as Wesley once idly speculated, fate now chose to play the wild card. The very day Wesley had made up his mind to tell Fulmer of his decision to leave Natchitoches, word came that Cyrus Hardoin had suffered a debilitating stroke and could not stand or speak. Two hundred fifty acres were snowy with cotton, and Wesley had to do what he could to bring in the harvest. His plans went unmentioned in the urgency of the moment. Fulmer, genuinely concerned for old Cyrus, was more frantic with worry than any of his men had ever seen him. After considering his options, he had no real choice but to entrust Wesley with the supervisory job even though he may have felt secretly it was still too much for him. The men liked Wesley, but he was young, and Fulmer had reason to doubt his leadership.

Fulmer's distracting worries proved to be near fatal. He pitched in and personally hauled cotton to the eastside cotton gin. But on a hurried late afternoon run in his Chevrolet truck, top heavy with an overload of cotton, it tipped over while crossing a shallow ditch at too high a speed. Fulmer was thrown across the cab, banging his head and side on the passenger door. He was groggy and bleeding when the men got to him. They stretched him on some of the loose cotton until he roused himself. Wesley gave him a dipperful of water, then deciding that his injuries were not life-threatening, asked Les Chaney to take him home in one of the wagons. Fulmer protested that he had to get the cotton to the gin, but Wesley would have none of it. "We'll haul it to the gin first thing in the morning, Mr. DuMont, and if the weather holds, we'll have this field picked clean in another two to three days. Just rest and leave it to us. That's what you pay us to do. And we'll do it."

After Les had driven Fulmer away in the wagon, Wesley ordered the cotton unloaded on a tarpaulin and with a dozen strong men and some stout ropes tied to the sideboards and through the cab they uprighted the truck, undamaged except for a few scratches. "It's quitting time," he told them. "Leave the cotton on the tarp and we'll reload it first thing in the morning.

It's too late to do anything else today. Go on home and sleep well. Tomorrow we'll make up for lost time, and remember Mr. DuMont and Mr. Hardoin in your prayers, if you are praying people and your good wishes if you aren't."

After the hands left, Wesley walked to the DuMont mansion to check on Fulmer and to ask about Mr. Hardoin. Fulmer had painful bruises but was not permanently injured. Mr. Hardoin's condition was unchanged. "I'll go over to his house after a bit," he told the DuMonts. "Is there anything I can for you while I'm here?"

"No, Wesley—" Fulmer started to say before his wife Martha interrupted him. "Yes, there is, Wesley, you can accept our thanks for sending Fulmer home. He needs to rest. It's a wonder he didn't break his neck when that truck turned over."

Helen came downstairs to offer her thanks. "Wesley, let me thank you too for helping Daddy. We're all worried about Mr. Hardoin, but do try to get Daddy to slow down a bit."

"Helen, Mr. DuMont is the boss and we're all out there to work for him, and to be honest about it, I don't think he would take kindly to my telling him how fast or slow to work. You can, but I can't. What I can say is that we got the truck back on its wheels and everything looks fine."

Fulmer chuckled. "Wesley, you're wiser than you are old. These women boss me around all the time, and there's not much I can do—or want to do—to change it. But seriously, I thank you for what you did. I was worried about the truck, and more so about Cyrus. I promise one and all that I'll be more careful. And I will say, too, that I'm pleased we're getting the cotton ginned as fast as we are."

"We all miss Mr. Hardoin, though, it's not the same without

him. I'm going over to his house to check on him. I hope I find him better."

Helen walked him to the door. "Thank you again, Wesley," she said softly. He turned as though to say something to her but thought better of it, nodded in acknowledgment, and left in silence.

Cyrus could move his hands, and his eyes were expressive, but he was still mute. "Dr. Bentley says it will take time for Cyrus to recover," Mrs. Hardoin said, her eyes glistening with tears that she tried to hide.

"We all miss you, Mr. Hardoin, and we want you back as soon as you are able. We're holding the place down for you, but we need you and we're all pulling for you to get well soon."

Cyrus looked earnestly at Wesley and responded with a slight hand motion. Then he closed his eyes.

After the way Wesley had handled the overturned truck and the injury to Fulmer, nobody had any doubts about him—least of all Fulmer. The three dozen men and a few women worked with a renewed zest, the weather held fair, and in two and a half days the fields were bare except for a few late-opening bolls that some of the women would pick in late November.

When the harvest was over and four hundred fifty cotton bales had been ginned and sold, Fulmer DuMont had sixteen thousand dollars in the bank, of which he cleared fourteen thousand after wages and expenses and expenses came out of it. He was delighted and asked Wesley to come by his house for something he had ready for him.

"Here, Wesley, this is for you," Fulmer said, gingerly handing him an envelope.

"What is it?"

"Open it and you'll see."

It was three crisp hundred-dollar bills.

"Mr. DuMont, you've already paid me. You don't owe me anything."

"I know that, Wesley, but this is not wages. It's what you can call a bonus. You got us through while I was bruised and laid up and Cyrus was down with that stroke. This is in appreciation for your good work."

Wesley hesitated, uncertain of what to do.

"Take it, Wesley," Mrs. DuMont urged, "you earned it and more from what Fulmer tells me."

"Now, Martha, don't you go getting too generous with my money," Fulmer laughed. "I get nervous every time you and Helen get that spending look in your eyes and decide to make a round of the stores."

"Our money," Martha corrected him, "and I vote we offer it to Wesley with our heartfelt thanks."

"Did somebody mention my name?" said Helen who had just come downstairs. "And what's all this talk about money?"

"We're talking about a bonus I'm giving Wesley. He worked like two men to get the cotton picked, ginned, and sold."

"So I heard, Wesley. I'm pleased but not surprised. You were always that way. But thank you."

"Now I say again, don't you two brag on him too much and give him the big head. I'll need him to be his normal hardworking self, come spring planting."

"I appreciate the bonus and the bragging, as Mr. DuMont says, but you may not be so happy with me when I tell you what I'm fixing to do."

"And what's that?" Fulmer asked in a more serious tone.

"I guess I'm going to leave Natchitoches. I've been thinking about it since Momma died. Now I don't have any family or things to tie me down here."

"But do you have family elsewhere?" Mrs. DuMont asked.

"No, ma'am, not any close kinfolks, and I don't really know the ones I do have. But on the other hand, I don't have bad memories in other places either."

The tone had changed, and all were silent for a moment.

"Wesley, I was going to talk to you later about this," Fulmer said, "but I'll just go ahead and tell you now. I'm offering you the overseer job. The doctors have told Cyrus that it looks like it'll be a long time before he can come back to his old job, if he ever can."

"Mr. DuMont, I appreciate your confidence in me, but I wouldn't feel right taking Mr. Hardoin's place even if I stayed in Natchitoches."

"Then you have made up your mind to leave?" Mrs. DuMont asked.

"I think so, ma'am. I believe it's time."

"Wesley," Fulmer said, leaning toward him to emphasis the point, "if it's Cyrus that's bothering you, I can tell you that he is not going to be hung out to dry. I aim to take care of him and his family and see to their welfare. He was worked for me all these years, and now I want to help him. He means a lot to us."

"I'm glad to hear that and I hope he'll be able to come back and work for a long time to come."

"Where will you go, Wesley?" Helen asked. And what about your things, the furniture and all? Have you decided?"

"No, I can't say I have. I guess I still have some kinfolks back in Tennessee and some others out west somewhere. One I heard of went north a long time ago, but we never heard from him again. Some of the Stokesburys that used to live around here moved out to West Texas many years ago, I'm told. Maybe I'll try to find them. As for the house things, I guess I'll sell whatever I can and give the rest away to anybody that can use them."

"Well, Wesley, you think about my offer before you do anything one way or another," Fulmer insisted. "I didn't tell you that you'll be making more money. The overseer job pays four dollars a day, and it's year-round, not just in the crop months. It's hard to beat that kind of money in this day and time."

"I do appreciate it and I will think about it before I decide anything."

"You do that, and we'll talk again."

Early the next morning, a Saturday, Les Chaney knocked on Wesley's door and told him that Mrs. DuMont wanted to talk to him.

"Mrs. DuMont? She say what about?"

"No, just that she wants you to come up to the mansion as soon as you can."

"You tell her I'll be right over," Wesley said, looking for his other shoe and wondering apprehensively if something was wrong.

"No, nothing is wrong, Wesley," she said in response to his first question thirty minutes later. "Please take a seat. I'd like to talk to you about what you told us last night."

"You mean about leaving?"

"Yes, about leaving."

"Well, ma'am, as I told you all last night, I will think seriously about the offer Mr. DuMont made, but to tell you the truth, I haven't had time yet."

"I know that, but there are some other things you might want to take into consideration before you decide."

"Yes, Ma'am?"

"Let's go back a way. I know in a general way what you agreed to when it came out that your father had sold Fulmer the farm and all. But Fulmer never filled me in on some of the details. A part of the deal was that you would not see Helen any more. Isn't that right?"

"I gave him my word."

"Not to see Helen anymore?"

"Well, yes, ma'am, and I guess you know his reasons."

"Yes, I knew that. Did you care about her?"

"Yes, ma'am."

"Then why would you agree to such a thing, if you cared for her?"

"Mrs. DuMont, I have to say with all due respect to you that the things we talked about that night were, as I saw them, confidential, and since I gave my word, I feel I can't say much more than I have without putting Mr. DuMont on the spot and betraying his trust."

"Then let me ask you this, Wesley: do you still have feelings for Helen."

"Yes, ma'am, you know we were friends from the time we played together as little children."

"I don't mean childhood friendship, Wesley, but feelings between a man and a woman, which is what both of you are now."

"What can I say, Mrs. DuMont? I have to keep the promise I made to Mr. DuMont, and so far I have."

"I know you have, but tell me the truth, Wesley. Do you love Helen? Tell me the truth."

He looked around, searching for another evasive answer, but the truth she had asked for broke through his defenses: "You asked for the truth, and the truth is what I'll give you, Mrs. DuMont. I love Helen more than my own life. I have always loved her. She means everything to me."

She drew back at the quiet intensity of his words and stared at him for a moment before responding, "Then you must tell her, Wesley, for she cares for you too, how deeply I don't know. She has never told me. But this is not something you can keep bottled up. You need to resolve it one way or the other. How you have managed to keep all this to yourself until now is something I find hard to understand."

"Because I gave my word to Mr. DuMont, ma'am, that's why."

"Your word is that important to you?"

"I decided a long time ago that I would be a man of my word. My word is my bond. I come from a family with a reputation for broken promises and I told myself that I would never break mine."

"I understand, but what if I gave you permission to override that promise?"

"With all due respect, ma'am, you can't. Only Mr. DuMont could do that because I gave my word to him."

At that moment Fulmer came down the stairs, still favoring his right leg, a reminder of the overturned truck. "Well, hello, Wesley, I didn't know you were here."

"I asked him to come over, Fulmer. I had something to ask him."

"Is that a secret or can the simpleminded man of this house know what it is?" Fulmer asked with a note of irritation in his voice.

Martha sighed and rolled her eyes, then realizing there was now no going back, she plunged full bore ahead: "It's about that promise you asked Wesley to make back when you bought the place from his father. I want you to release him from it."

Fulmer's face reddened. Wesley had never seen him really angry, but now he was afraid he was about to see the first demonstration.

"What Wesley and me talked about that day was between us. He promised me he would keep his word."

"And so he has. He won't tell me anything because he is a man of his word, but you, dear husband, have gotten no such agreement from me, nor will you ever as long as I am your wife," she retorted, her own temper ticking up a few notches. "Wesley has honored his word, and now I want you to honor him by releasing him from what you agreed to and the conditions you placed on him."

"And if I don't?"

"Then I'll think less of you and that will bring on consequences that you don't want. That's all I can say."

"But why, woman? What Wesley and me agreed on was between two men. Why are you asking me to disregard it now?"

"I have my reasons, Fulmer, and that's all I'm going to say at the moment."

"Hell fire and damnation!" Fulmer exclaimed in a rare outburst of profanity, "I'll not agree to anything until I can think it through. But I know that now that's it's started, I'll never hear the end of it. A woman can wear a strong man down to a nub quicker than a snowball melts in August. Wesley, you don't need to hear us arguing. I'll talk to you later."

"Yes sir, and thank you both," he said over his shoulder as he hurried out the door.

Later that morning Fulmer drove up in his Model-T.

"Wesley, you got time to talk over some things?"

"Yes sir, I'll bring some chairs out and we can sit under the magnolias. That way you won't have to climb the porch steps."

Wesley brought down the chairs. Fulmer settled himself carefully and leaned forward.

"Wesley, let's get right to the point. You heard what Martha asked me to do and that's why I'm here. I didn't want to say what's on my mind in front of the women folk."

"I understand, sir."

"Wesley, I asked you to stay away from Helen when we made the agreement about you and your mother staying on in this house and you working for me."

"Yes sir."

"Well, you proved to be a man of your word, and then some. You got us through the harvest this year with the best profits I've ever had. I have nothing but praise for what you've done. But I also have a riled-up wife, as you know, and that's about the most miserable thing a man can deal with."

"I hate to be the cause of that."

"It's not your fault. Fact is, I don't think it's anybody's fault. It's just the circumstances."

Wesley squirmed uneasily in his chair, not knowing what to say and not sure the direction Fulmer was taking.

"Wesley, let me be up front with you with a couple of questions. First, do you ever get the urge to drink?"

"No sir, never tasted the stuff and never wanted to!" he said so forcefully that Fulmer pulled back in his chair.

"Second question, what if right now I asked you to have a

glass of wine with me? Would you do it?"

"With the respect due you, no, Mr. DuMont, absolutely not. I know that wine in itself is not the problem; it's some of the people that drink it. But you know about my family, and I don't want any part of it. I don't condemn men who can have a drink and go on their way, but as for me, I made up my mind a long time ago that I would not tempt the Devil, so to speak. I never have felt the urge to drink and never intend to go down that road."

Fulmer stood up with difficulty and extended his hand. "That's good enough for me, Wesley. Consider that part of our agreement over, contract null and void, as the lawyers would say. And any friendship you may have with Helen is something between the two of you. The rest of what I offered you still stands, including the overseer's job I told you about last night. What do you say to that? Can we shake hands in agreement?"

"I'll willingly shake your hand, Mr. DuMont, but I need another day or two before I can give you an answer about the overseer job."

"You've got the time, and I hope you come to see it my way."

With that, they shook hands and Fulmer left.

That afternoon as he was trimming some new replacement rails for the low fences one of the mules had kicked down, he sensed someone behind him. It was Helen.

"Helen, I didn't see you come up."

"You weren't supposed to," she said laughing. "I slipped up on you so I could see what you're up to."

"Well, one of the mules knocked the fence down and I was trying to fix it."

"I hear you've been knocking down a few fences yourself."

"You're mean what me and your parents were talking about

this morning?"

"'Your parents and I', or have you forgotten what Madame Meuniere taught us in sixth grade about proper English syntax? But yes, Mr. Stokesbury, it is about that little matter. I happened to hear part of it up past the stairwell. We schoolteachers have to have good hearing, you know."

"And what did you hear?"

"Something about promises and keeping your word."

"Nothing else?"

"Nothing I will admit to hearing. Were other things discussed?" she asked with wide-eyed pretended innocence.

It was Wesley's turn to play coy. "Maybe."

"Like what?"

"Nothing I will admit to saying. What else did you think we were talking about?"

They both realized that they had resumed the playful banter of their earlier years and delighted in it. It was the eve of their happiness, which already was already beginning to sprinkle joy, like first drops of welcome rain after a drought.

"Did Daddy come over here a while ago?"

"To that I will give you a straight answer. Yes, he did."

"For?"

"To talk about certain matters that me and him—pardon, he and I—needed to clear up."

"And did you?"

"Did we what?"

"You know what I mean! Clear up those matters."

"Well, yes, I guess you could say we did."

"Was I one of them?"

"Yes, I guess you could say you were."

"And what did you say about me."

"Nothing directly, and that's the truth, Helen, but what he said made me a free man."

"Free man from what, or for what?"

"Free from a promise I made years ago; but for what, I still can't say. It's not up to me to say."

"You mean the promise you made to Daddy not to see me anymore? Momma told me about it."

"Well, since you already know, yes, that was it."

"Was that how you felt about me at the time, so little that you could just walk away and let Daddy decide for you? I was so angry with you."

"Is that when you started dating Robert Bourgeois?"

"Don't start answering my questions with another question. But yes, to be honest as I want to be about it. I had to get on with my life."

"I'm sorry about that, but there were things I couldn't say or do. I was glad, though, that you broke up with Robert."

"I had my reasons, he's a nice person but I was not in love with him. But since you seemed to lose interest in me . . ."

"Helen, you have to know that was never the way I felt about you, not then, not now!"

"Then tell me this, Wesley, how do you feel about me?"

"The truth?"

"The truth and nothing but the truth."

Wesley's hands were sweating and shaking, and his throat was dry. His whole life was packed in a confession he once thought he could never make: "Helen, I love you, always have and always will. I just couldn't tell you before."

"I know, Wesley," she said softly, putting her hand on his

arm. "I overheard you tell Momma this morning how much you love me, and they were the most beautiful words I've ever heard in my life. But I wanted you to tell me in person. A woman always needs to hear the words from the man she loves. I thought I would never get those words out of you, words I've wanted to hear—and waited to hear—for as long as I can remember." Then she laughed and added, "And even then I had to corner you in a barnyard to get them out of you. Just wait till I spread that story around Natchitoches. Now, Mr. Wesley Stokesbury, will you make your declaration of love a promise and give me your word to keep it? If so, I'll be happy and secure in the certainty that you will never break it, for everybody knows you are a man of your word."

"I promise."

"Then put that axe down before you hurt somebody and kiss me. You have told me how much you love me. I'll need a lot of time, you dear man, to tell you how much I love you."

They sealed their love with that barnyard kiss. He accepted the overseer job and they married in Helen's Catholic Church with Fulmer's blessing in December 1925. Cyrus Hardoin was able to attend. His speech was slurred, and steps were unsteady, but he insisted on being there for Wesley and the DuMonts. After the ceremony, people lingered to talk, among them Tom Bourgeois and Lou Tremont.

"Tom," Lou said in a low tone, "don't you reckon Wesley Stokesbury's head is swimming a little over all the money and property Helen is due to come into some day?"

"I wouldn't know, Lou, but it'd be human nature not to think about it. That's why my boy Robert keeps saying that's the real reason he's marrying her. He never did like him, you know."

"Could be for good reason. I don't know if you can really trust the Stokesburys. Now is Robert going to marry the Hardoin girl? I notice she was at the wedding with her grandpa Cyrus, just as happy as a fox in a henhouse."

"I guess that's because now with the DuMont girl married she's got Robert all to herself. They probably will get married, but I think it's more her idea than his."

"Speaking of Cyrus, you think he'll ever get over his stroke and back on his feet? He looked awfully shaky to me."

"I have my doubts. You don't get over things like that. Why he was completely paralyzed there for nigh on a week, they tell me."

"Nearly two weeks the way I heard it. Well, he's lucky that Fulmer's going to take care of him and his family, leastwise, says he is. People promise things sometimes and then renege on it down the road."

"That's the truth. But he's got the money. I will say this for Wesley Stokesbury, he's twice the overseer and cotton farmer lazy old Cyrus ever was. The way things are going, Wesley's going to make Fulmer the richest man in Natchitoches Parish."

"Yeah, no telling how much money he's got already, and Wesley will come into it someday. Who would have thought that the son and grandson of the most worthless men in this parish would end up being maybe the richest? You just never know how things will turn out, do you? Well, I guess I better go over yonder and pull Inez away from those gossipy old women and go tend my cane fields. My cotton didn't do all that well this year, but a feller's got to make a living. I'm having a hell of time getting that sly old Enos Filmore to give me a yea or nay on my cane. Ain't nothing easy in this world, is there? Anyhow, you stay in the traces, Tom, and I'll be seeing you."

"Yeah, you too, Lou. I need to get back and open up the store for two or three more hours. People like us that don't marry into money have to work for a living, don't we?"

"You got that right."

Four children were born to Helen and Wesley in a long and happy marriage in which they enjoyed riches, respectability, and the greater wealth of many grandchildren and great grandchildren.

The Acid Test

This latest disaster was too much even for chemistry professor Matthew Hayes. His family had been through too many calamities. For his daughters' sake he had tried to be strong long after his real strength was gone. But now he felt his spirit breaking; he could pretend no longer. He was out of options. He put his hands over his face and wept as weariness like death itself settled on his shoulders.

The ordeals began six years earlier in 1873 when his beloved wife Caroline first fell ill. He spent all his money and mortgaged his property, including his precious library, to provide the best medical care for her. But Boston's famed doctors were not good enough, and on Christmas day of 1874 she died.

For Professor Hayes it was as if a piece of the sky had fallen, or the earth had caved in, for she had been his love, his life, his strength. He had read many philosophical books on the meaning of life and death, but in the end none of them could tell him why he was left, and beloved Caroline was taken. He was also a man of faith, but only silence answered his anguished prayers for her recovery.

In January the university terminated him "for insufficient attention to classes and laboratories and unsatisfactory performance of assigned duties," the official letter said. Matthew did not appeal the termination. After all, the accusations were true, and the extenuating circumstances carried no weight. Although he received many private condolences for his loss, even from those who dismissed him, there was no public patience with his grief. News of his dismissal spread throughout academic circles, causing other universities to close their doors to him.

Creditors took his house and property in March. But he still had two assets: his health and his daughters, Ruth, 12, and Julia, 10. In both girls he saw the love that bound him to Caroline, and even though for himself he wished only to die also, for their sake he set aside his grief as best he could and tried to put his life and finances in order.

Through the good offices of a former colleague, an academy in Cleveland, Ohio hired him as a science teacher. But he no sooner relocated the family from Boston than the academy publicly declared its insolvency and closed its doors without paying its faculty. Handouts from a local church kept them from going hungry that winter.

For the next six years Matthew mixed manual labor with occasional teaching jobs. The hands that seldom had lifted anything heavier than a test tube or library tome now were calloused from rough carpentry. At night usually he fell asleep reading, and Ruth or Julia would come to take the book from his hands and gently cover him. This change in condition did not bother Matthew, for he had always been an unassuming person, but it pained him to realize that his daughters would never receive the excellent New England education he and Caroline had enjoyed. Money and means were desperately short, but the girls did not complain. Far from it; as so often happens when misery afflicts a family, they gave Matthew their unconditional love and support.

He heard that in the Reconstruction South there was a shortage of qualified teachers and decided that perhaps there he could resurrect his academic career. Remembering that some of his distant Hayes relatives had settled in Blount County, Alabama, before the Civil War, he made inquiries and reestablished contact with them. Indeed, they wrote, there is a need for educated men to help rebuild the South. Come. You will be welcome and we will help you all we can.

But once in Alabama, Matthew realized that the words of his relatives and their friends were more acts of courtesy than commitment. True, they were outwardly polite, especially his cousin Asa Hayes, now Probate Judge in the new city of Cullman, and Sheriff Thaddeus Roden, but even their politeness was limited and guarded. The mountains of North Alabama had produced many Northern soldiers and sympathizers during the Civil War, but the excesses of the carpetbaggers and Reconstruction abuses had converted many of them into embittered rebels long after the war itself was over.

Nevertheless, Asa set aside any reservations he may have had about Matthew's carpetbagger image and recommended him to the new Cullman Academy. Since there was no other candidate who came close to matching his scientific credentials, he was appointed.

Then the war began anew, except that in the Cullman Academy the North was impoverished and outnumbered.

"Why do we need a carpet bagging Northerner anyhow?" some of the parents complained when they heard about the hiring. And taking their comments to be permission to act, the students took it upon themselves to see that Matthew's days as their teacher would be numbered, and that number, they promised, would be as miserable as they could make them.

From the first day of class, swaggering Danny Ponder, 18, took the lead in tormenting the hated Yankee professor. The son of a cotton buyer, whose business was growing rapidly as settlers flooded into newly drawn Cullman County, Danny was the biggest and richest boy in the Academy. He was bored with classes and thought himself too old to be in school, but his father believed in education and would not let him drop out. Danny reacted by disrupting classes and intimidating the teachers.

Earlier in his career Matthew probably would have been unable to deal with a rascal like Danny. But his experience with working men had toughened him and to Danny's surprise, he stood his ground. As for Matthew, he realized that this could be his last chance as a teacher, and for his daughters' sake he could not let himself fail.

But Matthew was vulnerable. Danny soon discovered his weakness and exploited it with evil glee.

Matthew had only one threadbare suit to comply with the formal dress code of the Academy. Day after day he wore it, hoping that with care it would last until he could buy another at first payday. Aware of his poverty, the students made jokes about him. During each class and the experiments that followed he donned a traditional white laboratory robe, leaving his coat on a rack by his desk. At night in their small apartment Ruth and Julia would clean and press his clothes, carefully stitching tears and counting the days until their father was to be paid.

That week the lesson was about the chemistry and properties of acids. For demonstration purposes Matthew prepared a vial of hydrochloric acid. In an unguarded moment Danny emptied the vial on the back of the professor's hanging coat. It steamed and reduced the coat to tatters.

The students smirked and waited for the professor's reaction. Then they burst into open laughter as he folded the ruined coat and walked out of the classroom without a word. Matthew realized they were all against him. Danny had won; he was defeated. He might even be fired on the spot if Principal Meyer saw him without formal dress outside his classroom. The Principal disliked the "carpetbagger" as heartily as the students.

Ruth and Julia had not seen their father weep since their mother's death, and the sight dismayed them. The depth of their father's pain and shame all but overcame them. They looked at each other, ready to burst into tears themselves. But then Ruth reacted.

"No! No! We'll deal with this! Daddy, don't give up hope! We'll have you ready for class in the morning! I promise you!"

"But how . . .?" he asked. "I don't see any way. . ."

"Julia, iron his shirt and press his tie. Daddy, you rest in your chair and don't worry. I'm going out for a while. I'll be back soon. Don't worry about me. I'll be all right."

"But where are you going?" he asked, too tired to exercise a parental veto of her unexpected behavior.

"I'll tell you when I get back."

She returned two hours later with a coat.

"Where did you get that?" Matthew asked.

"From Mr. Hayes, the Judge."

"You went to his house?"

"Yes."

"You told him about me? . . . about us?"

"Yes, I told him the truth; I explained that we're going through some hard times. And then I said to him, 'You Southerners make such a big hurrah about helping your own, especially your kinfolk. Well, sir, we're here and we're kinfolk. And we may not talk like it, but now we're Southerners, too. So I came here tonight to see if you are as big as your words'."

"And what did Judge Hayes say?"

"Well, Daddy, you wouldn't believe it. He hugged me with tears in his eyes and said he'd never heard a girl speak more courageously. He apologized to me for being so distant and indifferent to us and said that it took a young girl, one of his own relatives, to make him see how unchristian he had been. Then he went to his closet, took out the best coat he had, and gave it to me. I'm not sure his wife approved, but she didn't say anything. Anyway, here it is!"

The next morning there was consternation in Danny's group when at the regular time Professor Hayes showed up in class—handsomely dressed—and announced in a calm voice that the class on acids would continue, to be followed by an examination on the material two days hence. Defections among Danny's followers commenced and continued all day.

And Danny's problems were not over. The very next hour as he was leaving his history class, a diminutive but angry Miss Ruth Hayes cornered the sizable but intimidated Mr. Daniel Ponder and in a clipped Boston twang proceeded to give him the worst—or was it the best?—tongue lashing of his life, punctuated at the end by a stinging slap to the face, which his classmates celebrated uproariously and he surely remembered to the end of his days.

With that the tide turned. Matthew and his family had passed the acid test. The Hayes—Northern and Southern—warmed to each other, the Academy and the townspeople forgot about carpetbagger labels and opened their hearts to their distinguished Professor of chemistry. On his own, Danny went to the Hayes home to apologize in person to the family for his behavior. The graciousness with which they received him caused Danny to become their most ardent defender.

Particularly of Ruth. Most men, the old saying goes, are won through their stomach, Cupid wounds others with his arrows, but in Danny's case, it took a slap to the face for him to discover his first love.

He and Ruth were sweethearts for a time, but their young love was not destined to last. The Academy soon closed its doors and Matthew moved to a school in Tennessee where he had a long and honorable teaching career. Both Ruth and Julia married teachers.

As for Danny, he followed his father in the cotton business, married a Cullman girl, and became a wealthy man. He always remembered Professor Hayes with great respect and Ruth with special affection. Though never to be his wife, she was always to remain his friend. Throughout their life they stayed in touch at Christmas, sharing news of their children, grandchildren, and great-grandchildren until Danny's passing in 1920.

Whiskey Runner

Floyd Howard was the best whiskey runner Cullman County had ever seen. People called his '48 souped-up silver Ford "The Gray Ghost." Its oversize bore engine, double-carburetors, and dual exhausts made ole Floyd the king of the country road racers and cock of the walk. Tall, good looking, fearless, and always carrying a wad of high denomination bills in his pocket big enough to choke a horse, he lived high, wide, and handsome. He strutted, swaggered, and crowed, but he backed up his words.

"If ye can do it, it ain't bragging'," he said.

He was too smart to get into down and dirty brawls. He kept his black hair combed just right, his pants pressed, and his shirts starched and clean. But if men crowded him too much or challenged him directly, he would take them out with a car tool upside the head or brass knuckles to the jaw. And talk was the pearl-handled switchblade he used to manicure his fingernails had done some late-night carving on unfriendly folks. They said he carried a loaded .38 pistol in a compartment under the front seat and that a certain smart talking Winston County whiskey maker who once tried to shortchange him walked with a gimpy knee because of it.

They also said a lot of girls were acquainted with the back seat of his Ford, and we younger boys all but drooled over the names of the beauties they mentioned. Maybe that part of his reputation was exaggerated. You know how things like that get stretched wider than the facts. But it was a fact that he always seemed to have a pretty girl snuggled up to him in the front seat as he rode up and down the Corn Road on Saturdays and Sundays. We younger boys would gather under the oak tree at Bibb's store just to see him race by ninety to nothing in a swirling cloud of dust. He always waved to us and sometimes even stopped to talk for a minute or two. He asked us to do little favors like being on the lookout for deputies patrolling the Corn Road. We carried out our duties religiously and felt like we were his accomplices and even strutted a little on our own because of it. Everything we saw him do we tried to imitate. For ole Floyd was our hero, the latest word in country style, the Alpha and Omega of all our rural ideals.

One day that I remember vividly Floyd stopped to get a cold drink at Bibb's store and came across the road to talk to us boys gathered under the oak tree. He asked if we were still going to school. Floyd had made it through three or four grades before he got smart and quit to make money.

"Not me!" Royal Brown boasted. "I done quit. I ain't got no use for teachers and books and all that stuff. I got better things to do with my time!"

"I quit two or three years ago," Earnest Sandlin said proudly. "We had too much farm work to do. I got my own cotton crop this year. I'm gonna get me a car this fall."

"Hey, way to go, Earnest! What about you?" Floyd asked, looking over at me. "Your name's Harold, right? I don't see you here as much as these other boys. I bet you're still going to school down at West Point."

"Yes sir, some. I'm still going some, every now and then, but I'm thinking of quitting pretty soon. I'm getting tired of that stuff."

Floyd laughed. "Now, Harold, you don't have to 'sir' me. Makes me sound old. Just call me Floyd like everybody else."

"Yes sir," I said like an idiot while everybody laughed at me.

"How far along are you anyway?" Floyd asked as he finished his cola and tossed the bottle out in the grass.

"Uh, about ninth grade," I squirmed, embarrassed by my advanced academic standing and feeling like a prime sissy.

"Ninth grade! Man, that's a lot of schooling. Instead of wasting your time at school, you could make yourself some money, have girls all over the place. Anyway, you must be some dumb shit if you ain't learned enough in nine years to do you," Floyd laughed.

I was mortified by his criticism. Everybody eagerly joined in to make fun of me. When Floyd laughed, everybody laughed.

That night at supper I made the announcement to my parents. "I reckon I'm gonna quit school. That stuff's for sissies."

"Well, I reckon not," Daddy said quietly. "You've been listening too much to that sorry bunch you're running with lately. I'll bet that whiskey running Floyd Howard's got something to do with it. He's filled a lot of young, empty heads with foolish notions. Now I promised your Momma here I'd see to it that you finished high school. And, young man, you're gonna finish, or you're gonna wish you had. Now I don't wantta hear anything else about quitting school. You hear me, boy? Just eat your supper and be quiet if you don't have anything better to talk about."

That was the end of my plans to quit school. But ole Floyd was still the kind of man I wanted to be some day. It would just take a little longer, and maybe too much education wouldn't do me that much harm. I said to myself that I would get over it, like the measles or the chickenpox I caught a few years back.

After Floyd's two-year run as king of the Corn Road, Junior MacBrayer's daddy, owner of the cotton gin at Battleground, bought his pudgy son a brand-new V-8 Rocket 88 Oldsmobile. Sleek, black, majestic, and swifter than a nasty thought, it quickly became an object of admiration to us Corn Road boys.

Junior started doing some crowing of his own by announcing to one and all that Floyd's old Ford clunker couldn't hold a candle to his Rocket 88. A challenge was issued. Floyd accepted, for manhood was at stake. Sides were taken, and the betting began.

Against their sentimental feelings for ole Floyd, all but his closest buddies put their money on the Olds. It was just common sense. Its engine was bigger, the coil springs were better than the Ford's old leaf springs, and because of its low-slung weight the Olds could take a curve better. Sure, Floyd was the better driver, they reasoned, but Junior was no slouch himself and he had a lot more machine to work with.

Junior was so confident of victory that he sent a condescending message to Lonzo that he could pick the time and place for the race. Floyd grinned and told the boys they better bet on him.

"I'll bring ole Junior down so many notches he'll have to climb a ladder to kiss a dog's ass."

"How you figure that, Floyd?" Edgar Will Blankenship asked him. "That Rocket Olds is one fast sonuvabitch. They say it's winning races all over the country. I don't know if you can keep up with him or not."

"Ain't the cars that win races, boys. It's the drivers, and' there ain't nobody that can take me on my home ground."

"Where's it gonna be, and when?" they asked him.

"I'll let you know," he said with a grin. "But remember what I told you boys: put your money on me unless you wanta lose it."

We all waited in suspense for Floyd's decision. He took his time, but finally, on Wednesday he sent word to Junior: "This coming Saturday at 2 in the evening. Three miles on the Corn Road, from the Blair Road fork to Doughball Church. And put up or shut up: $200. Winner take all."

Everybody and his dog were lined up on the Corn Road that Saturday afternoon (evening we called it of course) for the big showdown. Even the old men and women showed up. I didn't see the start, since Doughball Church was closer to my house. But folks said it was one hell of a beginning. The Olds was deadly fast on straightaways, but Floyd's Ford was jackrabbit quick on the starting line. And that advantage was all ole Floyd needed. It was no contest. Floyd got a twenty-foot jump on the hydramatic Olds and kept it all the way. Junior tried his best to get around him, but Floyd cut him off every time, throwing dust and gravel on Junior. Back and forth they careened across the Corn Road, Floyd's dust swirling so thick that Junior could barely see the road. When a rock flew up and cracked his windshield, Junior slid into the ditch down close to Oscar Pierce's house. The race was over.

Floyd eased into the Doughball grounds and waited for Junior. People crowded around to shake his hand. After several men had pushed his car back into the road, Junior came driving up, sporting a dented door, the front end knocked out of line— and of course the cracked windshield. Without a word, he handed Floyd two hundred dollars and sped back to Battleground to lick his wounds. After spending several hundred dollars in repairs, Mr. MacBrayer took the Olds away from Junior and demoted him to a lowly six-year old Chevy pickup.

Floyd and The Gray Ghost were still the champions. And

some people lost money because of it, and much of it went to swell Floyd's wad of bills. Our hero had won—even if some of us secretly doubted that he would.

Floyd lived with his mother in a big two-story house down on the Blair Road. Nobody seemed to know exactly who his daddy was, but people knew better than to talk about it to his face. He made most of his whiskey runs out of Winston County to bootleggers in dry but thirsty Cullman County. In the dead of night, sometimes running with lights out if the moon was full, people could hear Floyd's mighty V-8 tearing along the Corn Road or, if he smelled the law, one of many alternate routes. If things got too hot on the Corn Road or the Jones Chapel highway, he might detour south through bootlegger-friendly Jasper and swing east all the way over to Blount County. Sometimes he would do a northern run through Lawrence and Morgan Counties. He knew all the highways and byways like the back of his hand, every curve and rock, every mud puddle and sand pile. And if the law got too close or thought they had him cornered, he had log roads and invisible pathways where he could hide until they were gone. They said he could slide the Ford around on sandy roads and be headed in the other direction before lawmen could spit. And on a straight pursuit none of the law boys stood a chance. Floyd had left many of them eating his dust or working to get their vehicles out of the ditch. In his frustration Deputy Tom Turnbull, Jr. of Addison, once fired two bullets into the ford's trunk as Floyd sped away. We local boys pointed to the repaired holes with something approaching religious awe.

People talked for years about Floyd's fifty-mile run to the Tennessee line not long after winning the race with Junior. Lawmen spotted him on Highway 33 at Wren, southeast of

Moulton, and stayed on his tail at speeds topping a hundred miles an hour in places. Floyd's Gray Ghost was weighted down with a full load of Winston County wildcat and the Lawrence County deputies almost caught him at Red Bank up above Courtland. But he just managed to outrun them across the Tennessee River on the Wheeler Dam road. Alerted by the Lawrence County deputies, the Lauderdale lawmen were setting up a barricade at Elgin on Highway 72 when ole Floyd thundered by, sending barriers flying and lawmen running for their life. In the confusion, Floyd gained a quarter-mile lead and the Tennessee line was now only fifteen miles away. With pedal on the metal and a smooth highway, he beat them across the state line going away. By the time the caravan of Alabama lawmen reached the line, Floyd was nearly to Loretto on his way to Lawrenceburg, Tennessee.

Meanwhile, Tennessee patrolmen had rushed down to the state line to intercept the long line of Alabama pursuers.

"We don't need the Alabama law doing our job," they told the frustrated Alabamians. "Give us his description and tag number and we'll look into it."

But they didn't. Floyd lay low for a couple of days with some kinfolks up close to Amish country at Etheridge. Then when he saw that the Tennessee law had no interest in him, he worked his way east through Pulaski to the Huntsville Road, then south to Arab and, by night, on into Cullman to deliver his load. His customer wondered about the delay.

"Aw, had to take a little detour. Hope it didn't throw you off none," Floyd commented as he trimmed his fingernails with the pearl handled switchblade.

It was things like this that to us boys made Floyd a hero on his way to becoming a legend, or to hear the church-going folks tell it, an outlaw on the fast track to hell or the penitentiary, whichever came first. Later it turned out that there was some truth in both opinions. At the moment and at the peak of his notoriety, he was the worst of everything our parents preached against, which made him the best of everything we wanted to be.

But as they say, nothing lasts forever. Floyd had outrun the law, but now he was a marked man with a warrant out on him. It was getting close to election time, and there was grumbling that he was running loose and making fools of the Cullman lawmen. So Cullman County Sheriff Crant Waldrip made plans to bring him down once and for all.

Floyd knew all about it. Thanks to well-placed bribes, he had sources in the Sheriff's office and the Cullman police that kept him informed. The sensible thing for him to do would have been to disappear for a while. But lately he wasn't thinking all that straight. For ole Floyd had fallen in love with pretty Gladys Overton, daughter of Reverend Silas Overton of Sardis Baptist Church at Nesmith close to the Winston County line.

At first it looked like she was going to end up being just another name on ole Floyd's list of trophy girls. She had that dreamy look and things seemed to be moving her right toward the back seat. But when it came down to it, she balked, and I mean, balked completely.

"Floyd, I'm not about to get back there in your back seat, so ye can just stop your fooling and feeling around where you don't have any business. With me it's not gonna be like it was with the other girls. But I will be going to bed with you one of these days soon. I promise you that. You might as well get used to the idea, Floyd Howard, you and me are gonna get married!"

No girl had ever talked to Floyd like pretty Gladys, and it knocked him off his feet. He might be able to outrun the law all the way to Tennessee, but he couldn't resist the adoring but determined look in her pretty blue eyes. Probably he didn't know it at the moment, but his tomcatting days were over.

And his whiskey running soon would be.

Sheriff Waldrip's deputies surrounded him at the Wednesday night service at Sardis Church as he and Gladys were talking in the parking area after the service. Most of the congregation had left already. Cut off in both directions, Floyd looked around, considered his options, got out of his car, and calmly lit up a Camel as the deputies came running up. Gladys waited inside the car.

"We got the sonuvabitch this time!" hooted Deputy Hollis Skinner. "Watch him! He's tricky as hell! If he tries anything, shoot the bastard!" He had a personal grudge against Floyd. Before Hollis became a deputy, Floyd had beaten the crap out of him over a pretty Jones Chapel girl he claimed but who, so they said, was one of the girls who ended up in the back seat of Floyd's Ford.

"How you doing, Hollis? Anything I can help you boys with tonight?" Floyd said easily as the deputies approached with drawn pistols.

"We'll do the talking, Howard!" Hollis snarled. "Now just keep your mouth shut and stand away from your vehicle!"

"Glad to oblige. Here's the keys if you want them."

The deputies proceeded to search the Ford but found nothing.

"Hollis, he ain't transporting nothing!"

"He's dropped it off somewhere around here, and we'll find it. Look under the front seat. He carries a .38."

The deputy shined his flashlight, flashing the light accidentally on purpose up at Gladys' legs. "Naw, I can't see nothing."

"Goddamn!" Hollis muttered, grabbing the flashlight and looking for himself. "Where is it, Howard?"

"Where's what, boys? I'm not packing a gun. If you'd tell me what else you're looking for, maybe I'm could help ye find it," Floyd said, flipping the cigarette butt at Hollis' feet.

"The whiskey and the pistol, you sonuvbitch! Now where are they? You better tell us, if you know what's good for you!" Hollis warned him.

"Hollis, you need to tone down your talk. There are ladies around here. You can call me whatever you like as long's you're holding that pistol on me. Ain't like it was that time we had it out man to man over in Jones Chapel. You remember that, don't you, Hollis?"

Floyd shook his head at the pleasant memory as Hollis build up a pure rage of shame and frustration. He was about to pistol whip Floyd when Sheriff Waldrip drove up.

"Hello, Floyd."

"Good to see you again, Crant. Hope your family's doing well."

"Well enough, thank you. Did you boys find the stuff?"

"Crant, we didn't find nothing," Hugh Hudson admitted, "no whiskey, no gun. He ain't transporting."

"That right, Hollis?"

"Yeah," Hollis said grudgingly. "He must've unloaded it back down the road."

"Well, if he did, that's over in Winston County, and we're not going over the line."

"Well, I'll put the cuffs on the sonuvabitch and we'll take him into Cullman," Hollis said, removing the handcuffs from his belt.

"No, we're not, Hollis," Sheriff Waldrip contradicted him. "And you get this straight. You don't talk to a man, prisoner or not, using that kind of language. This is Mr. Floyd Howard to you. And if he's outsmarted you tonight about the whiskey, as it appears he has, well, we still have the warrant on him. But we have to follow the rules. We're the law and we can't break it. You understand, Hollis? You other men understand?"

"Yessir," they said sheepishly.

"Hollis?"

Hollis gritted his teeth and said "yessir" too.

"Crant, before you take me in, I need a little favor from you."

"What is it?"

"I've got Miss Gladys Overton in the car. You know her, Reverend Overton's daughter. Well, I need to take her home first. And just as soon as I do, I give you my word that I'll come back here and turn myself in. I'm responsible for her. Fact is, if she hadn't been in the car, I probably would've made a run for it."

"Where does she live?"

"Over towards Addison, about five miles from here."

Hollis spoke up. "Sheriff, that's in Winston County! You ain't gonna let him go over there, are you? Why, he'll run for it sure as hell's hot! I can drive the girl home."

"Crant," Floyd said calmly. "I'm asking you man to man. And I'm giving you my word man to man. I'll take her home and come back. You can send a car along behind me, if you like. But I don't want Hollis around her. He's got personal feelings involved in this from some things that happened a while back between us. You understand? I told her daddy I'd be responsible for Gladys, and I'd hate to break my word to him."

Sheriff Waldrip dropped his head and thought for a moment. Then he pulled Floyd aside to talk to him where the others couldn't hear. "Floyd, I'm going to let you drive the girl home. I believe you'll do what you say. If you don't, then I'm going to be the biggest fool in Cullman County and my sheriffing days will be over. But providing you keep your word, as I believe you will, I'll do what I can to help you get through this. I'd like to see you make something better out of your life, because if you don't one of these days you'll end up getting killed."

"I appreciate your confidence, and I won't let you down."

So Floyd drove off with Gladys. Thirty minutes later, just as the deputies were grumbling to one another that he had outfoxed Sheriff Waldrip, he came driving up.

Waldrip let out a long breath.

Now let me tell you how it all ended. Floyd got off with a six-month suspended sentence. The judge went easy on him, mostly because nobody had actually found any moonshine in his car, although there was circumstantial evidence and testimony that the court could not ignore completely.

Three things happened over the next few years that set everybody a buzzing with speculation and wonderment. First, it turned out that pretty Gladys was right: she and Floyd were married by her father at Sardis Church. They moved into Addison and set up housekeeping. First thing you knew, a baby was on the way.

But what floored us was what happened while Gladys and Floyd were starting their family. With Sheriff Waldrip's recommendation, Floyd became a deputy over in Winston County. We Corn Road boys didn't know whether to cry or celebrate. Our hero had gone over to the enemy!

And what an enemy he was to the bootleggers! Within a couple of years, almost single handedly he put such a dent in the whiskey running business that it never recovered. Moonshine went out of style, and thirsty drinkers started going to Huntsville or Birmingham. The Winston whiskey business just about dried up. In fact, beer and cheap wine replaced whiskey as the favorite drink in that part of the world. The whiskey drinkers of earlier generations were probably turning over in their graves.

But the biggest surprise was something that nobody saw coming. We could see him getting married. That was natural enough. And what better training to be a law officer in the North Alabama hill counties than first being a law breaker? That happened a lot. But who would have suspected that Floyd would become a man of God? Probably Silas and Gladys worked on him. Whatever the cause, Floyd went on to become a deacon at Sardis Church and years later after his law days were over, an ordained preacher in Addison. But if you think about it, maybe it was just a natural progression in his life. He got rid of whiskey first and then waged a considerable war against general sinfulness.

Still, maybe there was a little spark of the old Floyd left in the righteous preacher of later years. Now and then on a Saturday or after church on Sunday, he and Gladys would back out the old Gray Ghost, which Floyd religiously polished and maintained. And with their two boys and three girls all scrouged in with them, they would drive in grand style up and down the country roads waving to folks and reminding us of the old whiskey-running days in Corn Road country that were gone for good.

Witch Hazel

Old Hazel was a witch. At least some folks up on the Winston-Lawrence County line thought so, and Felix Hamilton, for one, always swore to it. He babbled about seeing old Hazel working one of her magic spells that made his hair stand on end. To hear him tell it, she was "messing' around with the pure old Devil."

It all happened back around 1928 or '29, as best I can judge from what folks told me. Felix lived with his deaf and dumb wife Dicey and their six feeble-minded children in a dirt-floor, pine-slab shanty up in the Lawrence County hills close to Penitentiary Mountain. Until his last mule died, he planted some cotton and corn like his ancestors, but the land his daddy and granddaddy farmed was now so gullied and stripped of topsoil that hardly anything came of his labors. Anyway, because he couldn't repay his last loan, the bank refused him more money for another mule, fertilizer, and such.

In the summertime, Dicey and the children picked blackberries and polk, pulled wild onions, and gathered all the hickory nuts they could find. That together with a little milk from their old cow, an egg or two now and then, and Felix's little hand-worked patches of Irish potatoes, black eyed peas, okra, and butterbeans helped them keep body and soul together. But foxes, hawks, and the hungry family devoured the last of their scrawny chickens, and the cow died of old age. For a time Dicey and the children stole watermelons, walnuts, and vegetables from the Valley farms until an angry farmer ran them back to the hills with warning shotgun blasts. Felix made a dollar or two here or there hiring out to chop or pick cotton, but he was so slow and clumsy that most farmers would only take him on if there were no other hands available. For a time he tried his hand at making whiskey on his daddy's old still, but when word got out that Felix might be trying to cut into their trade, some of the Winston County moonshiners came one night and chopped it up.

As times got harder over the years, Felix took to slipping down into the Bankhead National Forest to poach deer and turkey to keep food on the table for his family. Dicey, mentally stunted but maternally devoted, starved herself to keep her children alive, and folks reckoned that in a strong wind any of her children could "just up and blow away like a piece of fodder in a whirlwind." Ole Felix was no improvement over Dicey in looks and no more than a tad ahead when it came to sense. As one smart aleck put it, "If brains was water, they'd all would've died of thirst a lo-o-ng time ago."

His poaching turned out to be not much better than his farming. Not only did the deer and turkeys usually outwit Felix, but also the forest rangers knew the trails he took and caught him maybe three times out of four. Most of the time, he only had one or two shotgun shells and was not much of a threat to man or beast. All the same, he was a prime aggravation to the rangers, and they wasted a lot of time shooing him out of their jurisdiction. At first they warned and fined him. But since he never had a dollar to his name and couldn't really get it through his thick head why they objected to his hunting in the first place, to put him in jail, as they did once or twice, was to place his destitute family at serious risk of starvation. Senior Ranger Tom Turnbull, who had grown up in Lawrence County and knew about the Hamiltons, decided that legal ways wouldn't do any good with a dunce like Felix. So he started wracking his brain to come up with a better plan to put an end to his poaching.

Enter Witch Hazel into the story.

All kinds of tales circulated over the years about old Hazel and her strange ways. These would turn out to be helpful in dealing with Felix, but the facts about her were also pretty odd and not without a tragic turn. Choctaw on her mother's side, Hazel acquired an uncommon knowledge of medicinal plants and herbs from her Indian ancestors, and folks said she had a way with wild creatures that no purely white person could match. Old timers recollected that in her young years her Choctaw-Scottish bloodlines made for a fetching female who, if not beautiful, was comely enough to catch the eye of many a young man. One of them, Ray Milligan, one of Homer Stokes' renters from over in Morgan County, proposed marriage, and Hazel, much in love, happily accepted.

But about that same time, around 1890, Hazel's father, Silas Simmons, decided to leave Alabama and try his luck out west in Indian Territory. Since his wife was Choctaw, they could qualify for free land in the Territory and maybe get away from folks who looked down on her and their "half-breed" children, as they called Hazel and her two brothers, Harmon and Owen.

Hazel objected to leaving out of her love for Ray, but her father, who was angry at the whole community for the way people had mistreated his family, would not listen to her appeals and ordered her not to talk to Ray again. He auctioned off their farm over close to Hillsboro and the family boarded the train in Decatur, making their way to Fort Smith and then by wagon on into the Territory.

The farther they got from Alabama, though, the unhappier

Hazel grew. She begged her father to let her return, but he would hear nothing of it. They had been in the Territory only a few weeks when she slipped out one night in the middle of winter and walked all the way back to Alabama, a kind of Trail of Tears in reverse. By this time several months had passed without seeing or hearing from Ray, but she trusted in his sworn love, as she knew hers to be unwavering.

Finally she found Ray again—newly married to another woman.

We have no way of knowing how much Hazel grieved over her lost love. She was a one-man woman and, as far as anyone knew, never loved another. She had no interest in going back to Indian Territory, and her family made no effort to retrieve her. After her grief—or maybe because of it—she reverted to her Indian ancestry, spending a year or two with her Choctaw relatives in Mississippi. Returning to Alabama wearing her hair long and plaited in the Choctaw style, she moved into an abandoned log cabin just inside Bankhead Forest and in general shunned society. Even though her cabin was inside the federal boundaries of the forest, the rangers chose not to make an issue of it. As Senior Ranger Tom Turnbull put it, "Life's already been hard enough on her without us adding to her aggravations. Hazel's not gonna bother anything, and we're not gonna bother her unless the higher-ups make us."

Not that she went feral and cut off all contacts with people. Word got out that she was skilled in herbal remedies for all sorts of ailments. She had medicines for female troubles, consumption, and rheumatism; poultices for cuts and infections; roots to restore lost nature and strength in men; cures for worms in children and animals, and teas to thin the blood, relieve the fidgets, and help circulation in the elderly. There was even talk that she had money and gold hidden in the woods behind her cabin. People who came to consult her, some on the sly, said that she was friendly and talkative enough. Once or twice a year she walked down to Moulton to buy a few items. People would stare at her Indian dress and whisper about her, but she seemed to take no notice of them. When asked by some of the Hillsboro girls she had grown up with why she didn't come back to live with ordinary folks, she answered simply that she was satisfied to be where she was.

She also had a talk or two with Tom Turnbull about Felix Hamilton and his family.

"Hazel, I've tried talkin' to Felix," Tom said, shaking his head, "but it's like talking to a fence post. He can't understand things. But I can tell you this: if we don't do something to get him off that old rundown ridge of his, the whole litter is gonna starve to death. And another thing, my rangers are tired of messing around with him two or three times a week. I've told them to go easy on him, but one of these days one of them is just gonna kind of—ah—'accidentally' shoot him and be done with it. And if they don't, some of the lawful hunters might. That's why I wanted to talk to you about the mess. I don't want anything bad to happen to the dumb ole thing. Hazel, You know them and have some pull. Maybe you can do something. You think you can? I just don't know what else I can do without bringing real grief down on them. But I have to do something."

The problem was that, on his deathbed and knowing how addle-brained his son was, old Beason Hamilton told Felix to stay on the place no matter what. It was all he had and all he could leave him. And anything his daddy told him he took to be pure gospel truth. Daddy told him to stay, and stay he would.

Hazel promised to help when and if she could. She knew all about Felix's plight, as she knew many things other people were unaware of. Often she watched him secretly as he blundered through the forest, tripping over limbs, talking to himself, and scaring away the animals. It bothered her, too, she told Tom, that he disturbed the animals and made it harder for her to approach them.

Whenever she could, Hazel would take edibles and medicines to his starving family. Usually she came and went as silent as a shadow, always flanked by two big white dogs of unknown breed, which she had trained never to bark or make a sound except at her command. But when she did come to the door of the shanty to speak to the family, tears of gratitude would come to Dicey's weary eyes and she would give Hazel a fierce, clinging hug.

One day Felix got lucky and shot a big tom turkey known to feed and roost close to Hazel's place. But two young rangers heard the shotgun blast and were soon hot on his trail. Felix heard them coming and dragging his precious turkey and running as fast as his spindly little legs could carry him, he looked around in panic for a hiding place. When the rangers emerged from the forest into the clearing around Hazel's cabin where they expected to overtake Felix, to their surprise he was nowhere to be seen. They suspected he was hiding inside, but, obeying Tom Turnbull's standing orders not to disturb Hazel her cabin, they waited at a respectful distance, talking and making just enough noise for Felix to know they were around.

Hazel returned a while later with a tow sack full of herbs and roots. The dogs' ears twitched a warning, but she had already sensed the presence of the rangers. One of them came over and whispered to her about Felix. She nodded and went inside, forming a plan to deal with him if she found him there.

Sure enough, ole Felix was hiding behind a curtain she used to separate her sleeping area from her eating table and herbal apothecary. Turkey blood dripped on his ripped shoes and formed a little pool on the floor. She could hear his raspy breathing.

She made no sign, though, that she knew of his presence, but instead emptied her sack and began to stoke the fireplace fire over which hung a big iron pot. Then she started humming and making up mumbo-jumbo in what Felix thought was the ancient Choctaw tongue. Then she dropped assorted roots, herbs, and other unidentified things into the simmering brew.

"Ah-ah-ah!" she crooned, "Ah-ah-ah! Ah-i-ay!" Then the words became recognizable as she dropped more items into the pot: "a bat's wing for wisdom, a snake's head for power; a crow's beak for magic, a frog's eyes for second sight. Ah-i-ay! Ah-yah-hee! Ki-lo-shan-lo! Ki-lo-shan-lo!"

Then already trembling with fear, remembering all the witch talk about her, Felix heard her say these terrible words: "I'll throw in Dicey's arm for the thickening, Felix's ears for the seasoning, the head of their firstborn for the finishing, and this night my magic will be complete. I will catch and carve them in their sleep and boil them in my pot. Then I will be the mighty witch of the Choctaw nation, young again, even though today I'm but a bag of skin and bones!"

At these last words, Skin and Bones, the names of her two big dogs, jumped up and snarling viciously with fangs bared, they rushed toward the figure Hazel pointed at behind the curtain. That was more than ole Felix could stand. Dropping the turkey and the shotgun, he ran out of the cabin in terror, squealing like a stuck pig. Skin and Bones chased him to the edge of the woods, snapping at his heels and the seat of his britches. Then, on her command, they dropped abruptly to their bellies, their ears pointed towards the fleeing Felix.

The rangers laughed till tears ran down their faces as they watched Felix crash through the underbrush, yelling and cursing in terror. Even old Hazel chuckled a little.

Back at the shanty, a wild-eyed, winded, and terrified Felix rousted Dicey and the children and they set out at a trot toward Moulton. Before long, Tom Turnbull just happened along in his Model-T, gave them a ride, and even found them a place to stay in town. The next day he got Felix a job cleaning out stables and currying the animals in his uncle's mule barn—the first steady work Felix ever had.

The Hamiltons were better off in Moulton than they had ever been up on the ridge. Of course, town living took some getting used to, what with all the daily commotion and noise in the streets. They had never seen so many people. But the good thing was that the family didn't go hungry again. Eventually, some of their children even got some schooling, what little they could stand. But Felix always warned everybody about "that ole witch down yonder in the forest." After what he had been through, Daddy or no Daddy, under no circumstances would Felix ever go back out that way, not even to get his shotgun, which Tom eventually returned to him.

Tom also went over to Hazel's to thank her for her help, had a good laugh with her over the frolic, and asked her if there was anything he could do for her, concerned that she had no family or real friends and was getting on in years. He noticed that she was moving a lot slower lately and her braids were now snowy white.

No, she said as she thanked him, if he would just keep an eye on Felix and his family. As for herself, she had all she needed and was satisfied with things.

One morning, not many years later, however, contrary to her training, her dogs started an awful howling, and when the rangers got there, they found old Hazel dead amidst her roots and herbs. On her finger was a little trifle of a ring that Ray Milligan had given her more than 40 years earlier as a token of his love. They buried her with it on in an unmarked grave behind her log cabin and just outside the National Forest boundary. There was no ceremony, but Tom read some verses from his Bible.

As for Skin and Bones, they stayed loyally by Hazel's grave until the concerned rangers dragged them away forcibly to the ranger station. In time they accepted food and by night slept inside the fence on a bed Tom made for them. But for as long as they lived, as soon as the gate was opened in the morning, ole Skin and Bones would light out for the cabin and Hazel's grave, keeping faithful watch over them until the sun went down.

Monty's Mountain

One day in March of 1985—can't remember the exact date—Monty MacAllen propped his broom against a booth in the Nugget Diner and went over to pick up some papers that fell from a customer's pocket as he got up to leave the restaurant. He called to the man, but the guy was already out the side door. Monty shrugged his shoulders, put the papers in his apron pocket, and resumed his sweeping.

His was a crappy job, but since he cheerfully admitted that he was a crappy employee, it was a fair match. Jess, the restaurant owner, for some reason liked Monty and first tried him out as a waiter. But Monty was scuffy and surly with patrons, and when he refused to cut his hair that dipped into soups and drinks, Jess demoted him to bussing and cleanup instead of showing him the door. It worked; Monty was comfortable as a bottom feeder and had worked his way downward for years to get there. He groused at times to pretend he had problems, but he had no real complaints about life. (More on that later.) Jess deducted half his wage for an 8' x 8' room attached like a wart to the back of the restaurant. The rest of his money was enough for Monty's daily quota of beer with some to spare for occasional half-hearted vices he kept around from his California years. Food was no problem; there were enough restaurant scraps to feed two or three people as long as they didn't inspect it too closely or meditate seriously on what they had put in their mouth. Otherwise, Monty knew as well as Jess that there were several irregularities about his employment: no mention of social security, no insurance, no limit on hours, no federal or state deductions, no minimum wage, and no paperwork to show that he was even employed. Both were fine with the arrangement and by tacit agreement said nothing about it.

Now back to Monty's attitude about life that I mentioned earlier. He reached the peak of his existence while still in his teens and never expected to get that high again no matter how long he lingered in this screwed-up world. He had caught a glimpse of the real world at a peak moment and realized that the so-called normal world that most people huffed and puffed about so much about was nothing but a neutered imitation. Just short of eighteen and before the beginning of his freshman year at Princeton University, he ran off with a buddy to Woodstock and the pinnacle of his ambition. There for three magical days before the cops hauled him off on charges he swore were trumped up (but actually fell short of what really happened) he lived the orgy of his life, maxed out on music, sex, drugs, smoke, stimulants, and everything in between and besides.

After the Woodstock experience, Monty saw the rest of his life as a long slide down an incline. He had lived a high in several ways that he would never forgot but knew he could never reach again. The lows that followed were equal to it at the other end of the spectrum. No, don't jump to conclusions; the worst was not coming down from the drug high. That was a bummer in itself, but one he could handle. It was the storm that hit him when he got back home to face outraged parents, grandparents, and almost the entire clans of the MacAllens and Tremonts. That was more than he could deal with. After a week of their screaming, cursing, crying, and general damnation, he had had it with both sides of his family. He gave a middle finger to Princeton, hit the road, and never looked back.

Now, if I told you the whole story, you would probably say that he threw his life away with those decision. But isn't that what life's for—to threw away on things and people, good and bad? Don't answer the question. It's rhetorical, which I think means a false way of putting things.

Because of something that happened later, I need to make an exception in the case of Grandfather Gus MacAllen. Just before Monty walked out, Grandpa McAllen pulled him aside, gave him a rough whiskery hug, and told him to drink to his health now and then.

"Monty, I can tell you that when I was your age, I thought about doing the same thing you're about to do. All the MacAllens, at least the older generations, had a touch of wanderlust in them. Too much Irish blood to be stable, I guess. Of course, you have French blood from your Tremont relatives, so I don't know what kind of weird chemistry that creates. Probably nothing good, but make what you can of it, my boy, you hear? In my case, I was in love and your future grandmother had me already emotionally hogtied. I didn't care about all the money she was coming into as an only child, but, man, was she pretty! And still is, at least to these old eyes. So I stayed put, but you go on, Monty, and do it for both of us!"

Gus didn't explain what Monty was supposed to do. Not that Monty wanted to know; after all, the whole point was to have nothing definite to do so that everything indefinite would stay possible. Always keep your options open, as the cool people say. Anyway, Gus slipped his grandson a hundred-dollar bill and Monty hit the road. He never saw old Gus again, but now and then, or more truthfully, nearly every day, he did drink to his

Grandfather's health. Of course, a lot of it was probably after old Gus died and had no health left, at least none that we know of.

*****

For the next ten years or so Monty went everywhere and nowhere, if you know what I mean. If you've ever been on the road yourself without a destination, you know that the going drives you, but nothing is pulling you, so you end up going every which way but straight, a little like pushing a car without a driver at the wheel. I think I said that wrong; what I meant was you don't end up anywhere at all, and the more you go, the less you arrive. Anyway, take my word for it; that's the way it is, even if I don't explain it very well.

I know I've been reeling like a drunk in this story, but it's Monty's fault. He was the one who zigzagged around most of the known world for a dozen years (maybe it was ten or could have been closer to fifteen). You can't make something crooked straight without making it into something it isn't, or wasn't, or wasn't supposed to be in the first place. I read that again and it doesn't make sense even to me. So scrub it and I'll try to get back on track.

After all his wanderings Monty ended up in eastern Colorado, where we are now. Ah, Colorado, you say, mountains and scenery. Well, no, dummy; I said eastern Colorado, which is plains country like Kansas or Nebraska, only more so. Not a mountain in sight. Well, there's one exception to all that flatness. Keep that detail in mind because it has a lot to do with this story. That said, let's get on with the telling.

One morning head waitress Ellie, Ellie Branson, banged on his door at the inhumanly early hour of 8:30 a.m. "Monty! You awake?"

No response from Monty.

"Monty, I know you're in there, and I don't care if you've got sack company, get your ass up and open this door!"

Monty cursed Ellie and all her busybody tribe, but he opened the door.

"Yeah, what the hell is so important that you wake me up just when I was sleeping the best?"

"There's a man in the restaurant asking for you."

"I don't do men, Ellie. Not my style. You take care of him."

"Monty, one of these days I may just shoot you, put you out of your misery, and make everybody happy. Now get your butt in there and talk to the man. He looks sorta official, and Jess is nervous. Now hurry!"

Monty ranted on a bit but then threw on some clothes and went with Ellie. She pointed to a man in a corner booth, as out of place in the dingy diner as a condor in a chicken coop.

The fancied-up, suit-and-tie dressed man rose as Monty approached and asked, "Are you Mr. MacAllen, Montgomery Xavier MacAllen?"

"Who the hell wants to know?"

"I'm Sherman Stillwell, of Atterbury, Sanborn & Stillwell law firm of Denver, and attorney for the estate of the late Mr. Guthrie MacAllen," he said, offering him his card.

"So Grandpa Gus's bus finally stopped and he got off."

"Then you are the Montgomery Xavier MacAllen I'm looking for."

"I haven't used those names since I was a teenager. These days it's just Monty. So what do you want, man?"

The lawyer stiffened and drew back. Apparently, he was not used to being addressed without the usual formalities and titles.

"Mr. MacAllen, do you have proof of your identity?"

"I'm here. Isn't that proof enough?"

"No, I meant documentation: birth certificate, passport, military records, even a driver's license, things like that to prove who you are."

"Hey, I don't have to prove anything to you, Mr. Stillborn, or whatever your name is. You tell me what all this is about, or I'm walking."

"If you would step outside to my car, Mr. MacAllen, I'll tell you in private the purpose of my visit."

Inside the car, Stillwell unsnapped a briefcase and withdrew several papers which he scrutinized for a moment before turning to speak to Monty.

"These papers, Mr. MacAllen, are the death certificate of the late Mr. Guthrie Fitzhugh MacAllen, your presumptive grandfather, and a copy of his last will and testament, along with some appertaining documents. You, assuming you are indeed his grandson, stand to inherit an immense fortune from his estate. That, sir, to give you the short answer to your question, is the purpose of my visit."

"What do you mean by 'immense'?"

"To begin with, there are two principal properties: an estate in the Adirondacks and a mansion in Coral Cables, Florida."

"Yeah, we used to go up to the place in the Adirondacks in the summer. It was nice, but I don't know anything about Coral Gables. Grandpa hated hot places, so I'm surprised he would buy a house in south Florida."

"The Coral Gables bit was a ploy to test you. You passed; there is no such mansion."

"It's a good thing I'm in a pretty good mood today. A trick

like that could get you a bruised head, Stillwell. You'll notice that I'm a good bit bigger than you."

"Well, Mr. MacAllen, maybe it's a good thing I'm being patient with you despite your size and rudeness. You see, I'm a black belt in karate and can take care of myself, if need be."

"Okay, okay, Mr. Stillwell, I get your point. Can you see me backing down and shrinking to midget size already? Now getting back on task, I do have identification, if that makes you happy. But you said 'immense'. What else was there in Grandpa Gus's estate?"

"Approximately three hundred fifty-five million dollars in stocks and monetary assets plus additional properties, bonds, and investments that round it out to something on the order of three hundred ninety million plus or minus a million or two on any given day. Daily market fluctuations, you understand."

Monty whistled his astonishment.

"And who gets all that?"

"Well, your older siblings, Raymond and Susan, come in for about ten million each. Then modest amounts—a few thousand each—to approximately a dozen people who worked for him at one time or another. Some of them have passed on, which is a complicated process we're sorting out. As for the other family members, a dollar each and best wishes. Your purported Grandfather parted ways with most of the family years ago when he and his wife moved out of New York City. The rest and the bulk of the inheritance goes to you, assuming you can validate your identity and survive court challenges."

"Challenges?"

"Sure, the family will do everything they can to break the will. They're lined up to claim mental incompetence, forgery, underhanded maneuvers and pressures on your part, and other strategies if these are unsuccessful."

"But I've had no communication at all with Grandpa or the family for at least the last ten or fifteen years."

"That's what you say. They'll try to prove differently, believe me."

"What if I just walk away from the inheritance? I've lived without family or their money for most of my life and have managed to get by."

"For one thing, believe it or not, it would cost you money and probably court time to decline the inheritance, and for another, people would see a refusal as evidence of your complicity and guilt in defrauding your Grandfather MacAllen and the family."

"Holy shit! You're telling me I'm in a fight I didn't ask for over something I didn't want in the first place?"

"That's about the size of it, Mr. MacAllen. So, what are your thoughts? And while you're thinking, let me see the documentation you mentioned."

"Right now, I don't have a clear idea in my head. All this has me creeped out. But here's my birth certificate."

"Thanks. I understand what a shock this must be to you. My advice is to sleep on it, and I'll come by tomorrow and go into more detail to help you come to make decisions. Here are a couple of suggestions to think about in the meantime: first, big money can do big things—for you if that's the extent of your interest, or for a lot of people if you have a broader vision. And, second, somebody will end up with most of the money after the usual court costs, fees, and so on; that will either be you, which is what your Grandfather MacAllen obviously wanted, or the relatives that apparently crossed and angered him to such a degree that he disinherited most of them. Think about it. We've had a lot of experience with inheritances cases like this. But of course, I can't tell you what to do. My job is to do what's legally correct with your Grandfather's will and probate, nothing else. You have to decide about the other things we've talked about today."

"I do have one question up front, Stillwell. Grandpa lived in New York State, probably in his place up in the Adirondacks that he loved so much. So how come you Colorado lawyers are handling his will?"

"Your MacAllen grandparents did live briefly on the Adirondacks estate, but he moved out here to Colorado nine years ago after his wife died He passed away in Colorado Springs. His residence in that city is one of the properties mentioned in his will, one you are due to inherit."

"All that time and not that far from here," Monty said. "If I had known, I mighta looked up the old guy. He was good to me. Yeah, I woulda looked him up. Bummer I didn't know about it."

Monty walked around like a zombie all day.

"Damn fool must be on something," Jess whispered to Ellie. "Keep an eye on him, and if the cops happened to drop in, get him back to his room."

"Sure, Jess, but I think he's acting that way because of something that lawyer guy, or whatever he was, said to him this morning. Can't imagine what it was, and Monty's not talking, but he ain't been the same since all that."

That night he finished off ten beers and passed out without really sleeping. It was a night of flashing colors and worlds that spun around him. The next morning when he shambled into the restaurant with bloodshot eyes and wobbly legs a little after eight, Jess rolled his eyes and called Ellie over.

"Ellie, keep an eye on him. If he's too far gone, we may have to put him in his room till he's over whatever he's been high on."

"I think he's just plain drunk, or was, Jess. His trashcan was nearly full of beer bottles when I got to work this morning. But I still think he's rattled by something that guy told him yesterday, and he said the man was coming back this morning."

"Well, whatever to hell it is, I've just about had it with him. I've been easy on him up to now, too easy, I guess, but if he keeps this up, it's out the door with the asshole. He's starting to hurt our business."

Stillwell showed up a little later, and after coffee—two for Monty—the two of them went out to his car and talked for the better part of an hour. When Monty came back in, his steps were surer, and he stood straighter. He downed another black coffee.

"Monty, I'm gonna have to dock you for the hour you spent talking to that guy," Jess informed him. "The place is a mess, and Ellie and Jill are having to work their butts off because you keep slacking off."

"Sorry about that, Jess. I'll make it up to you and the girls."

Jess was mildly surprised; he had never heard Monty apologize for anything or to anybody. Maybe that's why he liked the bum; Monty did what he would like to do.

"Are you ready to get to work? The lunch crowd will be coming in pretty soon, and I need for you to clean up the mess and get these dirty dishes to the kitchen."

"No problem, but after the lunch rush I need to take the rest of the day off, in fact, the next three or four days off."

"Monty, what the hell is going on with you? You've been acting crazy, well crazier, ever since you talked with that guy yesterday and again this morning. They about to lock you up for something? You killed somebody?"

"Not yet, Jess, but it could be you if you don't stop asking stupid questions that I'm not going to answer."

"Well, I would appreciate knowing, if your lordship would tell me, why you need to take several days off? If that's your way of quitting and going on the road again, just tell me and we'll part friends—or at least not enemies."

"Nothing like that, and you couldn't guess the reason in a million years. But we'll talk later. Here comes that bunch from the lumber yard, so you better get ready with the hamburgers and beef stew."

After the lunch rush was over and Jess was making his tallies, Monty came and waited for him to finish.

"So, Monty, what's this about some days off? What are you up to? Whatever it is just leave me and the diner out of it."

"No problem with the Nugget, but I need to involve you just a bit."

"I don't think I'm going to like this, but before I say no, just out of curiosity, tell me anyway."

"Jess, I need to borrow three hundred dollars, a suit and tie, and a pair of shoes."

"You what? Monty, if you're thinking of dying on us, since you'd most likely be headed straight for hell, you won't need any of that stuff down there. It would burn up as soon as you reached the gate."

"Funny, but weak funny, Jess. Anyway, I'm not going to hell, not yet at least, I'm going to Denver, though in my professional experience there's not a whole hell of a lot of difference."

"What business you got in Denver?"

"As I said, you couldn't guess in a million years. But it is kinda important. So, can you loan me a suit, some shoes, and the three hundred?"

"Well, now I'm curious. Yeah, I have an old suit and tie I can let you borrow, but the money is something else. Maybe I could spring for fifty dollars? How's that?"

"Three hundred."

"A hundred."

"Three hundred, and I forgot, I'll need a white shirt too."

"Two hundred, max. And I guess I can scrounge you up a shirt."

"Three hundred. And I'll pay you back. Promise."

"Monty, your financial promises are worth about as much as a Confederate dollar. If I was to let you walk out of here with three hundred dollars, I'd bet another three hundred that I'd never see you again. Sorry."

Ellie by now was listening as best she could between trips to the kitchen and a lone patron. She came over after the man left, stuffing his dollar tip in her pocket.

"Monty, I'm not sure if being around you has made me crazy too, but I'll stand good for the other hundred. It sounds like this is something that means a lot to you."

"It does mean a lot, Ellie, and I will pay both of you back. Now Jess, I need to go shave, take a shower and clean up; then if it's all right I'll walk over to your house after you close up and pick up the shoes and clothes. And if both of you could have the money ready early tomorrow morning, I'll pick it up, too."

As he left, Jess and Ellie looked at each other, amazed and intrigued by Monty's strange behavior. He had always been crazy, which was bad enough but normal for him. Was he now doing something even more bizarre by going sane on them?

The next morning Stillwell was waiting in his car when Jess and Ellie opened the place at six fifteen. Incredibly, Monty came around the corner of the restaurant about the same time dressed in Jess's old suit and shoes and wearing a tie with a bad knot and one side of his shirt collar still turned up. Stillwell got out of the car. Monty asked Jess and Ellie for the money. She handed hers over without comment, but Jess released his reluctantly with a stream of profanity.

"Monty," he added, "you've got my two hundred and my clothes, even persuaded Ellie to contribute some honest money to your scam. Anything else we can do for you, Mr. MacAllen? Jess asked sarcastically.

"No, I'm good, but the suit's a little tight in the straddle, and I had better shoes than these when I was sleeping on Skid Row in Chicago. You sure you don't have something better for me?"

Jess added to his profane diatribe and disappeared into the kitchen.

"You ready to leave?" Ellie asked as she came over to smooth his turned-up shirt collar. "Did you find the socks and the note I left in a plastic by the door."

"Yeah, I'm ready, and yeah, the socks are okay. I'm riding up to Denver with that guy Stillwell waiting out there by the car. But I'll be back soon."

"Uh huh, sure you will, Monty. Just remember us whenever you don't have anything better to do."

"I told you, Ellie, I'll be back."

Sure you will, Monty, she thought as the car disappeared around a corner. How many times have guys told me that lie as they walked out the door? And not even a mention of my note. It surprised her that she could still care. Her eyes moistened, and she was glad she didn't have to speak to anyone at that moment.

A week later and no word from Monty, Jess and Ellie reached a verdict: he had scammed them.

"Well, damn it to hell, that's what I get for trusting him," Jess said, shaking his head. "Two hundred dollars down the drain. At least the suit and shoes were throwaways. How much did you give him, Ellie, was it a hundred?"

"Yeah, a hundred, money I couldn't afford to lose. I even bought him a pair of socks. I didn't want him walking around in Denver without something on his feet. But it aint the first time I've been lied to and used; that's been my history with men. Always getting mixed up with losers, and always losing. But you know something, Jess, I must be a total idiot, because I'm still not convinced we've seen the last of Monty. He could turn up."

"Trusting in your womanly intuition again, are you, Ellie? How's that worked out for you so far?"

"Just about a hundred percent."

"I getcha, a hundred percent right or wrong?"

"You already know the answer to that. If my barometer about men had worked, do you think I'd still be waiting tables at my age in a dump like this instead of living in a classy neighborhood with a nice family and a Mercedes in the driveway?"

"Hey, girl, don't put this old place down. It's kept us both going."

"Oh, I know that, Jess. I'm not complaining about the diner, or you, or anything in particular, just bitching a little about life in general, I guess. I had hoped for a better deal, but it is what it is. Still, you know, I always had a soft spot for ole Monty, even if he was crazy—or maybe because he was crazy—and sorta hoped that he might come through this time. But . . ."

"Did he take all his junk with him?"

"No, and that's the funny part. He left a bunch of crud in the room: all his old clothes, some pictures, and other things I thought he would've taken with him. I guess, though, that when you get right down to it, maybe he doesn't care about anything . . . or anybody."

"Well, Ellie, as you say, it is what it is, and we're the suckers in Monty's scam. Both of us shoulda known better. Hell, we did know better, didn't we? And we went along with it anyway. But, hey, here come the boys from the lumber yard, so you and Jill better get ready for them, and I need to get in the kitchen."

*****

In August of that same year, a sparkling new Cadillac pulled into the Nugget parking lot and a big, elegantly dressed man got out and went inside. Both patrons and employees stared. By his appearance it was apparent to all that he was out of his element. But when he spoke, Ellie recognized him.

"Ellie, I'm back, just like I told you."

"Monty? Monty! It's really you!" she said, ignoring a customer waiting for the Luncheon Special plate she was holding.

"Yeah, Ellie, it's really me. Now serve that man his lunch. He looks hungry."

Ellie slid the plate across the table and set the water down so hard that some spilled out. Then as man shook his head she ran on impulse to hug Monty.

"You really did, Monty! You came back just like you said, late, but you came back."

Jess came out of the kitchen and stopped in amazement.

"God Almighty! Is this who I think it is? Monty, is it you? But how? What? What's going on? And as fancied up as a crooked Washington politician. Did you rob a bank or something?" he asked as he came to give Monty a bearhug.

By this time everybody in the crowded diner was staring at Monty as though he were the prodigy of the age fallen from the sky. When things slowed down, Jess motioned for Ellie and Monty to step into the kitchen.

"Ellie, I see you have a new girl. Where's Jill? She still around?"

"Bobbie's the new girl. Jill got married, Monty, to a fellow she went to high school with over in Nebraska. I guess they dated some back then. He just happened to stop here one day, recognized her, and they reconnected, just like that. The rest is history. He's army, so they moved down to the military base in El Paso."

"Well, good for her. Hope it works out. And what about you, Ellie? What's going on in your life?"

"Hey, guy, are you sure you're the same Monty that used to work around here a little when he was sober enough? That guy never asked me what I was doing or cared about, or anything close to it, and he treated everybody else the same way—like crap."

"Maybe this will convince you that I'm the same Monty," he said as he took two one-hundred bills from his wallet and put them in her hand. "Will that settle my debt?"

"No, it was just a hundred dollars, and after all this time just think of it as gift," she said, giving him back the bills.

"No way. I owe you a hundred, and you can call the other hundred interest or appreciation, whichever."

"And if I refuse to take it?"

"Then you and all the customers here in the Nugget will hear me talk and act like the old Monty. You want that?"

"Monty, what I don't want is money you stole or scammed or maybe counterfeited. I may be a lot of things less than squeaky respectable, but I don't steal or lie, and I don't want to get in trouble with the cops. I've been down those kinds of road before through no fault of my own except gullibility, and I don't want to go there again."

"Ellie, this money is not hot or fake. It's mine and I came by it legally."

"How could you come by money legally? You never had a pot to piss in since I've known you. And now you come back here driving a new Cadillac and flashing money. That doesn't smell legal to me."

"Me neither," Jess chimed in. "But I'm not as picky as Ellie; I'll take my two hundred if you got it on you—and if it's not phony. But since you claim everything is straight up and legal, don't you think you oughta tell us what's going on and where you've been? We trusted you. Why won't you trust us?"

"You're right, Jess, you're both right. By the way, Jess, your old suit split down the ass and the soles came loose on the shoes. Next time I want better stuff. But yeah, I will tell both of you what I've been up to, but not till the place is empty after closing time. We have three or four hours till then, so while we're waiting, Ellie, I need something from you."

"What is it this time?"

"The pictures and stuff I left in my room. I know you're sort of a packrat, so you probably still have them."

"I haven't touched any of the crap you left. I'd guess it's still in the room, unless Jess threw it out. Did you?"

"I haven't even unlocked the door since Monty left; so, as far's I know his junk is still in there."

"Okay, now in the meantime, Jess, here's three hundred dollars for you, and the two hundred for you, Ellie. As I said before, consider the extra as interest or appreciation. If you don't want it after I tell you my story, you can give it back."

"Like I said before, I don't have a problem with taking it if it's legit," Jess said with a big grin.

Ellie took hers this time without comment.

Then Monty got the room key and two plastic bags from Jess and spent more than three hours going through his stuff. When he came out he dropped the heavier bag in the garbage can and handed the other to Ellie.

"Ellie, I want you to keep this for me until I get settled. Will you?"

"Sure, why not? We packrats can always use more junk."

By late afternoon Jess was making excuses to get the remaining patrons out. As the last two left, he put up the "Closed" sign and the three of them went out and sat in the Cadillac with its new car smell, Jess in the back and Monty and Ellie in front.

"Okay, Monty," Jess said, "tell us a story, one we can believe, like how you came by this Cadillac for starters, and these fancy duds."

"Okay, here's the real deal. I bought the suit and the car. Paid cash for them and I could buy a hundred more just like them if I wanted to. I've got more money than you can imagine, in fact, more than I can imagine myself. To make it short, I'm a rich SOB."

"The SOB part I don't argue with, Monty, but you either had to break the bank in Las Vegas or break into a real one, or you're lying through your teeth," Jess commented skeptically. "Which is it?"

"Yeah, Monty, where would you get that kind of money?"

asked Ellie.

"I inherited it."

"Inherited it!" Jess hooted. "You have to come up with a better story than that. If your family has money, how come you've been living like a bum for all these years? It doesn't add up."

"I chose to live the way I have, on the road and on the street. I never told anybody, but my family is, or was, rich, especially my grandfather. He's the one who left me a fortune."

"How much of a fortune, Monty, if you can tell us?" asked Ellie.

"Give or take a million here or there, how does three hundred fifty million plus sound?"

"So, you're telling us that just like that you went from being one step away from being a street person to a zillionaire?" said Jess. "You expect us to believe that?"

"Believe it or not, that's what happened. But, Jess, it was not just like snapping my fingers and the money appeared. In fact, these last three or four months have been a living hell."

"I'm not buying any of this bullshit you're throwing at us, not yet at least," Jess said, taking the hundreds from his shirt pocket and stuffing them in his wallet.

"What could be hard about coming into all that money?" asked Ellie.

"The problem, Ellie, was that everybody and his uncle in the MacAllen clan wanted it too, and it seems they hired every big lawyer between here and New York to break Grandpa's will and get it for them."

"That part doesn't surprise me," Jess commented, "big money, big greed, and big problems. So what did you do?"

"Nothing much on my own, just what the experts told me to

do, and especially what not to do. Stillwell—the guy that came out here a couple of times—and his law firm in Denver represented me. And they saved my bacon. If Grandpa had died in New York, we probably woulda lost the inheritance. Too much under the table corruption and inside connections back there. But since I qualified as a Colorado resident, the Denver bunch had the inside connections out here. They beat the New York crowd and got me my money just like Grandpa wanted. But it was nasty as hell and took weeks in court. Stillwell hired bodyguards to protect me 24/7. I thought it was crazy at first, but then he convinced me that all they had to do was arrange an "accident" of some kind to take me out and wind up with all the money for themselves."

"And then turn on one another in the process," Jess said. "Some smartass once said that power corrupts, but I've seen enough to know that money does it a lot quicker. But all that— lawyers, experts, bodyguards—must have cost a bundle. Right?"

"You said it, Jess, I don't know exactly how much, easily a million, probably more by the time you count up all the fees and expenses—and maybe some under the table bribes, too. Who knows? Hell, I don't know all that Stillwell and his crew did, and don't want to know. All I know is that they won the friggin' war for me against the New York sharks. So, I don't mind them gouging me a little. They earned it. But Jess, you sound like you're beginning to believe my story. Right?"

"I'm listening when I ought to be home having dinner."

"You don't eat at the Nugget? But you do the cooking."

"Eat my own cooking? You gotta be kidding. That would come under the category of cruel and unusual punishment, as your smart lawyers would say. My wife is twice the cook I am on my best day."

"Ellie, you've gotten awfully quiet," Monty said to her. "What do you have to say to all this?"

"Monty, what are you doing here?"

"Well, I'm sitting in my car talking to you and Jess. That's what I'm doing."

"No, Monty, I mean what you really are doing here in this little excuse for a town. Why did you come back? With all that money you claim to have, you don't have any real reason to be here. Me and Jess are just passing landscape on the road you're traveling now."

"That's where you're wrong, Ellie. You wanna know why I came back? I came back to see you two, maybe the only real friends and family I have. All those years I was a bottom feeder I didn't really like anybody, and I guess it was because I didn't like myself. I was seriously screwed up, as we all know. Now I see other possibilities. But coming back is not a sentimental journey. I'm going into business in this town—or really out east of here on six hundred acres of land I bought out there—and I want you to help me develop it, to work with me and for me."

"Work for you?" asked a slack-jawed Jess, "Doing what?"

"Among other things, the main one for me, building a mountain."

"Monty's Mountain, Monty's Mountain," Ellie repeated smiling. "It has a nice ring to it. And it's reassuring."

"Reassuring? I don't get it," Jess said, frowning at her description.

"Sure, Jess. It tells us that rich or poor, it's still crazy ole Monty inside that four-hundred-dollar suit."

"More like five hundred," Monty corrected her. "Yeah, I want to build me a mountain and some other things along with it."

"Like what?" asked Jess.

"Well, I'm not sure about everything yet; the mountain for sure, a couple of restaurants, probably a western type store, sportswear and hunting supply store, antique store, a motel, carousel, rollercoaster, train track, other kinds of rides, maybe a buffalo ranch, even a chapel, and some housing. The people that work there will have to live somewhere, and it's better if they don't have to drive in. Hell, I don't know what all yet, guys; I'm making it up as I go along. And that's where you two come in: I want you to help me plan and build a town. And as quick as we can find them, we'll need some civil and construction engineers, architects, and a bunch of other experts to design the layout and advise us on procedures."

"Monty," Jess asked, leaning over the seat now with obvious interest, "Why do you even want to build a mountain, as you call it, out there in flat country and a town where there ain't nothing now but prairie dogs and a coyote or two?"

"Because we can."

"Because we can," Jess muttered, shaking his head. "Is that a reason?"

"It's reason enough, Jess," Ellie reassured him. "I understand Monty's thinking."

"I'm thinking both of you—maybe me too—belong in a mental institution. Here we are on the wrong side of town, talking about enough money to buy both sides."

"So, are you two on board?" Monty asked.

"You sure you can pay us and are you gonna pay us?" Jess wanted to know.

"More than you ever made in your life."

"I think I'm in, Monty," Ellie declared. "When do we start?"

"Starting on my payroll September 1st, that's a week from today. Office work begins in about six weeks, as soon as I can get a building—maybe a temporary—set up on site."

"And how much wage are we talking about?" Jess asked.

"Not a wage, Jess, you'll be a salaried man from now on. White collar. You both will be. How does $75,000 a year and a car for starters sound?"

"You gotta be kidding. Is that one salary divided between the two of us?"

"No, Jess. Don't think stingy. That's seventy-five grand apiece per year. And I'll get my CPA to figure out the fringes: taxes, insurance, Social, deductions, and whatever to hell else needs to be included. He'll want you to fill out some forms. I'll bring them by tomorrow or the next day."

"You got a CPA?"

"Yeah, three as a matter of fact, and they're the best in the business. Without them, Jess, a rich dude's like a duck surrounded by a dozen hunters aiming shotguns at him." I've got lawyers, CPAs, bankers, and all kinds of people. Money attracts them like a dog attracts fleas. But I've learned you have to deal with them."

"You said a car, too, Monty," Ellie reminded him.

"Sure, got a problem with that?"

"Not really. Just that I've never owned a car and barely know how to drive."

"Well, start learning, Ellie. It's time. You're moving up in the world."

Am I really, she thought in a daze. Has my time really come at last?

"Okay, I guess, Monty," Jess said with misgiving in his tone, "but what do you want us to do in the meantime?"

"Something very specific: I want you both to start thinking about our town. Try to imagine it as you would want it to look. Make sketches or write descriptions. But keep the mountain central in your thinking. Okay?"

"Just one thing, boss, Jess said, putting an odd emphasis on the title, "I'll need to do something with the Nugget."

"Can you sell it?"

"Monty, you know the people around me. They don't have money, and a lot of them don't have enough credit to buy a crippled cat."

"Two ideas, Jess: why don't you and Ellie keep working there until we're ready to move on site, and, second, put it on the market right away. If it doesn't sell by then, you can just close it."

"But I don't own the lot. I lease it by the year, renewable in January."

"How much a year?"

"Well, uh, around five or six thousand."

"Exactly how much?"

"Forty-eight hundred," Jess said, looking at Ellie with distress spread across his broad face.

"Jess, you lying sack of pig shit!" Ellie said angrily. "Last time I asked for a raise, you told me the lease was six thousand a year and that you couldn't afford to raise my pay. Now the truth comes out! Liar, liar, pants on fire!"

"Well, Ellie, I may have fudged a little on the lease, and I'm truly sorry about that, but the rest was true; business was slow back then. I hope you won't stay mad at me."

"I'll think about it. But let me say something here and now to both of you: if the three of us are going to work together as a team of some kind, let's all pledge that we'll be upfront and truthful with one another. Okay?"

"Okay," they all said in unison and clasped hands in a mutual pledge.

*****

Once construction began, hundreds of people drove out to see Monty's Mountain—or Folly, as many called it—going up in slow stages. The very first day the site was opened to the public, an enterprising taco truck driver heard about it and followed them. He sold out in an hour. Next day more cars showed up and three taco trucks could hardly keep up with the demand. In no time Jess and Ellie saw the commercial possibilities of hungry crowds and had tents, tables, benches, and a half acre of porta-potties set up to feed and accommodate them. They brought Bobbie out to help the food service and left a permanent "Closed for Repair" sign on the Nugget. Businessmen and bankers from several towns also came by to assess how they might profit from the gawdiest and strangest project eastern Colorado had ever seen. As days passed, curious neighbors from Kansas and Nebraska started showing up to marvel alongside the locals at the noise, movement, and dust, and to gawk at the giant earth movers, cement trucks, water trucks, dump trucks, semis, bulldozers, and backhoes.

The engineers calculated that a thirty-acre base with an ample safety and clearance zone would be necessary in order to construct a man-made mountain eight thousand feet high. Since the high Colorado prairie at that location was already over forty-five hundred feet above sea level, the combined height would be approximately thirteen thousand feet, a respectable mountain by North American standards. They debated a lot among themselves. Nobody had ever designed a structure for a mountain.

In reality, "Monty's Mountain" was designed to be as a flattop pyramid with a perfectly square base and four slopes pitched at graduated angles to permit skiers of varying skill and daring to launch from three points. Monty, Jess, and Ellie agreed after consulting with the engineers that only two slopes would be designed for skiing; the other two would be for hikers and climbers.

Meanwhile, another construction crew was building the main office of MacAllen Enterprises, as Monty had named his company. Nearby, in a temporary structure, almost tripping over one another, crews of engineering experts, specialists, and technicians were designing streets, buildings, drainage, water and sewage systems, haggling with city, county, and state officials over regulations, roads, tax structures, abatements, and annexation issues. And slowly, inexorably, level upon level, Monty's Mountain kept rising on the flat terrain.

Seizing on the sheer size and extravagance of the project, the news media compared it to the pyramids of ancient Egypt and gleefully renamed Monty "Pharaoh MacAllen." They wondered in mock seriousness what sort of curses and devices he would place outside his burial chamber to thwart the graverobbers and befuddle the archeologists of a distant future age. As for pragmatic businessmen, they regretted what they saw as the waste of a great fortune and pointed out in somber detail how it could have been profitably used to develop the regional economy. Environmentalists began warning that the "mountain" was shaping up to be an ecological disaster.

As for Monty, he brushed all these groups aside with lighthearted but eloquent profanity describing their canine mothers, fatherless civil status, and a one-way ticket to an overheated eternal residence. Like kids in a sandbox full of new toys, he, Jess, and Ellie were having too much fun to take their critics seriously.

By late fall, work the mountain had become a race between completion and the cold. Now it towered seven thousand feet above the prairie, but as the tiers increased and distance between the corner turns shortened proportionately, it required more caution and took the machines longer to deliver their loads and come down. One truck slid over the edge on the return and rolled several hundred feet before coming to a precarious stop against a construction pier. There it was destined to remain in later times for tourists to gawk at, and for the remainder of the project, as a reminder to other drivers of the hazards. Fortunately, the driver survived with surprisingly few injuries, but the other drivers became more cautious and work slowed accordingly.

The cold won, but barely. The casement for the final level was in place but unfilled with stabilizing material when the first snow fell in mid-November. Work on the mountain ceased for the winter, but several buildings were finished, one of which now served as a temporary residence for Ellie and Monty. Jess came out from town on good days, but understandably spent the others in town with his family. He had grown up in the town and despite the good money he was earning, had not adapted to his new situation. He confided to Ellie that he was tempted to reopen the Nugget but did not want to be a drag on the project or disloyal to Monty.

"Jess, you need to decide one way or another," Ellie told him. "Monty's counting on you, and I doubt he would keep you on salary if you're here running the diner again."

"What about you, Ellie? I don't know about you, but I get

tired of people making fun of me for being a part of this thing. And I have to be honest with you. I miss the old diner. It was about all I ever did before Monty fell into all that money. How do you feel, Ellie?"

"Well, Jess, I don't miss the diner, to be honest with you. This thing with Monty and all the money he's paying me has given me a new lease on life. It's the most fun I've ever had. For the first time I can buy good clothes and live in a way I never could before. Life has been hard on me, or maybe I've been hard on life and just plain dumb in my decisions. I've told you about some of them. I don't want to go back to that. So I'm going to play out the string with Monty."

"You like the guy, don't you, Ellie?"

"Sure, I do, just like I like you, Jess. You're both my friends, though both of you can be a royal pain in the ass at times."

"With me, yeah, friends, but with Monty I think there's more. Am I right, or am I right, little lady?"

"Jess, you know more about me than you should. You know I've been suckered too many times to trust any guy too much. That's as much as I'm gonna say."

"I understand, Ellie, so all I can say is that I hope you don't get in too deep with Monty. You know how he is. He could walk away any day and leave you in the cold."

"Yeah, he's got all the credentials of a first-class SOB, but he's my SOB."

"That's what concerns me. I aint been the best of friends to you, but I don't wannta see bad stuff happen to you."

"Well, thank you, I think, Jess. It sounds like what my old dad told me about twenty years ago when I left home with the guy I thought I was gonna marry."

Spring came early. By June, Monty's mountain and much of the infrastructure, the Western theme store, the motel, and one of the planned restaurants were ready for visitors. Monty hired a publicist to promote a preliminary opening with the grand opening to follow.

It was successful beyond all expectations. All day longs trucks hauled in more food to the restaurant. The Western Store was nearly empty by early afternoon and Monty's Motel was full up and booked for weeks to come. Hundreds of people walked out and gawked at the mountain, particularly the truck perched high on the slope as though threatening to complete its plunge at any moment.

As more components of the complex, including a second motel and restaurant, came on line in the following weeks and word spread far and wide, tourists and money rolled in at a steady accelerating pace. "Monty's Folly," as many sober-headed folks called it at first now became the epitome of American entrepreneurial genius, according to economists. Within two years of operation, Monty had recouped his construction costs and was raking in the money: by the thousands daily and millions monthly. His work force soon doubled; his profits tripled.

There were immense growing pains. More water and electricity were needed in huge incremental amounts. There were charges that one or two of the contractors had hired illegals and fudged on their tax reports. Some tried to blame Monty for it. He responded with his usual colorful profanity. The environmentalists were beside themselves with rage. It seemed, so one group claimed, that Monty's Mountain and the town sprung up to support it had displaced a subspecies of prairie dog and called for the entire complex to be closed so that an exhaustive reevaluation of the environmental implications could be conducted.

On the other side of the ledger, financiers came forward with offers to purchase the complex. Monty waved them off—for a time, in fact several times. Then when his intuition—newly fine-tuned by experience—told him that real storm clouds were gathering on the future horizon, he called Ellie and Jess in for a conference.

"Hey, gang, two days ago I got an offer for the Mountain that I'm considering accepting. Look at the bottom line."

Jess whistled in astonishment. "Unreal, Monty. Is this offer for real?"

"Five hundred million?" said Ellie. "What's the catch?"

"None that my lawyers can find."

"Are they reliable?" asked Jess.

"It's Stillwell's bunch outta Denver. They got me through the inheritance mess when they could have made a fortune for selling me out under the table. Yeah, they're reliable. I trust them. The thing is—"

"But, Monty," Ellie broke in, "I thought you were in this thing because you were enjoying it, not primarily for the money."

"That's what I was about to explain. You're right, Ellie, I was in it for the fun of it. And aint it been a great ride so far? I thought nothing could top Woodstock, but this has. But Stillwell told me something yesterday that puts a different spin on everything."

"What?" asked Jess.

"What I'm going to tell you has to stay in this room. He's got word from a confidential source that in next year's legislative session—not in this one, luckily—there's a strong possibility they will pass legislation that could force places like this to suspend operations because of pressure from the environmentalists. As you know, they're getting politically stronger in Colorado. In fact, he tells me that the legislation will be aimed specifically at our place. Of course, the bill won't say so outright."

"Yeah," groused Jess, "getting to where you can't kill a grasshopper without some nut complaining."

"So, Monty," said Ellie, "You're thinking about taking the offer?"

Monty repeated her words: "So, Ellie, I'm thinking about taking the offer."

"While the getting's good, as they say," added Jess.

"While the getting's good, as they say," echoed Monty.

Monty sold the Mountain and more than doubled his fortune. He passed on ten million to Jess, who went home happy and built an upscale restaurant on the better side of town. But Ellie, who expected the same or similar treatment got nothing. She was visibly hurt, and her old pessimism about the men in her life came surging back.

"Well, Monty, thank you for everything," she said, rising above the familiar disappointment. "These years have been the best of my life. What will you do now? Where will you go?"

"Not sure yet what I'll do, but I am sure of where I'm going."

"And where's that?"

"Back to the Adirondacks and my Grandfather's estate. I was happy there as a boy, so maybe I can get centered again. I'll miss my Mountain, but they have mountains up there, too, and they're really beautiful, especially in the fall."

"I'm sure they are. Monty, I hope you'll be happy there. Maybe you can reconnect with your family, at least some of them, and not be lonely."

She kissed Monty on the cheek and got up to leave.

"Hey, wait a minute, we haven't finished talking."

"I think we've said everything that needs saying, Monty. Thanks again."

"No, not really, Ellie. I have something else to say."

"Okay, what is it?"

"I'm going home, or as close to it as I can get, but I was hoping I wouldn't have to go alone. How about coming with me?"

"I'm sure it would be pleasant, Monty, but I don't have anyone or anything in New York. I need to get on with my life out here somewhere, deal myself a new hand."

"Well, I can offer you a new deal, if you're not totally bummed out on me."

"You're still my friend, Monty, and I'll never forgot what you've done for me. What do you have in mind?"

"A husband and wife deal. Ellie, you have stabilized me. I know I'm a few years older than you, but I need you with me. Hell, let me skip the romantic bullshit and tell you the bottom line: Ellie, would you consider being my wife?"

Tears came to her eyes and her voice was shaky, but she got the words out: "Monty, I'll do more than consider it. I'll do it!"

And they did.

*****

Here I must confess that I am reneging on a promise I made to Monty. That's not his real name, and I'll keep that part of our agreement. But it seems only fair that I give him credit for his own story, which he wrote with Ellie's help. Through a mutual friend he learned that I was preparing this volume of stories and with considerable embarrassment for a man of his character asked if I would consider including it. I read the manuscript and agreed to accept it with minor editorial alterations such as toning down some of his raunchier language. Monty and Ellie—not her real name either—have two children and four grandchildren. Jess, they tell me, passed on last year. It turned out that Monty has the Midas touch, which works as well in New York as it did in Colorado: he turns everything into money. I couldn't guess how much he's worth these days, but a financial guru I know estimates his fortune to be close to a billion and a half. The guys that bought the Mountain were not so fortunate. They had a few good years before the State closed them down for violations of the new environmental legislation. To add misery to misjudgment, several lawsuits were filed against them that forced the company into bankruptcy. If you're thinking of going to see Monty's "Mountain," don't bother, it no longer exists. It seems that some kids jumped the chain link fence one night and climbed up to the stranded truck. It gave way as they were horsing around in the truck bed, rolled over several times and crushed one boy to death. After that the state hired a demolition crew to dynamite the mountain, and other salvage teams took down the dilapidated buildings. Today only a low mound of dirt, scrap, and concrete remains of Monty's dream. It's mostly plains again, but I can't tell you if prairie dogs have returned. Monty and Ellie have never gone back to the site. "It was fun while it lasted, but I don't want to see it in that shape," Monty says. They still spend most of the year on the Adirondacks estate, but since neither Ellie nor Monty have his Grandfather MacAllen's aversion to hot places, they spend their winters in Florida or at any of their several tropical residences. And Ellie drives that Mercedes she fantasized about back in the day.

A Love Letter to Camille

Several years ago, I got the following narrative in the mail. The return address turned out to be bogus and there was no information inside about the sender. After you read it you will probably agree with me that the man named Kindall—if there was such a man—could not have sent it. And I have no other information about who it could have been. This brief notation was included: "I send this in hopes that you with your contacts may know something that will make more sense of this than I can—which is none." It was not until I discovered a further bit of information appended at the end that I decided to include it with the other stories. Not that it solved the enigma about Kindall. If anything, it only added to the puzzle. Anyway, here it is. Make of it what you will.

*****

My name is Mancil Kindall and I once lost twelve years of my life. That's right, twelve whole years and maybe more, for nothing has been right since it happened. I don't mean I wasted those years in the usual doping and drinking that my Boomer generation was famous for. There's just a big empty hole in my life, like a piece of it had broken off and disappeared. Don't get me wrong; I had already done more than my share of that sixties stuff before any of this happened. In fact, if I hadn't gotten into trouble early on in Memphis, maybe none of this would have happened to me.

Not that anybody would ever believe my story, and probably you won't either. I can't blame you. I wouldn't if somebody else told it. All I can say for sure is that for a dozen years it was like I had fallen off the earth and it had gone on spinning out there without me. So, I'll tell you what I remember at the beginning and the end and let you make of it what you will. You guess is as good as mine—probably better.

It was early May 1967, the 8th to be exact, my twentieth birthday. But there was nothing to celebrate. Hungry, dirty, and dead broke, I was hitchhiking to Chattanooga along Highway 64 in south central Tennessee. I had run through my college money in Memphis, written hot checks, and piled up IOUs and bad debts everywhere I could. When bill collectors started calling home and my straight-laced dad found out, he was bent totally out of shape and cut off my funds. I had to drop out of school and get out of Memphis, even though it exposed me to the draft and the Vietnam war.

Before I quit to have a blast with friends, I worked for a couple of weeks as a roofer, and when I heard that housing construction was booming in Chattanooga, I decided to give it a try. I had to do something. My dad had always preached to me about the importance of money. For the first time I was beginning to believe he was right. Anyway, I needed to put some distance between me and the Memphis authorities before they picked me up for a stack of piddling to middling misdemeanors. This time, I promised myself for at least the tenth time, if I ever get out of this mess, I'll be more careful with money. But this time I really meant it.

I was mulling all this over and wondering where my next meal was coming from, when a black, pre-war Chevrolet in mint condition pulled over to give me a ride. For the past hour or so I had seen nothing on the old highway but a few old vintage cars. Must be going to a car show, I thought.

The driver, Frank Venable he told me later, was only two or three years older than I was, but he talked like a man from my dad's generation and his clothes were like a scene from a forties B-movie. Still, he would have been a good-looking guy if his hair hadn't been cut in such a hokey way. When I mentioned it, he had the nerve to laugh at my nice long mane. I dismissed these oddities as the local backwardness of a rural Tennessee country boy that the 60s had bypassed. I complimented on his '40 Chevrolet.

"41," he corrected me with a laugh. "Just traded for it this week. Hope you know women better than you do cars, city boy. Leastwise from the funny words you use and the nasty way you talk I guess you're a big city boy."

In the easy way that youth opens up to youth, we soon found ourselves sharing not only some welcome cokes and sandwiches but also the most personal and private things, which at that age usually has to do with girls. We were both still young enough to admire older women. Girls our age were fun, I declared, and maybe marriageable down the road someday, but mature women, hey, now there was the experience that could put hair on your chest and show a young guy what real sex was.

We compared love affairs as the Chevy dipped and topped the hilly terrain. My accounts were mostly exaggerations of half-truths, but I could tell that Frank's came sincerely from real experience. As our confidentialities deepened, he blurted out to me that he was on his way to deliver a letter to the love of his life, a woman five years his senior. There was only one main problem, my new friend explained: she was married, and her middle-aged husband was suspicious and dangerously jealous of any man who came near her. Consequently, their meetings involved elaborate deceptions. He showed me the letter and explained that he intended to deliver it to her younger sister Rosalie, who would then slip to is his lady friend Camille. Soon, maybe within a week, Frank and Camille planned to run away together. He explained that he had some money saved from his military service in the war.

"You already had a tour in 'Nam?" I asked.

"Nam? Whatta you mean 'Nam'? Naw, I was in the South Pacific along toward the end of the fighting."

Nothing he said made any sense, so we were silent for a few minutes.

"I just can't live without Camille," he said abruptly, "and she feels the same way about me. I've got to get her away from that crazy husband of hers and the pure hell he's put her through. If I don't I'm afraid he's gonna catch her and kill her. He knows something's going on and says he'll burn the house down with her in it if he ever catches her running around on him."

That kind of talk chilled my enthusiasm for the confidential mode we had drifted into. At that age I saw all serious topics as a vague threat to my laid-back view of life. I was all for love and sex as long as you kept it at the level of fun and games. But this sounded a lot more serious—and dangerous, and I was never overloaded with courage. Getting killed was heavy Vietnam kind of stuff; chasing some skirt was not supposed to be. And I cautiously told him so. But instead of changing the topic, Frank launched into a description of Camila's beauty and told me more about her than I needed or wanted to know. I tried to bring him back to our first frivolous talk, but he was too distracted to listen.

That distraction cost him his life and changed mine in an unbelievable way. Highway 64 was—and still is in long stretches—a winding two-laner. So when an old red semi topped a hill in the middle of the road Frank swerved too late to avoid a head-on collision. The impact crumpled the hood and shattered the windshield, then send us flying across the highway into a deep ditch. Luckily for me the car landed upright, and my door was still usable. I saw a flash of light and then blacked out momentarily as my head hit the dashboard. When I came to, the semi was gone, and there was a small smear of blood on my forehead. Otherwise, nothing seemed broken and I was not in pain.

I can't say the same for Frank. He was wedged between the steering wheel and the door and blood was flowing from a gaping wound in his chest where a piece of the windshield had impaled him. I was rattled by the suddenness of it all and uncertain how I could help him. Maybe, I thought to myself as I gingerly eased out of the car, if I can just get him out of the car. Frank guessed what I was about to do and stopped me.

"No, don't, good buddy," he wheezed through ruptured lungs. "Don't move me, I'm not going to make it. But there'll be people along in a minute to help me. Here, take the letter and promise me you'll see that it gets to Camille."

And with that he thrust the letter into my hand.

"Go to Weakley Road . . . not far . . . a little past Lawrenceburg," he gasped. "Easy to find . . . Ask folks where she lives . . . Big two-story house a mile off the highway . . . Camille . . . Promise . . ."

Those were his last words. I could not tell if he was alive or dead, but I suspected the latter.

At that moment two men in white uniforms and lights approached the door and without a word motioned me away from Frank. I could see a white glow up on the road bed, but I was too far down in the ditch to see an emergency vehicle. With professional help now on the scene and in charge, I was relieved and abandoned my feeble attempts to help Frank. I turned to gather my few belongings from the back seat. There was a large object against the door, but I did not want to examine it. The quicker I could get away from the tragedy, the better off I would be. When I looked up, Frank, the men in white, and the light were gone. But how could they have done all that so quickly. Those guys have got to be real professionals, I thought. It did not surprise me that they had not examined me for injuries. I guess they took one look and knew I was okay.

What to do now? One thing was certain: it wouldn't help matters to stay for long around the old car. If the highway patrol spotted me, they might implicate me in some way in the accident or else hold me on outstanding Memphis charges. At that point in my life I looked on all police people as my natural enemies.

That much decided, I got away from the scene as quickly as I could. Rather than risk being spotted on the highway, I walked for hours parallel to it through adjacent fields and pastures until finally wrapping myself in my old blanket and resting in a deserted barn until morning.

At daylight I made a decision. Frank had entrusted me with his letter for Camille. But, I reminded myself, I had not really promised him anything. After all, what was Camille—or Frank himself for that matter—to me? They had their problems and I had mine, and I couldn't see that mine would be resolved by concerning myself with theirs. And what difference could a letter make now? Besides, I dreaded the idea of having to explain to the woman that Frank was probably dead. Then there was her dangerously jealous husband; if I ran into him I might end up dead too. Sorry, Frank, but hey, man, I gotta get on to Chattanooga.

I had no appetite or thirst, so I left the drinks and sandwiches I was lugging in the old barn. After a while I got tired of carrying my belongings and tossed them aside too. I forgot that I still had the letter in my pocket.

The only problem now was that during the night I had gotten turned around and wandered so far from the highway I couldn't find it again. I walked for hours and when I thought I spotted it, it turned out to be Weakley Road instead. With appropriate profanity about my situation, I took it, thinking that it had to intersect with Highway 64. If I had to pass Camille's house on the way, so be it. She didn't me from Adam anyway, and now less than ever I had no intention of delivering the letter and giving an account of the tragedy. I pulled it out to toss it in the roadside weeds, but then hesitated for no conscious reason and put it back in my pocket.

Sure enough, I came within sight of the old two-story house a mile from Highway 64. I was hurrying by, eyes down, hoping to avoid human contact, when a young woman, pretty but dressed in an old-fashioned style, suddenly appeared in the road and spoke to me.

"Mancil, you have something for Camille, don't you?"

"What do you mean, ma'am," startled that she knew my name.

"You have the letter, don't you?"

"I do have a letter, yes, but who are you and how do you know my name?"

"I'm Rosalie. Come with me to the house."

"This is the letter," I said to her. "Here take it, but there's no need for me to go up to the house. You see, Rosalie, Frank's—"

"Gone," she said softly. "Yes, I know and so does Camille. It's all right, Mancil, but you have to keep your promise to him."

"I didn't make any promise to him," I protested.

"Oh, but you did, Mancil, not in words but you promised all the same by being there at the end when he needed you. Now you must come with me to the house to put things in due order."

"But what about Camille's husband? Frank told me he's a mean one. What happens if he sees me?"

"He's gone, too," she said.

I saw no reason to argue the matter any further with this strange girl, so I followed her to the old house. There I met Camille, a taller, prettier version of Rosalie. I understood at once why Frank had fallen so hard for her. If she was around thirty, as Frank had told me, her smooth young face made her look twenty. Only her eyes had a sadder, more mature cast.

"Welcome back, Mancil, I'm glad you brought me the letter. We were wondering if you would show up this time, the last time."

"The last time? I don't follow you, ma'am. I've never been here before in my life."

She smiled and held out her hand to take mine. Her touch was cool, and the sensation lingered long after she had withdrawn it. Yeah, man, I thought, no wonder Frank fell so hard for her. What man wouldn't?

"Give me the letter, Mancil, and, Rosalie, bring the box, please."

I handed her the letter. She opened, read it, and then pressed it to her lips. Tears glistened in her dark eyes. Rosalie gave her a box full of letters.

"Mancil, you don't remember, so I'll explain. This box contains the other eleven letters you have brought me, one each year since Frank left. This is the twelfth and last love letter. With its delivery you have fulfilled your promise that you intended to break. You made it harder on yourself—and us. But now you are free to go on your way. We're all free to go."

"I don't understand what you're talking about. I've never been here before, never seen you before."

"Everywhere you go is the last of other times. Mancil, now the ordeal is over, if you let it be over. Your work here is finished. The sooner you let go, the sooner you will be let go."

I had heard a ton of this kind illogical mumbo-jumbo from weed-smoking seers and phony gurus and thought no more about her words. Say the dumbest thing you can think of and gullible people will hail it as the deepest wisdom. But when Rosalie escorted me out to the road again, everything seemed altered in ways I can't fully describe. She said goodbye and went back into the old house. A quarter mile down the road I turned for a last look and saw what I swear appeared to be a deserted, burned-out shell of a building.

But I was in for an even greater shock when I reached Highway 64. Oddly shaped cars and trucks with strange names whizzed by. A few hundreds ahead I came to a combination service station-diner where several of the strange vehicles were parked. I thought I had misread the price of gasoline and hamburgers: ninety-five cents for gas and a dollar for a hamburger! How could stuff cost that much? They must be gouging folks because it's a long way from town. Inside I asked the attendant about the old house and the women that lived there back on Weakley Road.

"What women do you mean, mister? Aint nobody living there that I know of. That old house burned down about ten or twelve years ago. The two sisters that lived there died in the blaze. I don't remember their names. Some said the husband of one of them set the fire and then killed hisself. That's about all of know about the place."

My glance fell on a newspaper: May 8, 1979. Hey, my birthday, and I forgot all about it, but 1967, not 1979.

"What day is it?" I asked the man who by now was eying me in an odd way.

"Monday, been that way all day, mister."

"No, I mean the date."

"May 8th. It's right there on the front page."

"1967?"

"1967! Man, I wish! Those were my good old days. No, it's been 1979 ever since New Year's. Something the matter . . . mister?"

He probably started to say, "with you," but caught himself in time.

At that moment I saw a reflection in a hand mirror on the counter. I looked again and recognized myself—a weird version of myself. My face was fuller and broader than it was supposed to be, and the hairline was backed up nearly an inch.

For day my life was a kaleidoscopic swirl. I was still living in an earlier time but having to contend with a newer era. To get things in perspective again, I returned to my home in Jackson, Tennessee and tried to talk to my parents. They were older but seemed at first to be healthy. The main problem was they refused to talk to me. In fact, they ignored me completely. Not that I made demands on them. Since the accident I had lost my appetite and never seemed to tire or get sleepy. I didn't give it much thought; it seemed to be the new normal. I understood my Dad's anger; that had always been his nature and nothing I did ever really pleased him. But gentle, soft-spoken Mom? She acted like I didn't exist and seemed to be falling into dementia. One day I overheard her tell Dad that she was going out to the cemetery "to place new flowers on Mancil's grave." I tried to explain to her that I was alive, but she ignored me. Poor Momma, she was losing it, and I couldn't get through to her. In fact, I had lost them both. Dad ignored me but he didn't insult me any more either. It was all too painful for me, so after a few weeks I drifted away from home again.

I had many of the same puzzling problems with other people too, even my old friends. Many of them, especially busy adults, ignored me when I spoke to them and acted as if I weren't standing right there before them. They wouldn't so much as give me the time of day. Man, it really hurt my feelings, and sometimes I just wanted to level people with my fist. Some of the little kids, though, and a few of the old people would take the time to talk to me and answer my questions as best they could. But even they looked at me as though I was different from other people.

Finally, I started to adjust a little to my circumstances, but the adjustment did not mean that I understood any better what had happened. In fact, my bewilderment became total when I happened to see an old newspaper item dated May 10, 1947 concerning the demise of a certain Frank A. Venable, 23: "A veteran of WWII, Mr. Venable and a passenger were traveling east on Highway 64 when his vehicle plunged off the road and pinned him in the wreckage. Apparently both men died instantly. So far authorities have been unable to identify the passenger, who appeared to be approximately the same age as Mr. Venable."

What passenger were they talking about? They got their facts wrong. I was the only passenger in Frank's car and I'm here, alive and well, even if I am still confused about the dates. That part I don't understand at all: May 10, 1947/ May 8, 1967/ May 8, 1979. It's like three timestreams had crisscrossed or gotten tangled up in my life. Did my birthday have something to do with it? Am I having a bad trip from some of the junk I used to get high on? And which time is the real one, my real time? Where am I really. And bedamned if I know where I go from here.

*****

So much for Mancil Kindall's story. I laid it aside, thinking, as he himself suggested, that he had blown his mind with LSD, heroin, of other drugs popular with his screwed-up-sixties generation. Twenty-five years or more must have passed before by chance I saw his name again. While doing some historical research in 2007, I think it was, for a book I hoped to write about this part of Tennessee, I opened a history of Lawrence County, and by coincidence (?) an old newspaper clipping fell out. It was dated May 12, 1947 and read as follows:

Unidentified Accident Victim

The Sheriff's Office is asking for help in establishing the identity of the passenger killed in the wreck on Highway 64 near Lawrenceburg, May 8, 1947, which also claimed the life of the driver, Frank A. Venable of Lawrenceburg. First identified as Mancil Kindall of Jackson, Tennessee, the man's identification and driver's license proved to be false, and so far his fingerprints do not match any on record. State and federal officials have been notified and are investigating the case. Anyone with any knowledge about this man is urged to contact the Sheriff, Highway Patrol, or other police agencies.

The Talisman

I'll tell you in her own words what a very bright woman once told me: "Most of the time you never really know what's going on, at least we normal people don't." By graciously but mistakenly including herself in that category, I think she was trying to soften her conviction that generally speaking, most of us are on the stupid arc of the human circle. She certainly was not, and deep down she knew she was an exception as well as I did. Kindness is the source of as many lies as malice, only kinder ones. But I stray. Let me get back on task. She went on to say: "Where you would least expect to find it, in the loneliest and most forsaken places, evil may be busily sabotaging creation." Unpleasant thoughts, but since she's the Renée in the story, I'll concede her the right to say them. It begins with a letter from her cousin that came into my possession in 2007.

April 10, 1968
St. Catherine's Basilica
Siena, Tuscany, Italy

Dear Cousin Renée:
Your letter finally reached me here in Siena. And what a pleasant surprise it was to hear from you! Forgive my delay in answering you. For reasons that I shall not go into, it is not unusual for international mail to be delayed for weeks, first in Rome with its customary inefficiency and then in the Basilica with Father Francesco's strict censorship of outside influences.

Consequently, I receive very little news about America in general, even less about Louisiana and dear old St. Martinville. Indeed, *chère cousine,* I hear and speak English so seldom that it has become almost a foreign tongue to me. And our dear old French we learned as children from our older relatives and spoke *en famille* in those early days is also in shambles. As you can imagine, here everything is in Latin in the Basilica and Italian in the city.

Renée, I remember you affectionately as a bright and beautiful little girl, and never fail to include you and other members of the family in my devotionals. You were, as best I remember, about five or six when I left. (Somewhere among my papers I still have your photo.) I am delighted to learn about the solid progress you are making in your studies at Tulane University. Keep it up. If your experience is in any way like mine, everything worthy you learn will prove useful someday, and everything good you fail to learn will be a shortcoming somewhere in your life.

I fear, though, that in selecting me as a topic for your English paper on biography, you have made a poor choice. I am by no means a famous personality. The cloistered, secluded life I lead makes it all but certain that I shall never attain any notoriety— and besides that, I am the last person who wishes public notice. Nevertheless, since you asked me about my life and why I chose this pathway, I shall oblige you. You have my permission to use the information in any way you see fit, so long as you do so discreetly.

I remember clearly the day my double Great Uncle Daniel Bellechasse returned to St. Martinville. I think of it often because it changed my life forever and caused me to end up here in Siena nearly twenty-five years. Ago. It was a Sunday afternoon in July of 1952. With three other boys from St. Martinville I was leaning against the old Evangeline oak by Bayou Teche, laughing, boasting, and lying about things that were rare in our lives: cars, money, and—if you will pardon me the indiscretion for a man of my condition—girls.

"Who's that?" Louis Broussard asked, sitting up and pointing a stick he was trimming at an old man walking down the south side of the Church common with a walking cane in his right hand and a sack slung over his left shoulder.

"I've never seen him before," his brother Jules remarked. "Who is he? *Mon Dieu*, look how long his hair and beard are! He looks as old as Methusalah!"

"Maybe we can have some fun with him," Jacques Landry said with a grin. I'll bet he's as crazy as a loon!"

"Only crazy one I know of around here is you," I pointed out to Jacque, poking him in the side with my muddy stick.

"Hey, quit gouging me if you know what's good for you! You've been picking at me all day long and I've just about had a bellyful of it! Now you better leave me alone!"

"Or what? You think you're big enough to make me quit?"

"Big enough for two or three like you, butt face, and then some!"

I jabbed him again and he came at me. We scuffled and rolled in the muddy grass, kicking and struggled for advantage until I felt a sharp rap across my back and heard another pop against Jacques's head.

It was the old man wielding his cane. We looked up at the strangest face any of us had ever seen. It was creased by a thousand wrinkles and leathery as an old shoe. His full-length snow-white hair and beard flowed loose like a picture of a biblical prophet and his unblinking blue eyes flashed with indignation.

"Get to your feet, whelps," he ordered, "and don't insult manhood further by fighting like children! If you must fight, do it like men, not like puppies!"

Jacques and I were too startled to disobey him. We got to our feet as he scowled at us disapprovingly.

"Your names?" he asked in a gravelly voice, taking us all in at a glance.

"Our names?" we all repeated.

"Your names!" he thundered so forcefully that Madame Devilliers peered out of the near window of the old del Castillo hotel to see if we up to mischief again.

"You," he said, pointing his cane at Jacques, "who are you?"

"Jacques," he answered in a squeaky voice, thoroughly cowed by the old stranger.

"You have a surname?"

"A surname?" Jacques asked, looking around at us for help.

"Yes, a surname, otherwise called a last name by the ignorant, a vast category of humanity which I am beginning to believe includes all present."

"Landry," Jacques responded weakly.

"Landry," Hmmm. Yes, I remember the Landry family. "And you?" he asked, turning in Louis's direction.

"Louis, sir, Louis Broussard, and the ugly one there is my brother, Jules."

"And you, boy?" he continued, wheeling suddenly towards me.

"André Bellechasse, sir. *A votre service*, I added in my best French.

"André, so you're André. And you still remember a bit of French. *Très bien.* I think you're the one I'm looking for. They told me some of the Bellechasse family lived around St. Martinville. Who is your father?"

"His name was Henri, but he died in the war. My mother's dead too. I live with my grandfather, Antoine Bellechasse. There's just the two of us since Grand-Maman passed away."

"And would he be related to the Bellechasse family from Loreauville?"

"Yes sir, I guess so. They tell me the family used to live over there a long time ago before they lost their place back in Depression times."

"What was your great grandfather Bellechasse's name?"

"I don't know for sure; Ignace, I think, or something like that. He died a long time before I was born."

"And your grandfather? How is he?"

"Well, he grunts and complains all the time," and lately his hearing is going bad. But he's all right, I think. At least he was this morning when I left the house."

"Take me to him."

"Well, sir, I had planned to go on over to Louis and Jules' house for a while."

"Did you lose something at their house?"

"No, sir, not that I know of. But—"

"Then pick up my sack there and lead the way to your house. I need to speak with Antoine."

His tone was beginning to anger me. Who the heck did he think he was.

"I'm your uncle, boy, Daniel Bellechasse by name," he said, as though reading my thoughts. "Your great-grand uncle, to be specific, your great-grandfather's older brother. Now look here, André, you do as I tell you or I'll add more welts across your scrawny back to the one I already put there."

Annoyed but obedient, I picked up his sack and led the way across the Bayou Teche bridge and then on to our house a mile east of St. Martinville. For an old man he moved swiftly and the tapping of his cane so close on my heels made me nervous. Everything about him unnerved me. And I wasn't the only one.

Grand-père for one, didn't know what to make of Uncle Daniel, and I could tell by the look on his face that he doubted the old man was who he claimed to be. How could he be? The Uncle Daniel he had heard people talk about as a boy had left our Cajun country so many years ago that he was no more than a half-forgotten memory even in Grand-Père's youth. And even though he didn't know for sure how old that would make his uncle, simple arithmetic told him that he had to be years past a hundred. None of it made sense.

Nor did Uncle Daniel clarify matters. At supper that night in response to Grand-Père's question, he talked about travels and studies in foreign lands, many years in a place he called the "Middle East," and, later, a lengthy residence in Siena in Italy.

"Then it's true, as I was told, that you became a consecrated person, a religious?"

"Yes, a monk."

"Uncle Daniel, is that why you never came back to visit us? I don't recall ever seeing you, though I heard a lot about you from my father." He paused and continued, "Aunt Nicole used to tell me stories about your doings as a youngster. I guess you weren't always so devout."

Uncle Daniel slowly laid his fork across his plate and stared at Grand-Papa. "Aunt Nicole? Antoine, you know you don't have an Aunt Nicole."

"Well, somebody in the family must have told me," Grand-Papa stammered evasively.

"No, Antoine, I know what you're up to. You were testing me to see if I'm really who I say I am, to see if I'm lying. But you're the one who lied, not me. Well, to satisfy your curiosity, I'm not like I was back then, but I'm the same man I was ninety years ago when I left Loreauville."

"Ninety years! But, Uncle Daniel," Grand-Père protested, by my calculations, that would make you way over a hundred years old. How can a mortal man live so long?"

"The short answer is that we remain in this world as long as God has a reason for us to be here. The longer answer is that there are many things you don't know and wouldn't understand if I told you. And I myself understand very little. So just take my word for it. I am who I say I am, and I've come back for a reason that I may explain to you in part after you tell me what's happened to the Bellechasse family and other people I used to know."

They talked far into the night. I listened for a while, but when they switched to French, which was harder for me to follow, and to boring accounts of people I didn't remember or care about, I yawned, stretched, and went to bed.

Early the next day, hours before I wanted to wake up, Grand-Père rousted me out of bed with the news that I was to go down to Loreauville with Uncle Daniel.

"To Loreauville? What for?" I asked, yawning and rubbing the sleep out of my eyes.

"That's his business. He'll tell you what you need to know

about it. You just do what he says."

Uncle Daniel was waiting for on the front porch, impatiently tapping the doorstep with his cane.

"Mend your ways, André. You'll waste the best hours of your life and miss its main rewards by sleeping late," he said disapprovingly. "The world will pass you by if you're lazy."

"Yeah, I guess, I responded without the slightest interest in his advice. "Grand-Père says you want me to go down to Loreauville with you. How are we going?"

"We'll go the natural way, on foot. It's the way I travel."

"On foot! In this heat? Why don't we find somebody with a car to take us? It's a long way down there and with all the rain lately the mosquitos will eat us alive."

"Then you had better have some breakfast before the mosquitoes have theirs," he snapped, ignoring my question and comment. "And what strength you have left you'll need for walking. So don't dally. The matter is urgent."

"All the more reason to get a car," I pointed out to him.

Uncle Daniel smiled and patted my cheek with his shriveled, claw-like hand. It was the only gesture of softer affection he ever showed me.

"You seem to have a measure of common sense on occasion, André, but our affair calls for uncommon sense."

We started out. Instead of walking beside me, he stayed close on my heels, as he had the day before. Silently I cursed my luck. Stuck with this crazy old man who follows me like a noisy shadow, I thought.

"Not as crazy as you think, André," he said, tapping on the shoulder with his cane and scaring me half to death with his mind reading. "And for today and probably for a few weeks to come, I shall be as close to you as your shadow."

By early afternoon we reached the half dozen modest buildings that comprised the town of Loreauville. This was the end of the road and I was ready to rest and find refreshments.

"Well, Uncle Daniel, we made it. This is Loreauville, but there's not much to it. What is it you need to do here?"

"Nothing here, André; we're going on."

"On where? There's nothing past Loreauville but a farm or two and then the Henderson Swamp. No roads, nothing but a swamp full of mosquitoes, snakes, bugs, alligators, and God knows what else."

"You're right for once, André, God does know what's in there, and that's why we've come here. From now on you follow me. Remember I used to live here, and I know the way."

For all the good that does us, I thought. After a hundred years what does the old man remember about the swamp?

"Enough to get us to where we're going," he said, picking up my thoughts again.

"And enough to get us out?" I asked, remembering a time Louis, Jules, and I got lost in another part of the swamp.

He made no response except to set a blistering pace. I picked up the bag I had dropped on a bench and trotted after him.

If the mosquitoes were irritating on the road, they were vampiric as we made our way into the swamp. Despite Uncle Daniel's claim that he knew the way, we seemed to be following no visible pathway that I could detect. It was getting late, and the dread of becoming lost in the wilderness at night was only one of my concerns. At every step I was afraid of stepping on poisonous snakes that I knew infested the swamp. And then there were the alligators and, according to some people who claimed they had seen them, bears and panthers. God deliver us, I prayed silently, crossing myself.

"He will if we trust him," Uncle Daniel said without turning to look at me.

He ignored the mosquitoes and did not respond to my warnings about snakes or my anxious questions about the direction we had taken. He plunged ahead, letting the branches slap me in the face. To my relief we came eventually to water's edge. At least, I thought, we can't go any further.

I was wrong. Uncle Daniel paced up and down the overgrown bank until he spotted a bateau tied to a cypress sapling and hidden by overhanging vines. He ordered me in.

"Where to now?" I asked as I stepped gingerly into the rocking bateau.

"Ahead," he said.

He did the rowing, and as we glided through the dark water and moss-draped vegetation to the buzz of mosquitoes, the splashing of diving turtles and croaking of bullfrogs, I was amazed that he was still strong enough to row. Men of his generation had long since taken their final rest. I was in the hands of a man who by natural progression should have died many years ago.

"I'll rejoin my generation when my task here is finished. God allowed me extra time to complete a work," he explained, once again uncannily sensing my thoughts.

"A work?"

"A work," he repeated without further explanation.

After so many bends and turns that I lost all sense of direction, we came to an irregular row of seven huts all but devoured by the exuberant wall of foliage.

"We're here," he announced.

"What is this place?" I asked. "Do people live here?"

"The Attakapas people, a few of them that survived unnoticed here in the swamp."

"But Uncle Daniel, the Attakapas were cannibals! I've heard people talk about how they cooked and ate people they captured! I thought they were all killed off way back."

"Not quite. Anyway, the Attakapas are not the real danger here."

"Then who or what is?"

"Arnaud, their leader."

"Who is he?"

"You'll find out soon enough. Control your fears, or they will control you. Nobody's going to cook you today. There's good water in a spring beyond the huts. The evil contamination of this place hasn't reached it yet. Go and drink. It will lessen your hunger. And fetch me water in my cup."

He handed me a metal cup from his bag, and I cautiously made my way past the huts toward the spring. Despite Uncle Daniel's reassurances, I remembered what I had heard and read about the cannibals. But to my relief I saw no one. Maybe Uncle Daniel was wrong, I thought hopefully, and there are no Attakapas around here after all.

But he was right about the water; it was clean and cool. When I got back with a cupful for him, he was resting in the shade of a giant cypress and peering at a man rowing our way. Three men with long black braids emerged silently from the foliage and waited at water's edge. They seemed to take no notice of us. Attakapas, I thought with a shiver of terror.

"He has been following us," Uncle Daniel said as he emptied

the cup and returned it to his bag. "I expected him to come from the south, but he is as cunning in old age as he was in his youth. Hold on to my bag, André, and keep your distance from him—and your silence. It is time for me to deal with Arnaud."

The Attakapas secured his bateau, then went inside one of the huts. Uncle Daniel watched them go, shook his head, and muttered what I think was a prayer.

Then Arnaud approached us. Taller by nearly a head than Uncle Daniel, he was a racial mystery. His face was African black, but his features were sharply etched, and his hair was long and straight like that of the Attakapas. His arms and chest bulged with muscle and his stride was sure and quick like that of a strong man in his prime. It was only when he came close that I saw by his finely wrinkled face how incredibly old he was, perhaps as old as Uncle Daniel himself.

"So, at last you have returned, Daniel," he said in a low, guttural voice, "I was not certain you would have the courage to confront me."

"My years are many more and strength much less, but a promise is a promise and still binding; I have returned in my last days to keep my word."

"Indeed, our youth is far behind us and neither of us is as frisky as we were in the old days when we had our dealings. And who is this fine lad with you?"

I felt struck by a power almost like a physical force when he looked at me and was relieved when he turned away.

"Just a boy, Arnaud, sent to help an old man along the road."

"No, Daniel, now you try to mislead me. I can see that he's much more than that. But that's all right, you don't have to tell me. I have my own ways of knowing things, if you remember."

"Yes, I remember. I see you don't live here with the Attakapas any more. Have you given up your tawdry business of voodoo charms, cures, spells, and talismans?"

"I moved on to more important things as my powers increased."

"Yet I knew as soon as we got here that you have been leading the Attakapas back to the old devilish ways that destroyed them before."

A flicker of anger twisted Arnaud's features.

"I'm teaching the lore they forgot, the wisdom that made them strong and feared centuries ago before people like you taught them misleading things."

The confrontational tension between them was intensifying, and I promised myself that if I ever got out this place I would go straight to Father Augustin to confess my misdeeds and gladly do whatever penance he ordered for me.

Arnaud, I hoped that I would find you changed from your evil ways after all this time, perhaps even repentant. But I see that the Evil One still has you more enslaved in old age than you were in your youth."

Arnaud laughed scornfully. "And I hoped, Daniel, to find you wiser, yet I see that you are more misguided as an old man than you were as a young fool. You still believe the empty promises of the Galilean."

"By the grace of the Almighty, yes," Uncle Daniel responded emphatically. "Anyway, we are not here to change minds and trade insults, but to exchange the talisman as we agreed so many years ago. I have brought it back as I promised I would. And I have complied with all the conditions you set when you gave it to me for my protection and keeping."

"Arnaud leaned forward and his eyes gleamed. "Then give it back to me, miserable little man! You have had it too long in your possession!"

Probably I imagined it, but Arnaud seemed to change before my very eyes, to grow larger, more imposing. In contrast, Uncle Daniel seemed even older and more shrunken.

Uncle Daniel nodded and told me to get it for him from the sack. "It's in a mahogany box, a little brown box, André."

The box seemed heavy out of all proportion to its size. Uncle Daniel took it and handed it to Arnaud.

"Unlock it for me if you will, André," Arnaud said with a mirthless smile. "My hands are too old and stiff for delicate tasks."

éI was about to turn the small key when Uncle Daniel reached out and grabbed my hand with a grip unimaginably strong for one so old.

"No, André, don't open it! Give it to me!"

He took the box and gave it back to Arnaud who was visibly annoyed.

"Daniel, you make such a show of a trifle. I meant the boy no harm."

"Maybe not now, but in the end, you knew he would have been touched, perhaps contaminated by its dark resident power. It took me years to understand the depth and scope of your evil, the masters you serve, and the real motive behind the talisman you prepared for me in my youth."

"You understand nothing," he said sarcastically as he caressed the box. "You contemptible followers of the Galilean never do. You asked me for a talisman to protect you in your travels. And I obliged you. You have no reason to complain now. My only requirements were that you open the talisman at the proper coordinates of time and place and return it to me upon your return."

"You're right, Arnaud, I understand very little. It is true that with the help of your corrupt spirits you forged a talisman that afforded me a false protection in my travels. But that was only a vehicle for a greater evil. I was incidental to your purpose, a useful fool, a witless agent, sent on a mission to contaminate and destroy."

"And like many other fools, you served our purpose," Arnaud laughed. "If you exposed the talisman as I instructed you, then my mission is accomplished as my masters planned. For once opened in many strongholds of the Galilean, the dark power attached to the talismans began its work and cannot be stopped. Everywhere you see its effects—the collapse of the Galilean creed, the proliferation of doubts, and the approach and triumph of the dark force. As for you, Daniel, your misspent life is over. I have no more time for you and your ignorant nephew."

"True, Arnaud, my life is nearly over, but so is yours, and yours will happen sooner than mine. Your stipulation was for me to open the talisman in the monastery then bring it back to be reopened and reset for other purposes. Now you must do so and suffer the consequences of its power."

"And so I shall open it, Daniel, so I shall, but not to suffer consequences as you erroneously believe but to enjoy the fulfillment of my mission. The unbreakable link with that despicable monastery was established many years ago. Now it needs only a second opening of the talisman for its annihilation to be complete. Nothing you or anyone else can do can alter the fate of that Galilean monstrosity."

"Arnaud, the dark masters have lied to you, as they lie to all their servants. They keep no promise of reward or gratitude, but at the end gleefully inflict punishment on all: those who serve and those who fail. Now before you die, hear what really happened to the talisman. Yes, I opened it, as I promised, naïve fool that I was in those days. But by the workings of powers mightier than yours, I did so in the presence of saintly Father Benedict. By his prayers and the intercession of the Brothers, the dark force was stymied, and its fury held in check. Now you open it to your peril but open it you must. And well you know that the dark force always has two potential targets: the first is the intended victim, but if thwarted, the sender is the second."

"You lie!" Arnaud said in a raspy whisper. "You puny servants of the hated Galilean cannot stand against the power of the dark masters!"

He fumbled to insert the key, opened the box, and held up a metallic pentagon that shone like polished silver. There was a flash and then for an instant something darker than the swamp seemed to flutter over us. Then it slowly dissipated, and all seemed normal again. The murky swamp water rippled for a few seconds and grew still. For a few more seconds we waited in an unmoving, suspenseful tableau. Then a smile spread across Arnaud's wrinkled face.

"You see, old fool, how wrong you were!" he sneered. "You see how weak your so-called 'holy men' are! You—" he started to say.

But before he would finish his boast he gasped, and his face contorted in pain and terror. For a moment he clutched his chest, then he fell, writhed uncontrollably, and died. From the hut where the Attakapas waited a long wail of loss and despair arose. It made chills go up my spine.

*****

I was not sure what I had witnessed. When I asked Uncle Daniel about it, he reassured me.

"Arnaud was living under a delusion, the eternal delusion of evil. He entrusted his life to the occultic masters. But in reality, their power is limited to the actions of the furious elemental spirits and misguided mortals that serve them. When I went to the Monastery and told Father Benedict about the talisman, he guessed its purpose, for he had been forewarned of it in a dream. He and the brothers prayed and then I open the talisman only in his presence. He did not think it would be prudent for the brothers to gaze on something that might tempt them in some way. Higher powers held the elementals in check and turned them to the destruction of the one—Arnaud—who had summoned them. Nothing happened to Father Benedict, to the monastery, or to me. The redemptive work goes on, in which the monastery has a small role. But without Father Benedict's intervention, there was a good chance—that is, a bad chance— that great harm could have been set in motion. But compared to the enlightened powers, those of the talisman are negligible."

"But Uncle Daniel, you saw what happened to him. If the talisman had no real power, then what killed the man lying there on the ground?

"Oh, it had power, but much less than Arnaud believed. Most of the power of evil is our fear of it. On the natural level, old age killed him, André, the same mortal decline that will soon claim me. But on a higher level, he also suffered a spiritual death. At the higher, unseen level, everything real is also spiritual.

"If you knew all this and had that much power you could call on, then why did you bring me along to this place," I asked, staring down at the corpse. "What am I doing here?"

"For three reasons, André: first, to keep you from mischief you would have gotten involved in today that eventually would have caused great harm to several people. And second, because I am nearly blind and needed you to be my guide. My natural forces are precariously overextended. I live on borrowed time. Most of what I perceive is by second sight, not with natural vision. But it requires an exhausting concentration that I cannot maintain for long. The third reason is that if you remember what you have seen and heard here, it can teach you a great deal about your future work. You don't know it yet, but some day you'll travel some of the same roads I have, and I must teach you what I can in my few remaining mortal days. I know for a certainty that you have a work to do in this world. We all have a work to do, whether we know it or not, whether we do it or leave it to burden someone else. You have been summoned, André, but you have not yet heard the voice. You will in time."

How could Uncle Daniel have known that Louis and Jules had been urging me to join up with them to break into the old Monfort mansion? Nobody lives there these days, they said, but demented old Hervé Monfort. Just think of all the gold and guns they say he has. And probably money besides. I have to admit it was a tempting prospect.

"Don't even think about it, André," reading my thoughts again. "If you boys were to break in, Mr. Monfort would probably shoot at least one of you. He's not as demented as Louis claims. And regardless, your lives would be ruined."

I was embarrassed and ashamed. To change the subject, I asked what we should do about Arnaud's body and the Attakapas men. I was afraid they might think we murdered him.

"It's best for us not to touch the body. The Attakapas will dispose of it in their own way. Probably no trace of it will ever be found. And then they, too, will drift away. Arnaud promised to restore their power if they would serve him. But it was a false promise; their age is over. New people rule the world, and someday their time will also pass, and others with different ways will replace them. As for the talisman, it is now devoid of all enchantment and only a trinket that I am about to drop in the water."

"Can I have a look at it first?"

"Better you don't," he said as he turned from me and dropped it. "Come on, André, let's be on our way. The residue of wickedness hovering about this place is a torture to my spirit. It needs to be exorcised, but that is not our affair. Our business here is finished. Let's get out of the swamp before it gets too dark for even your young eyes to see. When we came here I had some hope that I could help Arnaud, but it was too late, eternally too late. Poor man!"

His last comment seemed out of place.

"Why should you care, "Uncle Daniel? You said yourself that he served demons and meant to hurt you."

As we—or better, he—rowed through the twisting turns of the swamp, he explained his comment: "True, André, but there is another side to Arnaud's story that I haven't told you. He and I never spoke of it, but I know he was my blood brother, my half-brother. He was, I know now for sure, my father's son with a woman of mixed race, African and Attakapas. But because of it he was an outcast from all three groups. Yet he was a young man of great mind and talent, and because of his gifts and embittered by his status, he took the first steps toward evil."

After a pause, he added, looking me in the eye: "as many of us are tempted to do at weak moments."

"Maybe I could have helped him if I had reached out to him when we were young. Maybe, but I was too comfortable in those early years, too cowardly and indifferent in those days to do so. And by the time I tried, he had slipped too far to turn back. Would that I had prayed more for him. God forgive me and have mercy on his soul."

I was stunned by his revelation and for a long time could think of nothing worthwhile to say. By then I was totally lost; the darkness seemed as oppressive as it was appropriate for the mood I was in. But as he said, Uncle Daniel knew the way out—in a double sense. At last we reached open country, but I was so hungry and morally deflated that I felt I could not take another step.

"Do we have to walk all the way home on this same road? I'm not sure I can make it."

"Yes you can, André. And by this experience you may start to learn that a road is never the same road twice, and no trip is ever like another. You get out of a journey what you put into it, and in this way you make a new road every time you travel it. True roads and real journeys are trips of the spirit. Someday you will discover for yourself what I am telling you. Already you are not exactly the same boy you were when we left this morning."

Uncle Daniel, I learned later, was known in Italy and the East as Brother Andrew, his second name (the same name I took later in my religious order). He lived another three weeks, and lucid to the end of his mortality, taught me lessons that I am still trying to understand.

✶✶✶✶✶

Renée, all this will seem alien and bizarre to you, as it did to me at first. For six months after Uncle Daniel's death, I busied myself with milder forms of fun and friendships and tried to put the experience with Arnaud and all it signified out of my mind. But in the end, it was no use. I could not be again the same person I was. Uncle Daniel was right; I felt a calling that grew stronger with each passing day.

You probably know most of the rest of my story, if you have read my bio or talked to members of our family. The day came when I could no longer avoid my destiny. That's when to the astonishment of the family, I announced that I was leaving to follow it. So here I came and eventually and here I have remained. In a bizarre way, Uncle Daniel and I have exchanged places: he is buried back in St. Martinville and here I am in living in Siena as Brother Andrew. In my imperfect way I am trying to carry on his work.

Affectionately,

Your devoted Cousin André

Title: *Louisiana Rogue*

- Author: Harold Raley
- Publisher: Lamar University Press
- Paper Back: ISBN: 9780985255275
- eBook: Kindle
- Pages 306
- Publication Date: April 2013

This wonderfully entertaining picaresque novel by Harold Raley falls in the tradition of rogue literature established by Tom Jones and other early novels. Set in the nineteenth century, Louisiana Rogue will take you on a wild, fast-paced romp through all levels of Cajun society in the 1830s. The title page says the book promises to tell "The Life and Times of Pierre Prospère-Tourmoulin, Picket-pocket, Thief, Gambler, Fugitive, Undertaker, Barber, Doctor, Priest, Prisoner, Bandit, and Count; Latterly penned in his hand for the gentle reader of leisure, Spanning the years 1831-1839" and claims to be translated by Peter Tourmoulin.

Title: *The Unknown God: Mysteries of Deity, Time, Space, and Creation*
- Author: Harold Raley
- Publisher: CreateSpace
- Paper Back: ISBN: 9781466273184
- Pages 142
- Publication Date: October, 2011

In his powerful Introduction to The Unknown God, religious thinker and writer Harold Raley makes this unusual request of the reader: "Suspend, if you will, everything you know about God. Put aside for the duration of this reading your traditional theologies and hear a new and more reverent way of thinking about God. When you return to your old understandings, they will have deeper meanings, unless those you once professed were meaningless to start with. If you are unwilling or unable to do as I ask, read no further. This message is not for you. The truth it contains will find you later when it is ready for you and you have been made ready for it." To approach Deity from this radically new perspective--arguably the greatest advance in theological thought of modern times--is to expose and shed light on the baffling paradoxes, improbable notions, and misleading errors not only about God but also about time, space, creation, and immortality. In each of these categories this book offers stunning new insights that incorporate not only the efforts of classical theologians but also the latest discoveries in science. Outline in these advanced insights is a new understanding of human life. By the law of corresponding identities, Raley explains, a more elevated theory of God necessarily means a more elevated theory of mankind. Each of the many themes and aperçus packed into this slender volume could have been a hefty tome. With pristine eloquence Raley reduces them to the essentials, believing as he does that clarity of style is courtesy to the reader.

Title: *The Light of Eden:*
A Christian Worldview

- Author: Harold Raley
- Publisher: John M. Hardy Publishing
- Paper Back: ISBN: 9780979839122
- Pages 196
- Publication Date: May 2008

An inspiring vision of richer Christian life and thought. In the tradition of C. S. Lewis and G. K. Chesterton, this extraordinary book is both a spiritual adventure and an intellectual feast. Packed with illuminating insights and written in beautiful language, The Light of Eden introduces its readers to a vast treasury of creative ideas, innovative concepts, and possibilities contained in Christianity.

Title: *The Spirit of Spain*
- Author: Harold Raley
- Publisher: Halcyon Pr Ltd
- Paper Back: ISBN: 9780970605498
- Pages 212
- Publication Date: October, 2011

The Spirit of Spain brims with aperçus and revelations, many of them controversial, others startling, all engrossing. From Roman Hispania to the most recent Spanish trends, Professor Raley narrates the unique story of Spanish civilization. Examples of his original thinking include a "phenomenology of Spanish history," a new theory of the Spanish Renaissance, new concepts of Spanish patriotism and nationalism, and a reinterpretation of Spanish "Stoicism." As the book unfolds he also takes many sidelong looks into Hispanic America and offers a new explanation of Spain's relationship to Moslem Al-Andalus and modern Europe. The book culminates in a radical analysis of "Quixotic life" and its unsuspected significance for the post-modern age.

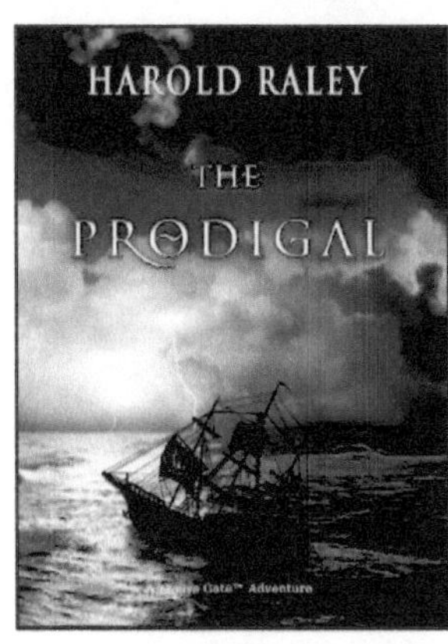

Title: *The Prodigal*

- Author: Harold Raley
- Publisher: Mouse Gate Press
- Paper Back: ISBN: 9781590953402
- eBook ISBN: 9781590953419
- Pages 96
- Publication Date: October, 2016

In the tradition of Crusoe and Sabatini, The Prodigal is a story of the shipwreck and struggle for survival of a young ship's carpenter who escapes one captivity only to fall into more dangerous circumstances. The story unfolds from Boston to Mexico, Cuba, Africa, and back again. At critical points a mysterious stranger intervenes to lend a hand and guide him to his destiny.

Title: *Barefoot On A Frosty Morn*
* Author: Harold Raley
* Publisher: Mouse Gate Press
* Paper Back: ISBN: 9781590953426
* eBook ISBN: 9781590953433
* Pages 352
* Publication Date: October, 2016

Barefoot on a Frosty Morn is a literary and genealogical tapestry of several families over three centuries. The genealogical threads stretch back to England and France and unfold in step with America's continental expansion. The families crisscross north, south, and west as the tapestry grows in richness and complexity. A final episode sheds light on the earliest roots of the story. The reader has a perspective only partially available to the personalities immersed in the stories. Episodes are woven around some American milestones: the Revolution, the Civil War and WWII. These resonate and enrich but do not hinder the genealogical flow of the novel. In its conception and execution *Barefoot on a Frosty Morn* is unlike any writing before it. It surpasses the limits of history and narrates the essence of the American vision of life.

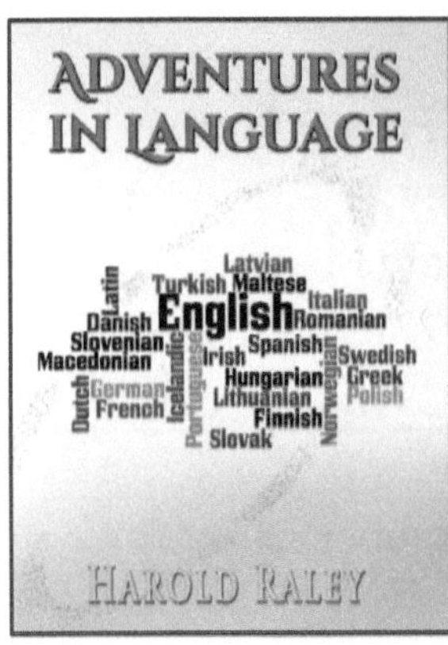

Title: *Adventures in Language*
- Author: Harold Raley
- Publisher: TotalRecall Publications
- Paper Back: ISBN: 9781590955321
- eBook ISBN: 9781590955352
- Pages 216
- Publication Date: October, 2017

In these *Adventures in Language* linguist Harold Raley explores fascinating features of English and many other languages in different cultures and historical eras.

Even though at times I point out obvious errors in the languages as they are currently structured, I realize that the rules of grammar and usage in English or any other living language are, or can be, subject to change. This may not be true of, say, ancient Sanskrit, but then we note that despite its perfection—or perhaps because of it—ancient Sanskrit ceased to be a spoken tongue many centuries ago.

Over the ages thinkers have pondered the qualities that define humanity and set mankind apart from other species. In my view, no stronger case than language can be made for human uniqueness. Animals can communicate and mimic but they cannot speak. Language, sung, recited, or spoken, is archly human, and for that reason also deeply mysterious, beautiful, and fascinating.

Title: *Points Of Light*

- Author: Harold Raley
- Publisher: TotalRecall Publications
- Paper Back: ISBN: 9781590955369
- eBook ISBN: 9781590955376
- Pages 238
- Publication Date: October, 2017

These *Points of Light* centered on the beauty, humor, and mystery of human life present many perspectives flowing out of the unifying philosophical premise that life, not physical reality, is the foundational reality in which all others are rooted.

A noted thinker once said that clarity is the courtesy an author extends to the reader. Insofar as my abilities permit, I have tried to add another kindness: word economy, which I understand to mean saying as much as possible in the fewest words. In those cases in which there is neither clarity nor economy, I alone take the blame.

Title: *Memories of Appalachia*
- Author: Harold Raley
- Publisher: TotalRecall Publications
- Paper Back: ISBN: 9781590956496
- eBook ISBN: 9781590956052
- Pages 296
- Publication Date: 2020

A celebrated philosopher once said that in order to understand anything human we must tell a story. However, this human narrative is not about what we are. That kind of information is the business of science, which teaches us about our physical nature. But the real story of our life, the human portion, is who we are, and it begins where science and nature end. Biography, not biology, is the true human narrative.

No one can write our narrative for us, and no one should. For we are the novelists of ourselves, the composers of our personal melody of life. Daily we add pages to our story or notes to our song. Animals, our only flesh and blood companions in this world, are what they are by Nature's decree, but we humans are who we become primarily by our personal choices. This means that of all God's creatures, only we have the freedom—and therefore the responsibility—to choose how we live our life, and if necessary, to reconsider, to rectify, to repent and rewrite our story if it is sordid or change our tune if our music is discordant.

I take these distinctions to heart in this writing. It is the story of the things I did for the first twenty years of my life and what happened to me as I did them. In a general sense, this is the description of any life, great or small, and mine conforms to the pattern with nothing exceptional to recommend it. Mine is the unremarkable tale of an obscure life in an obscure place. Yet I cannot dismiss it as insignificant, for that would imply that I am judge and jury of life's meaning, which I am not, not even of my own life, most of all, my own life.

Harold Raley

Title: *Tides of Fortune*
- Author: Harold Raley
- Publisher: TotalRecall Publications
- Paper Back: ISBN: 9781648830068
- eBook ISBN: 9781648830075
- Pages 202
- Publication Date: 2020

These are tales of fortune and forfeiture, happiness and hazard, love and deceit. Some stories are set in specific times and places but not confined to them. Others arise in the mere vastness of the world and belong anywhere applicable or nowhere definitive. For wherever there is human life, there are the yearnings, dreams, possibilities and impossibilities we call tales and stories. For this reason, I do not think of myself as their creator, but only their author or perhaps their channeler. I say this because the people who come to life in this book do not always behave as I wish and plan. I push and they push back. Which is why I am as surprised as the next person by what they decide to do and who they choose to be. Perhaps their way is best. For if the decisions were left up to me, most likely I would be their tyrant. As it is, I end up being their friend.

Title: *Tattletales*
- Author: Harold Raley
- Publisher: TotalRecall Publications
- Paper Back: ISBN: 9781648830044
- eBook ISBN: 9781648830051
- Pages 260
- Publication Date: 2020

A celebrated philosopher once said that in order to understand anything human we must tell a story. He spoke a profound truth, and it is important to understand some of its implications. Art, including musical and literary art, tells us very little about what we are. That kind of information is the business of science, which teaches that we are mammalian animals, first cousins to the great apes. On the other hand, art has much to tell us about who we are. It reminds us that we are persons, or better said, men and women, who daily add pages to a private narrative, or notes to an inimitable life melody. We are the novelists of ourselves. If we exist at a primary level as biological creatures subject to nature's laws and limitations, on a different plane we live as unique biographical persons whose mission is not to remain at nature's mercy but to humanize the world with artifact and artistry, creed and creativity, song and story. The thirteen tales in this book are modest examples of the high art of being human in a rich alchemy of styles, times, and climes.

www.ingramcontent.com/pod-product-compliance
Lightning Source LLC
Chambersburg PA
CBHW020615110726
47899CB00002B/517